An *of*

the NHS

Marion Andrews

Grosvenor House
Publishing Limited

The right of Marion Andrews to be identified as the author of this
work has been asserted in accordance with Section 78
of the Copyright, Designs and Patents Act 1988

The book cover picture is copyright to Inmagine Corp LLC

This book is published by
Grosvenor House Publishing Ltd
Link House
140 The Broadway, Tolworth, Surrey, Kt6 7Ht.
www.grosvenorhousepublishing.co.uk

A CIP record for this book
is available from the British Library

ISBN 978-1-78623-047-8

To Mike who inspired me to begin.
To Jan, Jill, Alison and Helen, my wonderful flatmates
whose friendship has lasted a life-time.
To my family whose love and support I depend upon.
To Holly without whose encouragement, IT and editing skills
this book would have never come to fruition.

5. 7. 2018

To Jane,
On the 70ᵗʰ anniversary
of the NHS - Happy Memories!
Lots of love,
from Elaine xx

Contents

Chapter 1:
The Beginning

It is said that nurses are born, not made, and the idea made me wonder; how old do you have to be to decide what you want to do with your life. I'd wanted to be a nurse since I was seven. Where the idea came from I can't remember; but I recall the look of surprise on my parents faces when I announced it during Sunday tea. Later the BBC's Emergency Ward 10 confirmed my decision. I was going to be a nurse. There was no doubt in my mind. Now standing on the threshold of the Nurses Home in London, eleven years later, I wasn't as sure.

The red brick building had a broken, crumbling look and the rain falling from the leaden sky made the black and white tiled steps treacherous. It was May. With sinking spirits, I turned to my mother. We smiled superficially, and made polite conversation to hide the pain we felt.

"Look at that doorbell!" she said, a little too brightly, "I bet that's been around since the last century. If only it could speak". It was easier to pretend this was everything I'd dreamt of doing, rather than to listen to the voice of doubt inside 'Leave; just go. It's all a huge mistake'

Six months previously I had sat in front of the Matron of this large teaching hospital "Why do you want to be a nurse?" she had asked, staring at my unmade-up face.

"I want to help people get well." I had replied. It sounded trite.

"People don't always get better you know, they sometimes die."

I'd nodded vigorously to show I understood, willing her to believe me. I remember nothing else, except that the hand beneath the starched white cuff of her navy dress was large and strangely rough, almost like a farmer's, when she shook mine as I stood to leave. I carried this image with me; to remind me of that day, should it be the end of my dream. Later it was replaced by a feeling of pure joy, when the postman thrust a thick buff envelope through the letterbox informing me that I had been accepted to train to become a State Registered Nurse.

The door opened and we stepped into another world. The scene within was far from the quiet exterior. Two women, in matching navy dresses bustled in and out of an oak-panelled booth, clutching clipboards. The taller approached and without introduction or smile barked "Name?" She didn't even look at me.

"Nurse Cooper" I replied shyly.

She consulted her list. "Room 427. Lunch is at one". Clicking her fingers, a young Spanish girl in a dull orange overall appeared and guided us to an ancient iron lift.

As we stood waiting for the lift, another girl, accompanied by a couple, I guessed were her parents, entered the hall. Sister, clipboard in hand, strode towards them. The gentleman shaking the rain from his mac, smiled extending his hand, "Good morning. Nasty day."

It was as if he didn't exist. "No men allowed I'm afraid. You may wait in the lounge."

She indicated a large, insipid room in which beige vinyl covered easy chairs, blended with brown carpets and blinds, like an old sepia photo. Taken aback he seemed about to object, but noticing glares from his wife and daughter, exited and flung himself into one of the chairs by the window. Mission accomplished, Sister commenced her standard welcoming speech. "Name?"

Room 427 was just as I imagined. For years I had read and re-read any books about nursing, fiction or non-fiction, and now I considered myself an expert. It was small and rectangular, furnished with a single iron bedstead, a wardrobe, a table which served as a desk and a wooden chair. By the window was a sink with a glass shelf above, containing a chipped tooth-mug. The brown theme of the lounge continued with cheerless beige walls. On the bed, stiff white starched sheets were topped by rough blankets and a pale green bedspread with the words "Hospital Property" woven into its fabric as if it was in danger of being stolen. A bold printed notice on the door stated that "The fixing of posters to the wall with cellotape is strictly forbidden".

Mum looked close to tears. "You'd better go." I said "I'll start to unpack"

She nodded and we clung to each other. "Be good Joy" she instructed "Eat properly and darling, please ring. You know where we are if you need us". I nodded, not trusting myself to speak, and with that, she left.

My trunk, so carefully packed at home, lay by the window. On the bed were piles of grey-striped uniform dresses, white starched aprons, stiff white collars and finally a strange semi-circular piece of starched white material which I presumed was a nurse's cap. The bed was hard and for a moment I felt overcome and alone. Tears pricked my eyes and I rubbed them furiously defying them to spill down my cheeks. Struggling to undo my trunk, I rummaged through it, trying to find something familiar and mine alone. Anything that did not have a label attached telling me what I could or could not do with it. Previously it had seemed ridiculous to bring my childhood Teddy, but now he seemed perfect as I pulled him from the trunk and sat him on top of my pillows.

There was a knock on the door. It was the girl I had seen downstairs. She smiled as she introduced herself.

"Hello, I'm Mary. Have your folks gone too?" I nodded. "Well I think we are neighbours." she continued "Can you remember where the dining -room is because I'm sure its lunchtime."

I shrugged "I'm sorry but I can't remember either" adding "I'm Joy, by the way", and suddenly we were both laughing as if we had known each other forever.

"Are we supposed to put our uniforms on?"

"Goodness knows" Mary replied "I can't remember a thing Sister said. I was so worried my Dad was going to make a scene."

"He did look cross" I agreed adding "Perhaps he should have made a fuss. Anyone would think this was the dark ages."

Suddenly the door opened, revealing an anxious face. "Can you help me?" a voice began. "I've just arrived and that Sister downstairs said I had to be in the dining-room at 1pm. I don't know whether to put my uniform on and, for the life of me, I can't remember where she said the dining-room was."

Mary and I laughed. "That's what we've just said" I ventured. "Let's stick together. Between us I'm sure we can find the dining-room and they can't chuck us all out, if we should have put our uniforms on. They're supposed to be short of nurses aren't they?" The newcomer's face softened as she smiled.

"Great," she began "My name's Jane, by the way, How about you?"

We began our search for the elusive dining room. Mary the tallest and most senior, by a year, led the way. Her long brown hair, tied in an elegant French pleat, gave her an air of confidence. Jane and I, unaware that our short hair had been completely flattened by the rain, scurried after her eventually creeping into the room, feeling self-conscious. Inside were several tables around which girls, not in uniform, sat looking uncertainly at the watery beef stew, accompanied by soggy over-cooked carrots and lumpy mashed potatoes that was lunch. These, we presumed were our new colleagues.

After lunch we were shown to Classroom 1, on the ground floor of the nurse's home. We sat in groups, around the grey formica tables that served as desks in the stark room. There was little to distract us; no pictures on the walls or any form of decoration, just the standard beige paint I'd seen on every wall so far. Excited chatter echoed around the room, the noise level rising as we shared stories and details of our lives.

Suddenly the door flung open and a short, large-bosomed woman entered and stepped onto the raised platform at the front of the room; immediately there was silence.

Miss Barnett, as she introduced herself, looked like an Oxford don. Her worn tweed suit and permed dark hair made it impossible to guess her age. "Good afternoon ladies" she began "Welcome to Preliminary Training School or PTS as it is usually shortened to. I hope you have all found your rooms and enjoyed luncheon." We sat upright, as if to attention, not knowing quite how to respond as she continued. "I am your Principal Nursing Tutor. I will be responsible for ensuring the training you receive at this hospital is one you will be proud of throughout your life. This is the beginning of an adventure. Perhaps, at this moment, you are wondering if you have made the right decision; I would like to reassure you that we pride ourselves on taking each individual and moulding her to become, at the end of three years, a true professional, proud to be called a State Registered Nurse." She paused and if I had of been holding a flag I think I might of waved it, so strong was the emotion inside me.

The door opened again to admit a woman in a dark green uniform with the frilled cap of a Sister. She smiled benignly at us as Miss Barnett continued. "Our first task is to provide you with your uniforms and for this I leave you in the capable hands of Sister O'Reilly."

"Afternoon ladies" Sister O'Reilly's soft Irish accent was a pleasant change from her predecessors BBC enunciation. "I'm afraid my next request will mean you get out your maps again." She looked around the room and finding a sympathetic face continued, "I'm glad to see I'm not the only one who finds this place a maze." She paused then continued "Right. This is the plan. You are to go to your rooms and change into your striped dresses, black stockings and regulation shoes, then return here with an apron, your cap and an old toothbrush in a mug of water." She clapped her hand "Go. Be back in 5 minutes".

Breathless we arrived back clutching our tooth mugs. Our first lesson was to learn how to attach the stiff white collars to the dresses using collar studs. This complete we watched, as Sister picked up the half-moon of crisp white material, which was to become our cap. First, she dipped the toothbrush into the mug of water and brushing gently she dampened the strip of material that held the drawstrings. These, once freed from their starchy prison, were somehow gathered up to create delicate butterfly- like ruffles at the back of the cap. With another twist of her hand she folded over the front edge to form the front, and like a magician produces a rabbit from a top-hat, she displayed a beautiful nurses' cap. Then it was our turn.

I realised then that not everyone was as "new" as me. Within minutes, a group of girls were clipping neat caps into their sleek smooth hair, whilst the rest of us struggled to produce huge pancake-like caps that were more suitable for the stage than a hospital. Phrases like "Do you remember that patient who haemorrhaged post-op?" or "I assisted Doug put a drip up on him. Honestly that guy was a complete Wally" drifted over as I watched with awe. Would I ever use medical words so casually? I doubted it. Later I discovered they were

'Orthopods'; they had completed a two year orthopaedic course which allowed them a 6 month reduction in their general training.

The room filled with chatter as we admired our head gear. At 3pm Sister said above the noise "Nurses it is now tea-time. Please be back here in ten minutes." Jane stared anxiously at her new fob-watch. "I think I'll miss tea" she began "I can't face finding the dining room again. I don't want to be late back".

The conversation was overheard by Val, one of the orthopods, who grabbed her arm; "Miss tea? Rule one if you are to survive as a nurse is never, under any circumstances, miss tea. Follow us." She turned and swept out of the classroom to join her friends. We obediently trailed behind and in the dining room, gulped down stewed tea, our eyes continually straying to our watches. Val's group, however, looked very relaxed; just as we were beginning to become agitated, convinced that our nursing career was over before it had even begun, with a great scraping of chairs the Orthopods stood up and left. We hurried behind, noting landmarks. Entering the classroom, Val turned to us once again. "The second rule of survival is never be early for anything". I glanced yet again at my watch. It was exactly 3:10pm.

That night, I tried to gauge my feelings about the first 12 hours of my new career, but my brain felt numb. The narrow bed was uncomfortable, the mattress hard and the regulation starched sheets with perfect envelope corners trapped your legs, as if in a vice. The noise of nurses coming off-duty echoed along the corridor. A door slammed and there was a screech of high-pitched laughter; it was as if the building had energy of its own, and suddenly I was overwhelmed with the feeling that I, at last, was part of this new, rather frightening world. Without more ado, I slept.

It seemed only a moment later that I was dragged from my dreams by the shrill ring of my alarm clock. I washed and dressed into the still unfamiliar uniform and made my way into the corridor. Jane and Mary were there already.

"Hi did you sleep?"

"Your cap looks great."

"Still can't remember the way to the dining room."

"Follow us". Greetings hung in the air, as door after door opened along the corridor to reveal bleary-eyed new nurses, who at that moment were anything but anxious to begin Day 2 of the introductory course, but begin; it did.

Our first job was to collect the necessary study books from a visiting bookshop, set up in the basement. We each left with a stack of books, including 'Anatomy and Physiology for Nurses' and, 'Ballieres Book of Nursing Procedures,' which seemed obvious; but when we were offered "Notes on Nursing "by Florence Nightingale, there were raised eyebrows and comments of "Haven't we moved on since the Crimean war?" and "Isn't this a bit old-fashioned?"

Frank James looked anxious as he entered the room to be faced with 54 pairs of female eyes. He came from South Wales, although his welsh accent had long been lost and replaced with a London lilt. It was good to note that not all our tutors were old and female. Frank was different, not only by gender. He was friendly, approachable and not bad looking, wearing his white coat over a fashionable shirt. Smiling, he introduced himself. "Good morning Nurses. I am your tutor specialising in Anatomy and Physiology. I look forward to instilling into you the marvellous workings of our bodies."

He paused and in that brief moment Val leaned over and whispered loudly to her neighbour. "He can instill anything he likes into me."

A ripple of laughter crossed the room. Frank obviously heard too, because a dusky pinkness spread from where his red hair met his forehead, across his face and down towards his neck, deepening as it did so. We were amused. So it seemed not only did we have a male tutor who smiled, we had a male tutor who blushed. The possibilities seemed endless.

Frank, recognizing the need to re-assert his authority, continued "Today we shall be studying the heart and its functions. Open your books please. Chapter 2." For the remainder of the morning we were introduced to the heart and circulatory system on a level unequalled by any previous biology lesson I had experienced. It was both fascinating and terrifying. There was so much to learn, where did we begin? By lunchtime our brains felt numb, and incapable of absorbing any more information.

The queue in the canteen was long and as I reached the stainless steel counter, I saw the reason for the delay. Lying encased in coagulating dark brown gravy were slices of Ox heart. I stared at it, noting its various valves and chambers. I didn't feel hungry anymore; just sick. Even the stodgy tapioca seemed too much to stomach. I turned away and joined Jane queuing for a mug of tea. "Couldn't face heart; not after this morning" she said grimacing. "Nor me" I replied adding "I have biscuits in my room". We disappeared upstairs noticing, as we did so, most of our set were doing similarly.

An hour later, feeling fragile we arrived in the practical room. "Come in girls" Sister O'Reilly said "This afternoon we shall be learning the art of bed-making. This is a practical skill you need before we let you loose on the wards." She smiled continuing "Now I know it's a Friday afternoon, and I expect you are all itching to meet up with your boyfriends but first we have work to do."

She moved towards the first bed in a row of five. "Could I have a volunteer please?" Val stepped forward. "That's what I like" said Sister O'Reilly, removing her stiff white cuffs and rolling up her sleeves. "It's better to volunteer than be commandeered. Now nurse follow me."

Val faced Sister and they stripped the bed of its pillows, sheets and counterpane placing them on a steel rack they had extended from the foot of the bed. Val was obviously an experienced bed-maker; it was as if she and Sister were dancing partners. Val, slender and agile, contrasted with Sisters stiffer movements but they moved in the same rhythm as they gathered up the bed linen, remaking each bed. Their movements exactly mirrored each other.

Finally they presented the perfect regulation hospital bed. Three pillows stacked neatly on top of each other with their openings facing away from the door; the bottom sheet taunt and wrinkle free with envelope corners folded at a neat 45 degree angle. A plastic and a draw sheet protected the middle third of the mattress. "So handy in case of accidents" Sister O'Reilly explained, tapping the side of her nose and fluttering her eyes. The top sheet was next, followed by a cotton blanket and counterpane, which were folded under the top sheet to an exact measurement of 18 inches. The couple stood back to admire their achievement.

"Now it's your turn." Sister instructed, turning to us. For the rest of the afternoon the room was filled with shrieks of dismay, which degenerated into muffled laughter as the bed-making dance, which had looked so simple, was revealed to be a real art. Although Sister had at first seemed easy-going, we discovered that nothing short of perfection was good enough. She inspected each of our offerings rigorously, pointing out crinkled sheets, sloppy corners or too small a turnover. "Strip it and make it again" she commanded. There was to be no compromise. Exhausted and hungry at the end of the session, we were rather pleased with our achievements, but our triumph was short-lived.

"Right then girls" Sister began "You seem to have almost (she emphasized the word) picked that up. Next week we'll see how you manage with a patient in the bed." She rolled her eyes and turned to leave the room calling over her shoulder. "Have a nice week-end girls. Be good. See you next week"

It was our first week-end in London. I woke trying to feel excited, but found, to my horror, a strange sensation like an ache which started in my chest and rose to my throat. I'd been gradually more aware of it since leaving home, but there was no disguising it that morning. Perhaps without the discipline of getting up and being kept busy all day, it refused to remain hidden. I lay in bed determined to have a lie- in, but in the end found it was better to get up. I met Jane and Mary at breakfast and as we pored over maps of London and planned our day of exploring the West End, the pain began to ease.

Our first initiation was to find our way via the underground. Jane took control. She had lived on the outskirts of London and was familiar with 'the tube'. "Follow me" she instructed as we entered Warren Street station.

Mary looked anxious. "You sure you know where we are going?" she asked as we made our way down the steep escalator and when Jane nodded she continued to mumble "Good name Warren Street. It's just like a warren." She looked amazed when the tube actually arrived at Oxford Circus. "Well done" she began, but then became quiet as we pushed our way through the crowds.

Oxford Street, when we exited, did not disappoint. Crowds of young people in bright coloured clothes swarmed towards the fashion shops. Music blared over the loudspeakers and there was a party-like feel to the day. We joined in, determined to be part of the crowd. A new shop called Top Shop had just opened; we'd been told it was 'the place' to be, so we headed there first. The shop was huge and stretched over several floors, each full of racks of multi coloured clothes.

Mary pulled on a red military jacket. "Look at this" she struggled into it and rushed to the nearest mirror "What do you think?" she asked giving a twirl.

"You look great Mary. You must get it." We replied.

She searched for the price ticket, then quietly took it off and returned it to its hanger. The moment was gone. She pulled on her old waterproof coat. "This is more me" she declared "the red one would have been hopeless in the rain."

Our next stop was Carnaby Street. Names like Mary Quant, Biba, Twiggy, previously fantasy, became real. We were surrounded by 'beautiful people' in miniskirts with knee-high boots and flowers in their hair. It was intoxicating. Where did we fit into all this we wondered as we searched the rails full of skirts priced according to their length in inches?

We sat in a café to sip strong coffee and 'people watch'. This was a new start for us after all. But something didn't feel right. Our clothes felt drab and old-fashioned. Mary spoke first. "Trouble is" she began "I don't know about you but".... she hesitated "I don't want to sound mean or like an old fuddy duddy, but I haven't got much money and..." her voice trailed off.

Jane finished the thought, "You're right Mary. Goodness knows how much we actually get, once they've taken off board and lodging, but I don't think my budget will run to a new wardrobe."

I nodded; there was nothing left to say. It was a shame to let it spoil our fun though. "Tell you what "I began "We'll just window-shop today and pretend we're trendy, How about that?" "Done" we all agreed trying not to look at the tray of Black Forest Gateau, glistening with cream and black cherries that beckoned us.

The rest of the day passed in a blur of shops and walking. Now we had assessed our financial state it seemed rather foolhardy to spend all our money on tube fares. Walking was cheap; so we did; stopping only when we were too tired to go any further. It was tea-time when we arrived back at the Nurses Home and it was good to sit in the canteen, drinking mugs of tea and discovering that at the week-ends we were allowed a thin slice of cake. It was Madeira. It was dry, and nowhere near as tempting as the Black Forest gateau, but to us, it tasted heavenly.

Dining in the canteen on our first Saturday of independence seemed wrong. We huddled around the table trying not to look conspicuous. The on-duty nurses eyed us sadly as they ate. We heard snatches of their conversation. "Wouldn't catch me here unless I had to be." Escaping to the 'new girls' lounge we found a few of our set watching TV. "Have you had a good day?" we asked. There was a general nodding of heads, but I wondered if they shared the same niggle I was aware of. It had started in the canteen. I felt tired and hungry and suddenly I was longing to be at home, in my own bedroom with my parents downstairs and no concerns about money or what I was going to eat. It felt almost like a physical pain in my chest rising slowly to my head; it reached a crescendo and began to die away leaving me feeling fragile and tearful. Later I would discover that it was homesickness and it would affect most of us at some time.

Chapter 2:
The Road to the Wards

Anatomy and physiology of the respiratory system may sound a dull subject but Frank was a good teacher and, by the end of his lecture, I was hooked. The knowledge that in a few weeks I might be caring for someone whose illness made breathing difficult, made learning the complex way the whole act of breathing came about, much more relevant and exciting. We were comforted, also, by the thought that lungs were unlikely to appear on the lunch menu.

Our practical sessions in the afternoons also became patient focused. Sister O'Reilly divided us into small groups saying; "Right who's going to act as patient?" There was a pause until she added "Don't assume that patients do just as you tell them. Each one is different and will need individual care. It's called holistic care; I'm looking for someone who enjoys being awkward".

Mary's hand shot up and Sister took her aside and whispered instructions. Mary got into bed. "This patient has a soiled bottom sheet, which needs to be changed" explained Sister, demonstrating how to roll the sheet so it could be changed in that situation. When she had finished she said "Now, it's over to you"

As Jane and I approached, Mary started wailing "Ooh no Nurse. I can't move: you'll drop me."

Jane stooping low tried to reassure her. "No dear. We won't drop you. We're nurses. We never drop anyone."

But Mary wailed even louder "Noooo. You'll roll me out of bed. Help. Police."

All efforts to turn Mary on her side and put the new sheet in position ended with us collapsing into a giggling heap, caps at strange angles as Mary clung to any body part she could find. Sister allowed us these moments of hysteria realising perhaps that similar struggles with real patients would come soon enough. Eventually, the sheet was in place and a pink-faced Mary, allowed Sister to inspect that everything was in order.

Sister clapped her hands, "Not a bad effort Nurses" she said "But that was the easy part; your patient was co-operative". A cry went up around the room causing her to correct herself. "Well perhaps not completely co-operative but at least they were able to move. On the wards you will be required to move patients who are unable to move at all. That will be the next part of our lesson."

Lifting-aids and hoists were not part of standard hospital equipment so, it was essential to learn to move patients without hurting them, or ourselves. Most of our set were only 18, many of us slim and some not much taller than 5 foot; there was, of course, no weight restriction for our patients.

Sister divided us again into small groups; the largest nurse in each group became 'the patient' and the other two nurses faced each other across the bed. Mary was our patient. She snuggled down the bed looking mischievous. "Oh nurses, I can't sit up. Please do my pillows for me" she began.

Sister strode towards us. "This lift is called the 'Australian Lift' and it is ideal for this situation." Mary looked alarmed, as Sister enlisted Val as her partner and pushed Jane and I aside. They stood facing the head of the bed and linked their nearside hands under Mary's thighs. "Put your hands across our backs" Sister instructed Mary sternly and when she meekly did so, they moved their outer legs forward and with a resonant 1...2...3.. propelled her towards the top of the bed so forcefully she struck her head on the metal backrest. Mary grimaced but managed to not cry out as Sister said, "You'll have noticed how Nurse Lake and I kept our backs straight at all times. This is most important, the move is made using the strong muscles of the legs; a curved back is a weak back. Forget that at your peril. Numerous nurses have been forced to abandon their career" she continued "Because in a time of stress, they lifted badly and injured themselves." She smiled kindly, "Now it's your turn" she instructed "Remember keep your back straight and lift using your legs. Off you go."

Jane and I facing each other turned towards the head of the bed. Jane was quite short so we struggled to grip our hands together under Mary's thighs. At first only our fingertips met, but we burrowed our heads into Mary's flesh as she protested "Mind where you put your face.", and "Oh you're pinching me."

From the depths of Mary's dress I heard Jane exclaim "Never mind you; what about us" then came a muffled "1....2...3..." and Mary moved a fraction of an inch. Jane's flushed face came up for air "Dam" she exclaimed. "We'll have to do it again".

Once again we positioned ourselves, back straight, legs flexed.. "1...2...3..." this time with a great cheer from Mary, she was propelled up the bed, making sure this time that she did not bang her head.

"Well done. Now it's my turn" she shouted and we spent the rest of the lesson practicing our new skill. Now this was what I imagined nursing to be. Sister watched us quietly. As the lesson ended she asked "Any questions, girls?"

Caroline's cheeks were flushed and she shifted uneasily. At only 5 foot tall she was the shortest in the class. Sister noticed and asked "Nurse Lincoln have you something to say?"

"Well" Caroline began hesitantly, "It's just I really struggled because I am so short and I wondered how I would manage if I had a six foot something patient, who weighed about twenty stone?"

A titter of laughter spread around the room, but Sister looked very serious. "That is an excellent question". She smiled at Caroline. "You are right. It will be hard, but I must stress you are nurses and your job is to care for your patients, whatever their weight, and if a patient needs moving that is what you must do. You have been taught the safest way to do this. The rest is up to you." Caroline looked alarmed, but one look at Sisters face told us she was being serious and no-one dared to challenge her. Nurses it seemed could do anything.

Next session we were to learn how to give a blanket bath. Sister stood beside a trolley on which was laid a green plastic bowl, soap, 2 flannels and a plastic tooth mug and receiver. On its lower shelf were 2 towels, a nightie and a neat pile of clean starched bed-linen. "May I introduce you to Annie" Sister began as she stood beside a life size plastic model, usually associated with resuscitation, but today dressed in a floral nightie.

"Today she needs to be washed in bed. Can I have a volunteer?"

Helen offered. Sister turned to Annie "Good morning dear. We are going to give you a wash. Can we take off your nightie?" That done she turned to us. "Nurses tell me what you notice. What should be our priorities?"

"Well it's quite embarrassing to be naked." Someone offered.

"Chilly too" from another.

"Exactly" Sister replied. "We need to preserve dignity and warmth." She covered Annie with a blanket and asked "Do you like soap on your face dear?" She continued, exposing one part of the body at a time, moving the towel to expose the area she needed. Front completed, Helen supported Annie as she was turned onto her side whilst Sister washed her patients back, taking particular care of the pressure areas on her sacrum. Finally Annie was helped into a clean nightie, her sheets were changed, her hair combed, her teeth brushed. She was settled back into the pillows and if she could speak I'm convinced she would have said she was very comfortable. I doubted that all patients were so compliant. Sister smiled at us and said "It won't be long, Nurses, until you are caring for patients like this on the wards."

I could hardly wait.

The next day we arrived in classroom one, to find Sister assembling a large trolley containing stainless steel receivers filled with syringes and needles. "Right nurses," she explained "today we will be learning how to give an injection". My heart sank as she continued "First we will watch a film demonstrating giving an intramuscular injection". I felt tiny beads of sweat break out on my forehead. This was the day I had been dreading. I took a deep breath. Since the age of 9 I had developed a phobia of injections; the mere mention of one made me tremble. I remember the origin of this fear quite clearly. I was the first child in my class to have the Polio vaccination. Children are cruel and I recall being told by another child "The needle is massive; it goes in one side of your arm and out of the other. And I should know because my auntie's a nurse." The group gathered around me nodded in agreement.

Later queuing to receive the dreaded injection I remember a feeling of pure terror. I stood with my arm exposed and when the nurse gave the injection I said, to everyone's amusement "It didn't hurt". Then I fainted. Since then every time I had an injection, I fainted.

Now 11 years later I wanted to be a nurse. Trying to be clinical, I watched as the nurse on the screen, drew up the drug and injected it into the patient's thigh. I felt the familiar symptoms begin. A mist, punctuated by bright flashes of lights, began to descend and I was aware that my heart was racing. Breathing deeply I repeated to myself like a mantra. 'I mustn't faint. I mustn't faint'. The next thing I remember was a figure standing over me and someone saying "Lift her legs onto the back of the chair". I felt myself being moved and slowly the room came back into focus. Jane and Mary stood above me looking anxious and Sister was kneeling at my side. "You fainted Nurse" was all she said.

I lay still, waiting for the lecture to begin. How could I expect to make it as a nurse if I couldn't even watch a simple injection being given? But Sister just helped me into a chair and smiling asked "Do you feel better now?" I nodded and she continued "Good, well don't worry about it. You'll get over it"

I sat at the back watching the others carefully drawing water into their syringes and tentatively stabbing into the sandbag, that was supposed to replicate human tissue. I felt a total failure.

That evening feigning tiredness I went to my room. "You're not worrying about fainting are you?" Mary asked kindly. "It could happen to anyone you know."

"Of course not" I lied "I'm just tired – I think I'll have an early night."

Once alone I felt distraught. I'd have given anything to jump on the train and rush home to my Mum. Previously I had discussed everything with her. Now it seemed my world was about to fall apart and I couldn't face the thought of ringing her because I knew I would cry. I felt such a wimp, but eventually decided that writing her a letter might help.

I got out my pen which had been a leaving present from my old colleagues and fresh tears spilled onto my cheeks. They had been so impressed with my plans to be a nurse. What they would say if they could see me now, I wondered. Hanky in hand I began;

Dear Mum,

Thought I'd drop you a note to say Hello and get you up to date with everything that is happening. It's hard to know where to begin. We are doing new things every day. It's good to be part of a big group of girls; there are 53 in my set and I can't wait for you to meet some of my special friends.

I am missing you and Dad today. It's been a bit dire. Thought I ought to warn you that I'm not sure nursing is my "thing" after all. Everything seemed to be going well, but there's so much to learn and today it was injections. I fainted Mum. You know what I'm like. I don't mean to worry you. I'm fine and everyone was very kind but, well how can I be a nurse if I faint when I see an injection?

Anyway I thought I'd better warn you. I don't want you to be too disappointed with me if I come home. Sorry to worry you. Miss you lots. Love Joy x.

It took a long while to fall asleep and when I did I dreamt of huge hypodermic needles and always, I saw myself lying on the floor in a deep faint.

Next day Sister O'Reilly greeted me "Come with me Nurse Cooper. There is something we must do." I followed, fearing the worst. Was this the end of my dream? She led me into the practical room "I could see you found yesterday difficult" she began "So I thought today a little bit of private tuition might help."

In the corner was the trolley used yesterday. For the next hour I repeatedly drew up water into the syringe, connected the needle and stabbed the sandbag. Sister watched carefully, showing me how to position the syringe to accurately measure the dose required; how to flick the syringe with my finger to expel any air; and how to stretch the surface of the sandbag prior to injecting the needle. "I've found that seems to make the injection less painful for the patient" she explained.

By the end of the session, I felt elated. I could give an injection. Maybe, my phobia would be cured too. I rushed to my room and tore up the letter for Mum. I felt very grateful for Sister's kindness.

The day had at last arrived. We were to spend a whole morning on the ward. We could hardly contain our excitement as we walked in a snake-like queue through the underground passages that connected the nurse's home to the hospital. Sister, our escort, dropped 2 nurses off at each ward we passed.

Mary and I were to go to a men's surgical ward. Sister guided us through the heavy ward doors where a bright-eyed Staff Nurse, blonde hair pulled into a tight bun under her cap and her tiny waist accentuated by a very ornate silver buckle on her belt, bustled towards us. "Staff Nurse" Sister began "you have two fine young nurses for the morning. I leave them with you". She turned and left.

Staff gave us a quick nod of acknowledgment, and led us towards a trolley piled high with green plastic bowls. She smiled "We are very busy this morning, we have 6 patients going to theatre and 8 had their op. yesterday. These patients will need help to get washed." She pointed to two men in their mid-thirties in adjacent beds. "I suggest you take one patient each, start giving them a blanket bath, and then I will send someone to help you finish". She thrust a bowl into our hands, pointed us in the direction of the sink and with that she disappeared. We filled our bowls, trying not to look too terrified and made our way towards our allocated patients. I introduced myself shyly, as I pulled the screens around the bed of my patient.

His name was Gordon and he was recovering from an inguinal hernia repair the previous day. Wearing standard hospital striped pyjamas, he was lying with his head resting on a stained pillow; an unruly mop of ginger hair highlighted the pallor of his face. I checked the name above his bed.

"Mr. Terry?" I began. He opened his eyes sluggishly

"Call me Gordon, Ducks" he replied.

I smiled; feeling encouraged "I'm to give you a blanket- bath." Opening his locker I began to search for his toilet things.

Gordon watched my every move "You're new aren't you?" I nodded, hoping he would not discover just how new I was and that he was, in fact my first experience of washing anyone, other than myself.

"Do you like soap on your face?" I enquired and when he nodded I rubbed a little soap on the flannel and began to dab tentatively at his unshaven face. He was silent, as I worked but I felt his eyes follow my every move. I struggled to take his jacket off and had just finished washing his chest when he spoke.

"There's just one thing I would like you to do for me Nurse" he hesitated then continued "Could you cut my big toenail. It's really giving me jip. It keeps catching on the bedclothes?"

Warnings flashed through my mind as I tried to remember if cutting toe-nails was something a nurse should do. Something associated with diabetes was niggling me. I felt my face go pink, as I struggled to reply, realizing at the same time that the only part of him left to be washed was covered by his trousers and how was I supposed to take those off on my own? Perhaps cutting his toe-nail was my easiest option.

Suddenly the screens parted and a flustered looking nurse joined me by the bedside. "Sorry" she began "I'm Nurse Briggs. I got held up in the bathroom with Mr. Franklin." She raised her eyebrows and grimaced. "How are you getting on here?"

It was Gordon's turn to look uncomfortable as I explained. "I've washed the top half but Gordon has asked me to cut this toenail and that's as far as I got."

She turned to look at Gordon, who avoided her eyes. She laughed "Well you must be feeling better Gordon. Got your sense of humour back?"

Flipping back the bedclothes, she exposed the offending toe. It was nail-less. I must have looked puzzled because she continued "Don't worry he's tried it on us all. It's your little joke isn't it Gordon?" He looked rather sheepish as Nurse Briggs continued "Gordon knows that nurses aren't allowed to cut the nails of diabetic patients, which he also is. So nail or no-nail it is a definite no."

I made a mental note of that piece of information, as Gordon obediently lifted himself, allowing Nurse Briggs to remove his trousers and complete his blanket bath. She threw me the towel. "I'll wash, you wipe" she instructed. "I'm not a piece of crockery you know nurse" Gordon objected as we helped him into some clean pyjamas and then into his chair. We smoothed his unruly hair into a slightly tidier style with a side parting.

A broad-shouldered man, in a white coat entered the ward. He was clean shaven and his head was bald on top except for a long strand of hair which had been combed neatly across the baldness and brylcreamed securely into place. He was carrying a tray containing towels and what looked like razors and combs. He stopped at the end of Gordon's bed. "Shave sir?" he asked.

Gordon looked alarmed "I had my op yesterday. Don't you remember?" he began. "You shaved me down there". He lowered his eyes discreetly.

The man laughed "Don't worry. Of course I remember, but I was thinking of your face today." He moved slowly towards Gordon with an outstretched hand. "Sorry, I should have introduced myself" he began "I'm Cecil, the hospital barber. I visit the wards twice a week for all sorts of shaves." He winked before continuing "Now let's begin again. Would you like a shave?" I left Cecil lathering Gordon's face enthusiastically.

Collecting more bowls and water, I headed towards the next patient on my list. Nurse Briggs stuck her head around the screens, just as I was helping Mr. James out of his open-backed op gown. "I'm just taking someone to theatre" she whispered "can you manage for a bit?" I nodded looking more confident than I felt. But it was only a wash, I reasoned. What could go wrong?

Mr. James was in his late 60's and his prostate gland had been removed surgically last week. He had appeared to recover well from the operation but had developed a chest infection, which although treated with anti-biotics and physio had left him feeling weak and tired. In report, Sister had explained that he needed TLC, (which I discovered much later stood for tender loving care). I introduced myself and began to wash him, encouraging him to talk about himself.

I soon discovered he was married and had two sons who were both policemen. He had retired a couple of years before after working for 50 years in the clothing department of a famous London store. All was progressing well and I was beginning to feel quite accomplished. Mr. James spoke very quietly and I had to lean my head towards him to hear him. Only the groin area was left, but as I began to wash his penis I was horrified to see it rise and extend to previously unimaginable proportions. I stepped back in alarm. This was my first contact with the male anatomy and in my naivety; I thought I was witnessing a medical emergency. Picking up the towel, I flung it over the offending part and retreated from the curtains not knowing what to do. Where was Nurse Briggs?

At that moment, Staff-nurse appeared. I rushed to her and described as calmly as I could what had happened. She looked at me strangely, but reassured me saying "That does happen sometimes. You know men. Just hang a towel on it and it usually subsides."

She hurried off leaving me to return to a rather pink-faced patient. The towelled off area had now returned to normal proportions, but the poor man looked totally wretched and avoided all eye contact. There was a rustling of curtains and to my relief Nurse Briggs entered. "Everything alright?" she asked. I nodded and together we helped the embarrassed man into clean pyjamas without any further problems.

Nurse Briggs looked at the clock "It's almost time for lunch. About time too. I'm shattered." I nodded weakly. I couldn't believe the morning had gone.

"What time do you leave today nurse" Staff-nurse asked, as a porter pushed the huge steel dinner trolley onto the ward.

"I was told lunch-time Staff, but" I was about to offer to stay but she interrupted "Well that's about it then. Thanks for your help. Good luck with the rest of your course. Bye"

Suddenly, Mary was by my side and we were being ushered out of the big swing doors. We hadn't seen each other all morning and there was so much to say. We didn't stop talking until we had to eat lunch. Even then only the fact that the meat in the stew required us to concentrate or choke stopped us from comparing notes.

Our ward visit had excited us all and I could hardly wait for PTS to end and our 'real' careers begin. It was in this mood that we eagerly opened our first payslips. For our first month, after tax, and board and lodging had been deducted, we had each received £12. There was a general muttering among us. "How do they expect us to live on that?"

"It can't be right."

"Tax, surely we don't pay tax? We're students after all."

Val, as usual took control. "I suggest we all take a trip to the wages office "she suggested. Nodding militantly we left en mass and arrived at the wages office, clutching our pay slips.

One of the senior accounts clerks, in a shiny grey suit which matched his receding silver hair listened to Val's speech sympathetically. He smiled sadly as he looked at our incredulous faces and explained that yes, we did have to pay tax and no, he was afraid there had been no mistake. After deductions, £12 was the correct amount. We shuffled away, muttering as we went. "Ridiculous. They can keep their Job!" Other derogatory phrases were bandied around but most of us knew in our hearts, that even with such a poor salary this was the career for us. After our day on the ward we could hardly wait until we finally finished PTS and became real nurses who worked on real wards with real patients. How eager we were.

Chapter 3:
St. P's

My first ward was away from my friends, in an outpost of the main hospital; and it was entirely my fault. We had been asked to let the tutors know if there was a particular group of friends we would like to stay close to for our first ward. Like a fool I didn't respond. I can't think why, except, that perhaps, I thought it would all work out for the best.

Now sitting in the back of Dad's car the familiar knot of anxiety began to churn in my stomach. It was a Sunday afternoon and we were heading for my placement on a men's surgical ward, in a small hospital specializing in Neurosurgery and Geriatric care. It was regarded as an integral part of the main hospital and although only 3 miles away, as the car pulled into the main gates, it could have been a million.

Later, lying on a hard bed in a strange room I wondered again how I could have been so stupid. Fighting back tears, I thought of Jane and Mary, chatting excitedly about their forthcoming "first day" on a ward, with all the buzz and familiarity of the main hospital, whilst I was here, knowing no-one.

My room was quite pleasant I decided, reflecting on the pastel shaded walls with coordinating soft blue curtains; a welcome change from the beige I had become so used to. Outside, the large grassed area which led from the nurse's home to the wards contained raised flower-beds. Brilliant red Geraniums contrasted with pastel coloured roses meandering along the edge of the concrete path. Flinging open the window, the scent of honeysuckle drifted into my room; a significant improvement from the cabbage smells of the main hospital.

I had also acquired a shiny silver electric kettle, standing proudly alongside two new blue-striped mugs and my old cake tin complete with Mum's homemade chocolate cake; my favourite. Yet I was still here alone; tomorrow at 7.30 I was to start on Ward 3, men's surgical and all I wanted was to be back at the main hospital with my friends. As I continued to feel sorry for myself, there was a knock on the door and outside stood Megan Jones and Clare Summerfield. They were Orthopods, now in my set, who had previously worked together in Wales.

"Home Sister told us you were here" Megan began, smiling "First to arrive eh? You're eager." I hoped they wouldn't notice my tear-stained face; if they did they were too kind to mention it.

Instead, Glenda said, "We didn't really get to know each other in PTS, but since we're in exile here, we thought we should have a cuppa and pass our last night of freedom together." Why not? Clutching my cake-tin I joined them.

In her room Megan was examining an old army jacket. It was scarlet with shiny brass buttons and a row of military ribbons across the chest. "I saw it at Portbello market this morning and I just had to have it" she said.

"Isn't it fabulous" then without waiting for a reply continued "I thought it would look good hanging on my wall". She hung it on a waiting hook, then reached into a paper carrier bag and took out 6 large oranges and put them in a wooden bowl. "And these" she continued "are the final touch to show-off the coat. Look at the colours."

I nodded politely trying to catch her enthusiasm. Coffee was made. Mum's cake devoured and the oranges brief career as 'l'objet d'art' ended as we ate them. From somewhere a bottle of wine appeared, and we christened my new mugs; suddenly it was bedtime. I returned to my room transformed from the miserable creature that left it; no longer alone and anxious, but part of Set 175. Tomorrow come what may, we would be there and ready to greet it.

Any feelings of euphoria disappeared when at 6:30 the following morning, a deafening ringing of the rooms alarm woke me. Breakfast here was definitely superior to the main hospital, but even the smell of frying bacon couldn't tempt me, and I nibbled cautiously on piece of dry toast. I kept looking at the clock, scared of being late, then I remembered Val's previous advice about never being early; sure enough at precisely 7.27, chairs started to scrape as the entire early shift, exited for the 3 minute walk to the wards. With racing heart, I joined them.

The ward was laid out in the classic 'Nightingale' style with its 28 beds lining the wards outer walls and central partition. Standing at its entrance behind the breakfast trolley I was conscious of 28 pairs of eyes watching me. Nurse Bowers, her white starched belt identifying her as a first year student probably only three months ahead of me, took pity on me.

"You our new PTS nurse?"

I nodded. "Nurse Cooper."

"Follow me" she commanded. "First Job is to give out breakfast."

I approached the first bed. "Hello would you like cornflakes or porridge?" The patient, a young man, the label above his bed stated that his name was Stuart, shook his head. "It's ok nurse. I'm down for a boiled egg this morning."

A second year nurse, in a striped belt was passing. She was glamorous with shiny blonde hair which bounced as she walked. Stuart's eyes followed her and speaking loudly so she could hear said "That is if blondey over there hasn't left them in too long again and turned them into golf-balls."

She turned looking severe "Its Nurse Stephens to you" she began "and I'll have you know my boiled eggs are the best."

The glint of humour in her eyes betrayed her. Stuart continued with his teasing "I think I'll reserve judgment."

She disappeared into the kitchen, but the mood for the day had been set and if a witty reply could be found, one was given. By the time the trolley had reached the end of the ward my "no-belt" status had been noticed and the patients whispered to each other "She's new." "Just started." I tried to look professional and ignore the comments, but they were onto me.

Later we assembled in the ward office for "Report". Sister Scott introduced me and said "It's good to have you here and I hope you'll enjoy working with us. If you have any concerns please don't hesitate to talk to either Staff-nurse or myself." I smiled trying to look confident, then listened carefully as Sister discussed each patient in turn, identifying their condition and any specific treatment they needed.

Report over Staff nurse took me to one side. "We have put you to work with nurse Bowers this morning. You are to do the washes. Stay close to her. She will explain how we work".

It did not take long to discover how the ward routine was organised and made to run like clockwork. Each nurse worked according to her seniority and ability. In later years, this method of work was labelled 'Hierarchal 'and 'Task Orientated' and replaced, in many cases, by 'Holistic Care' where each patient was cared for by a 'named nurse'. On ward 3 every nurse knew her place.

Heading the team was the ward co-ordinator; a trained nurse, usually Sister or Staff-Nurse. She was responsible for the overall shift. She took report from the Night Staff; allocated and oversaw the care needed by the patients; dealt with family and patient enquiries; liased between nursing and medical staff, as well as dealing with physios, occupational therapists, barbers, chaplains, cleaners... the list was endless. The co-ordinator kept up-to date facts about each patient at her fingertips. One of her first jobs of the day was to visit each patient on the ward, to enquire how they were and listen to their questions and concerns. On the whole, patients loved to be heard in this way; it made them feel valued and cared for.

Next Staff-nurse held the drug cupboard keys and gave out the medications, usually doing the drug-round with a student and, if time permitted using the time as an opportunity to teach. She often did the wards dressings, generally helping in the care of the patients and the supervision of the student nurses.

Second and third year students, (Striped belts) as it was a surgical ward, usually prepared patients for surgery, accompanying them and collecting them directly from the operating theatre. They performed the necessary 'observations' or 'obs' when the pulse rate and blood pressure were recorded to ensure no complications went unnoticed. Striped belts took charge of the ward in the absence of trained staff.

The 'underlings' in the nicest sense of the word, were the junior nurses (White belts and No- belts), who cared for patients basic needs and did whatever they were told to do to the best of their ability, or there was trouble.

Nurse Bowers took me under her wing. Bill had been washed earlier by the night staff. Four years previously he had been knocked off his motorbike, by a bus, fracturing his neck and paralyzing him from his neck downwards. He was only able to move his head and had been a patient on ward 3 for over a year. He had been transferred from a provincial hospital for a series of operations to debride and graft a huge pressure sore on his sacrum. I had learnt the theories about the prevention of pressure sores in PTS; now I saw the reality of what can happen without proper care. It is hard to imagine that lying in one position can cause so much trauma, but if a patient is not moved regularly the underlying area is starved of its blood supply. Initially it becomes red and feels uncomfortable, but if ignored the underlying tissues break done and become necrotic; sometimes to the extent that the whole area, right done to the bone becomes one huge wound.

The mainstay of our hospital policy was that a patient's position was changed every 2 hours. It was a serious event for a patient to develop a sore, as it was thought to be due to bad nursing care. Any nurses deemed to be negligent or accused of not carrying out the correct preventative measures would be summons to Matrons office; a terrifying thought.

In paraplegic patients, such as Bill, the problem is intensified because they are unable to move themselves at all or feel the discomfort that warns of a sore developing. Bill's sores were now healed and he was on the waiting list to be moved to a rehabilitation unit, but the list was long. Our task was to manage his care and prevent further sores from developing. The physiotherapist visited regularly and had given us a regime which meant we moved Bills limbs through a range of passive movements to reduce his muscles wasting. In addition Bill needed to be fed, washed and his bowel and urinary output managed.

Bill was Scottish and as I made my way to the sluice to collect the trolley of wash things he called me over. "Nurse" he spoke quietly and I had to lean my head next to his mouth. He said just one word "Bottle?"

I didn't understand what he meant. Bill began to get agitated "Bottle" he repeated, opening his eyes wide and trying to jerk his head to direct my gaze. Still not understanding what he needed my eyes scanned the locker top and I picked up a bottle of squash and showed it to him.

"Do you want a drink?" I asked.

"NO, Bottle, bottle" he repeated. His eyes looked down towards his lower body, so I cautiously lifted the bedclothes.

"Yes, yes" Bill encouraged. Then I saw a urinal wedged between Bills thighs to collect the urine as it dribbled from him, completely out of his control. He looked relieved. Is it alright?" he asked.

I looked at it and could see nothing wrong. "Yes Bill all ok" I replied. "Thank you, nurse. Thank you" he said sounding very grateful.

Later I recounted the episode to Nurse Bowers "Oh yes. He's always asking for us to check that. It's his mantra. You'll learn." It seemed I would.

I felt strangely confident as I pushed the trolley onto the ward. The green plastic bowls and receivers with the multi-coloured beakers reminded me of our first visit to the ward in PTS. It was reassuring. Nurse Cooper bustled up carrying a jug containing delicate pink mouthwash. "Great Job" she began, surveying the trolley "That looks about everything. Let's get started."

One of the most common operations carried out on ward 3 was 'Repair of an Inguinal Hernia. The inguinal canal is the channel in the groin through which the blood vessels to the testicles pass. A Hernia occurs when part of the bowel protrudes into this channel, usually appearing as a painless swelling in the groin. Although harmless in itself it was usually repaired surgically because if the bowel twisted the condition became an emergency, needing immediate surgery.

Gary, Pete and Dave were 3 young men recovering from the operation, in adjacent beds. Apart from extensive bruising in the groin area, they were relatively fit and seemed to be enjoying their hospital stay. We set them up to wash and shave independently. Today, we were to get them out of bed.

"Now then lads" Nurse Bowers began "Ring the bell when you've done as much as you can and we will come and finish you off."

Gary was quick with his reply "Finish us off. I thought you were supposed to make us better."

The others joined in the general laughter and it was several minutes before Nurse Bowers could make herself heard above their banter. "Fine" she continued "You know what I mean, joke taken, but listen as this is important. Before you get out of bed you need to wear a scrotal support. And "she added as an afterthought "Whatever you do don't get your dressing wet."

This information had a mixed reaction. There were cries of "You can fit my support anytime Nurse" and "Get out of bed?? You must be joking it hurts to just move."

We left them to wash as we had instructed and Nurse Bowers led me to the cupboard to introduce me to the world of scrotal supports. Stacked in neat piles were boxes of the devices, an adjustable elastic strap went round the abdomen and a mesh pouch supported the scrotum rather like a woman's bra supports her breast. Nurse Bowers sorted through them deftly "The trick is getting the right size" she explained.

The sizes varied considerably ranging from an S for the smallest to an XXXL for one that looked as if it would fit an elephant. We selected some mid-range ones and after demonstrating how they fitted, left one with each of the men. Initially all was quiet, but gradually we heard sounds of laughter from behind the screens. "Everything alright?" Nurse Bowers asked.

There was more laughter until eventually Pete answered "I don't know what you're trying to do to me nurse, but it's too small by a mile."

Nurse Bowers 'tutted' and disappeared behind the screens. She examined the packet then said "Well it says it's a large. I'd have thought that was fine for you."

Pete gave a wink. "You don't know me Nurse. I bet I need an extra large."

Once again we disappeared into the cupboard, but by now Gary and Dave had joined in the mayhem, each demanding the next size up. For a while chaos reigned as from behind the screens there were shrieks of laughter and cries of "It's no good lads, I'm going to need an XXL." And "Perhaps they don't make one big enough for me." Eventually the contest ended and each one of them became silent as fitted appropriately, they had to get out of bed. Laughter turned to "Ooh" and "Ouch", but they did get up and sat meekly as we made their beds. I realized then how great part laughter played in recovery and how humour helped our patients survive all the indignities they had to endure.

For the next few weeks on the ward my life seemed to be an endless round of dealing with the men's basic needs. All previous modesty and ignorance about how the male species functioned disappeared. I became proficient at "bottle rounds", collecting the used glass urinals from each bedside and exchanging it for a clean one which I carried in a special crate, rather like a milkman delivering milk. When needed there were bedpans to provide, assist the patient onto and finally take away and clean. For all these things we relied on the faithful bedpan washer, which with a loud clatter and several eruptions of steam cleaned the bottles and pans. Life would have been even more difficult without it. Having to clean manually would have been far worse, but when standing for the 20th time that shift, face reddened by the dubious smelling steam and waiting for the machine to stop, so I could load the next

2 in, it was hard to remember that. Our starched white aprons were our only protection against splashing and with no disposable rubber gloves available the repeated washing of our hands often made our skin red and sore.

Another prerogative of the junior muses was the "back-round". Visiting hour had just finished and most of the patients were still in bed. It was almost the end of a very busy shift when Nurse Bowers found me. "It's time for the back-round" she said. She disappeared into the sluice and emerged looking cross. "Typical" she began "The jar of back rub is empty. We'll have to make a new one." Collecting a large specimen jar from the cupboard, she took it into the kitchen. I followed to find her stabbing at the jars lid with a large tin-opener. She laughed "Yes this is how we do it. Technical isn't it."

Next in the utility room she mixed equal parts of arachis oil and surgical spirit in the jar, and she screwed the lid on tightly, and shook the jar vigorously mixing the oil and the spirit to make a pale cloudy solution shimmering with tiny goblets of oil.

The patients knew the procedure; those who were most immobile or ill didn't resist as we gently turned them onto their side and shaking the contents of the jar onto our hands, rubbed the solution vigorously into the skin of the sacrum to "restore the circulation". We moved from bed to bed. The more agile of our patients turned onto their side and bared their behind in readiness. Elbows and heels were also scrutinized and given a rub if at all red or dry. The system would be denounced in later years. Cries of "What about cross-infection?" or "Rubbing, damages the epidermis" would ring out, but at that time it appeared efficient and reliable, and incidents of pressure sores were virtually nonexistent in the hospital.

It would be no exaggeration to say that nurses, on the whole, were regarded by the general public, as 'angels'. The National Health System with its principle of free care at the point of need was popular. Nurses, though poorly paid, were held in high esteem by many who regarded Nursing as a vocation, rather than a career. Perhaps it was as because of this, we sometimes were able to enjoy a few 'perks'. Several London Theatres, for example, regularly sent their spare tickets to the hospital so that we could enjoy a free night out.

One afternoon I was in my room after an early shift, when I was summoned to the telephone. "Are you free tonight?" Mary asked.

"Actually I am "I replied "Why?"

"Well get your best clothes on and catch the transport over to the main hospital immediately" Mary instructed "because tonight we are off to the theatre." She paused for effect then continued "I've got free tickets to see 'The Mousetrap'.

I rushed back to my room, searching frantically through my wardrobe for an outfit that would label me as a 'regular theatre-goer'. My favourite dress needed a wash, so I chose a straight grey skirt, with a plain turquoise top. The colour suited me and by the time I had carefully applied some make-up, I felt good. Mary, when we met, was wearing her 'posh frock'; a floral number with dainty frills around the skirt and sleeves.

We had never been to the theatre before and arrived early, so we went to the bar and ordered Pepsi's. Sipping our drinks on plush velvet seats we were stunned at the sheer luxury of the place. Chandeliers glistened and soft velvet curtains trailed across the tall arched windows. Mary nudged me "Look over there".

In the corner two men dressed in black tuxedos, with dazzling white shirts and dark crimson velvet cummerbunds, were smoking cigars and laughing with the two ladies who sat with them. A waiter arrived with a bottle of sparkling wine, pouring it into shining tall glasses.

"I bet that's Champagne" Mary whispered.

I nodded, trying not to stare but Mary's observations continued. One of the ladies was wearing a fitted black dress which flashed and sparkled like a firework as its sequins reflected the chandeliers light. A grey fur stole was thrown casually over her shoulders. "Mink." Mary hissed but was interrupted by an announcement on the intercom warning that the performance was due to start.

We're in the stalls" Mary said, consulting the tickets.

The usher smiled and showed us to our seats. We settled down, but just before the curtain rose, we heard a volley of laughter as the 'champagne drinkers" entered and sat in the row behind us.

Mary pulled a face "I can't imagine how much these tickets cost" she whispered jerking her head towards our neighbours adding "I hope they don't know that ours were free."

For a moment I felt nervous, like a child caught doing something forbidden. I couldn't believe that we were surrounded by 'beautiful people' who must have paid lots for their tickets; what if... ? But there were no 'what ifs'. It was ok and I gradually relaxed and enjoyed this new experience.

It had been a wonderful evening, and we didn't want it to be over. Mary suddenly stopped. "I don't know about you Joy "she began "but I'm starving."

Of course, we had been so excited about getting to the theatre we hadn't actually eaten since lunchtime. We were passing a Wimpy Bar. "Let's go in here" Mary suggested "Hamburger and chips is cheap, and perhaps we could even have one of their milkshakes, Whippsys, I think they are called; Chocolate... Its heaven".

Inside we got our meal at the counter then found a red-formica topped table to enjoy our hamburgers, striped from the griddle, topped with greasy caramelized onions, stuffed inside a dry-looking white bread roll and finally wrapped in a white paper serviette. On the side was a cardboard box containing a pile of straw-coloured thin strips of fried potato. They smelt wonderful.

"These chips are a bit thin" I remarked.

"Chips? These aren't chips." Mary replied "these are fries. French fries to be precise. They're very superior to chips."

She took a slurp of her extra thick chocolate milkshake. It was so glutinous it needed an extra wide straw and even then Mary's neck muscles worked furiously as she drank. She lifted the top from the hamburger and inhaled deeply murmuring "Lovely... All it needs is a bit of tomato ketchup to give it that final touch."

I passed her the large red squeezy plastic tomato and she held it over her meal and squeezed expectantly; nothing happened. She tried again; still nothing. Looking cross she began to bang the container on the table.

"Dam things blocked" she said, repeating the bang but this time adding a squeeze to the process. As she did so a fountain of livid red tomato sauce shot into the air, and arcing like a missile, landed neatly on the back of the white trench coat worn by the man on the next table. Totally oblivious to the fact he now looked like a stabbing victim, he continued to eat. We stared at the coat, transfixed.

Mary was the first to react, her eyes scanned the room but it seemed that no-one was paying us any attention. "Eat up" she hissed "We need to leave."

I raised my eyebrows, trying to convey my silent question. "Should we tell him? Apologise?"

Mary shook her head, took one final slurp of her milkshake, grabbed the wrapped hamburger and container of fries and headed for the door. I followed, trying to look innocent, but feeling very guilty. We headed down the street eating our food in big mouthfuls, expecting any minute to hear shouts coming from the Wimpy Bar, but there were none. Our only reminder of the incident came later when dreadful indigestion prevented me from sleeping; but that particular eating venue remained out of bounds for at least a year.

The next day on the ward, I recanted the story. The patients seemed to like to hear of 'life on the outside 'and joined in, laughing; repeating it to their visitors later. I realised how I had transformed from the scared 'new girl' not many weeks before. I loved this Job. Every day was different; holding a new challenge.

My next first was giving an injection. I was dreading it; the fear still not entirely erased from my mind. Yes, I had injected a sandbag correctly, but could I inject a real patient and remain upright?

Staff Nurse took me aside saying "Mr Rider is going to theatre soon and he needs his pre-med. You haven't given an injection yet have you?" I shook my head, apprehension building. "Well" she said "this is a good time to start."

Together we unlocked the cupboards to get access to the phial of Omnopon and scopolamine usually prescribed prior to surgery. Omnopon is morphine based and therefore was controlled by the Dangerous Drugs Act (Known to us as DDA). The act demanded all drugs categorised as DDA's were stored in a special locked cupboard, within a cupboard. Each & every use had to be recorded and two nurses, one of which was trained (a State Registered Nurse), had to count all the ampoules and sign that the correct number were present. There was only one set of keys to the cupboard and these were usually kept by the trained Nurse in charge of the ward. "Who's got the keys?" was frequently heard during a busy shift. Woe betide anyone who left the ward in possession of them.

Staff nurse counted the ampoules and together we checked the patient's prescription. All was correct. Staff continued with the paper work while I drew up the medication. After rechecking the prescription we placed the syringe and a cotton wool ball soaked in surgical spirit in a receiver, and went to the patient's bedside.

Mr Rider was to have surgery to remove a malignant tumour from his large bowel; naturally he was very nervous. Ready for theatre, his screens had been drawn and he had bathed and changed into an open-backed gown. Rules required that no jewellery was worn and dentures had to be removed; he had put them in a pot on his locker. He was a well-built man, almost 6 feet tall, used to being independent and in control. Now he looked vulnerable and afraid.

Staff-Nurse took his hand "We're just going to give you a small injection in your thigh" she explained "it will help you relax and make your mouth dry, which is what the anaesthetist wants."

He nodded "OK, do your worst Nurse."

Inside my heart was pounding, but I forced myself to smile reassuringly and selected a site on the upper, outer area of the thigh. First I cleaned the area, and then with trembling hands stabbed the needle in at right-angles to the skin. It went in easily. I gently drew back the plunger to ensure I had not punctured a blood vessel, and then slowly delivered the injection. When the syringe was empty, I quickly withdrew the needle and massaged the area briskly with the cotton wool saying. "There all done." "Is that it Nurse?" he asked. " I hardly felt it. Thank you"

I felt elated. I had given an injection. A big smile crept over my face.

"Well done" Staff said "The first time is always the worst. You did very well."

My next 'first' was much more challenging and sad. Bert had been on the ward for several weeks, and it had become obvious that he was not going to leave. He had initially been admitted for surgery for a probable cancer of the stomach, but when the surgeon had operated it was obvious that the cancer had spread throughout his abdomen and no operation would cure that. The doctors had explained the situation to his family; it had been a hard time for them all.

Initially, the plan was for Bert to go home to enjoy some quality time with his family, but it soon became obvious that this was not to be. The wound was problematic and was not healing properly demanding regular dressing changes. He couldn't eat much and tired very quickly. Bert's wife, Sarah, a timid woman in her early 70's was distraught. Although she longed to have him at home, she feared she wouldn't be able to care for Bert in his current state.

Things came to a head when Bert became too weak to get out of bed. The doctors met with the family and he was moved to a side room, allowing visiting hours to be relaxed and giving the family the privacy they needed. For a few days Bert became king of the side ward, receiving a steady flow of visitors, who all wanted a chance to say their good-byes, give support or just pay their respect to a colleague, relative and friend. Bert must have been a good man, because he had many visitors and well-wishers. Sarah would sit at his bedside, face glowing with pride as yet another bunch of flowers arrived for her beloved Bert. But he grew weaker and soon the only visitors he could tolerate were his wife and Sally their daughter.

One day, coming on duty I felt the tension in the air as soon as I entered the ward. People spoke with hushed voices and the general atmosphere was sad. There was no joking or pranks that day. In report we learned that Bert had deteriorated further, his wife had been called in and he was not expecting to live the day. Bert died peacefully at 5pm. Sarah and Sally were with him. They held his hand and whispered his name, willing with every fibre of their being that he would not leave them, yet knowing that inevitably, he would. The blinds in the cubicle were drawn, the lamp switched to low. It was as if the world held its breath and waited. When the time came a silence descended on the ward that was tangible. The family left after a while, cups of tea could no longer sustain them as they huddled together in their grief.

Hospital life however continued. There were still patients to care for, tasks that needed doing. Despite this we snatched time to support each other. We'd pass in the sluice and whisper "You OK?" Sometimes a weak smile and a nod answered the question, at others a tear would escape and drip silently onto the starched bib of our apron or be brushed away impatiently by the back of the hand. On that day I saw very clearly the qualities a Ward Sister required. Although responsible for the everyday running of the ward with all its inherent disciplines Sister was also a warm, compassionate nurse. I watched as she cared for Bert's wife with sensitivity and concern and saw her gentleness with her staff and the patients, who although no-one said a word, seemed troubled and upset by Bert's death.

She called us into her office "I just wanted to check that you are all coping today" she began. "Bert's death was expected I know, but that doesn't make it easy and it is alright to feel upset. His wife was very grateful for the excellent care he received and I would like to re-iterate that and say thank-you too".

She went on to organise how we could cope with the extra work the death involved. She took me to one side. "Nurse Page, am I right in thinking this is your first experience of a patient dying?"

I nodded and she continued "Well I would like you to assist me to prepare Bert for the Mortuary."

Feeling very nervous I collected everything we would need on a trolley, and, Sister and I entered the heavily screened cubicle where Bert lay. We worked in silence, washing Bert and dressing him in the standard hospital shroud, its starchy, frilled ruffle-like collar framing his face like that of a chorister. His limbs were straightened and eyes gently closed to ensure he looked at peace. The bed-linen was changed and Bert was wrapped in a white sheet, secured down its edge with strips of thick white Zinc Oxide plaster.

Bert's belongings were cleared and placed on his locker ready to be packed and listed in the wards 'Patients Belongings Book', with copies that would be given to his family when they returned the next day to collect the Death Certificate. A large brown cardboard label, on which all Bert's details were written, was attached to his body. As a final gesture, Sister selected a single flower and laid it carefully on top of, the now enshrouded, Bert.

Our task completed, we pushed the trolley back onto the main ward again to an uncanny silence. Sister disappeared into her office and emerged to whisper to the assembled nurses, "The porters are on their way, please draw the screens."

Silently we dispersed, drawing the curtains around each patient's bed. No words were spoken, none were required, the patient's faces and eyes seemed to acknowledge what was needed and for that short time, no bells rang.

The porters arrived looking sombre and tense: this time there were no jokes to tell or gossip to recount. They pushed a low, grey metal box-like trolley into the cubicle where Bert lay. Once inside the box was opened and with great care Bert's body was lifted into the trolley and the lid was closed. A further hand-written card containing Bert's details was handed to the senior porter, who nodded to acknowledge everything was in order. Sister, with bowed head led the sad procession from the ward, into the lift and thence to the mortuary; we remained at the entrance of the ward our young faces reflecting the sobriety of the occasion; the patients, hidden from view,` tensed as the squeaking wheels of the retreating trolley broke the deafening silence.

Somehow the shift continued and I was relieved when it was time to go off-duty. That day it was good to live in the Nurses Home, surrounded by others who understood the feelings stirred up by Bert's death. At first all I wanted to do was flop on my friend's bed and discuss what had happened over the inevitable cups of coffee. But after supper Megan and Glenda decided that a distraction was necessary. "We need to go out." Megan began "I know it's been a sad day, but you mustn't let the ward take over your life."

Glenda produced a newspaper and suddenly we were on the way to the cinema. There we allowed Omar Shariff as Dr. Zhivago fill our minds and our senses. As the credits rolled I was not sure if I was crying for Bert or the film, but whatever it was, Megan had been right; it was right to have gone out.

Sleep came hard that night. Brought up in a Christian family; my parents were actively involved in the local Baptist church we attended. My father was a deacon and a Sunday school superintendent. My whole home life had revolved around 'church' and I had become a Christian too. I had arrived at the hospital feeling I knew what I believed about life and death; now I was less sure. As I lay gazing at the ceiling, waiting for sleep I couldn't help but question my beliefs. Life somehow didn't seem so simple now.

Chapter 4:
Geriatrics

I felt sad. I had spent 12 weeks on ward 3. Today was time to move to Ward 5; female Geriatrics. First wards were special. I would miss its informality and friendliness. Ward 5, too, promised to be an entirely different experience, and if rumours could be believed, not necessarily a good one.

1967 geriatric wards were the backwater of the medical world. Most patients were there to receive long-term care where chronic illnesses and associated confusion made treatment difficult. Few beds were available in nursing homes and since most patients were not well enough to go home they had been on the ward for months and in some cases, years.

I had the week-end off before starting on "Geri's" as it was unofficially called. At home I was spoilt by my parents, enjoying hours of sleep, cherishing the now, unaccustomed feel of soft, clean sheets and a sprung mattress. Having breakfast in bed with sunlight streaming into the room; drinking tea and eating warm toast with lashings of golden butter dripping from it, did little to prepare me for what lay ahead.

The first thing I noticed was the smell which hung in the air like mist hovering over a stream in winter. It defied all attempts to mask it with sprays or deodorizers, catching in the back of your throat and making your eyes water and sting in protest. It was an aroma you could eventually accept, yet never completely ignore. It was well-known that the first thing nurses from these wards did when coming off-duty was bathe and change out of their uniform.

The ward consisted of 4 six-bedded rooms leading from a long, central corridor, and 4 single rooms which housed patients too ill or disruptive to be nursed with others. Sister sat, in her office at the wards entrance.

She smiled briefly as I entered. "You're our new nurse I presume?" I nodded politely. "You'll be with Nurse Meredith today. Make sure you follow her very closely."

As if on cue Nurse Meredith entered, her striped belt stretched tightly across her ample waist. Sister, looking annoyed, said "Nurse Meredith, you're here at last." She glanced at the ward clock then continued. "You're on today with Nurse Cooper; it's her first shift so you'll need to take her under your wing. You are very fortunate; Staff-nurse Pearson is doing a split, so they'll be three of you." She glanced once more at the clock then continued "We'd better get on with report, we haven't got all day."

Nurse Meredith looked at me over the top of her black-framed spectacles and I thought I saw the briefest of winks. She handed me a piece of paper and for the next 10 minutes I scribbled frantically, trying to make sense of what Sister was saying. The moment report was over, Sister and the rest of the early shift disappeared to lunch, leaving me alone with Nurse Meredith. Turning to me, a smile lit up her face. "Hi. It's Anna to you.

Hope you are feeling fit. You need to be strong on this ward."

Laughing I replied "I might be strong but I'm not sure I can bear the smell."

Anna sniffed tentatively "Oh you'll get used to that." I must have looked unconvinced because she laughed and touched my shoulder briefly "Come with me. You'll soon find out about smells."

She disappeared into the sluice and emerged with a huge stainless steel trolley, on top of which stood a shiny wash basin, soap, a roll of brown cotton wool and a collection of huge plastic tubs of cream. On the lower shelf was pile upon pile of white bed linen and folded garments, some plain, some of which looked as if once, before being subjected to a vigorous laundry regime, they might have been floral. All had a slit running down the back, beginning just beneath the shoulder blade.

Pushing the trolley we entered the six-bedded ward at the far end of the corridor. "Afternoon Ladies" Nurse Meredith began. Silence, except one lady dressed in a garment identical to those on the trolley. She was bent forward in her armchair, rocking rhythmically and with each movement she said one word "Joe?" She repeated the name like a mantra. Anna knelt at her side and gently stroked the lady's soft silver hair which was tied back from her face with an old pink satin ribbon. "Bessie, Bessie" Anna spoke directly into the woman's ear "It's time you went to bed for a rest. Is that ok?"

Bessie stiffened "Is that you Joe?" she asked.

Anna tried again "No Bessie it's not Joe. You're in hospital. Can you remember? We want to help you into bed for a rest? Will you help us?"

Bessie looked into Anna's face as if trying to understand. She became agitated "Who are you? I don't know you? You're not Joe."

"No Bessie we're not Joe. We're the nurses. Can we help you into bed? Wouldn't you like a little rest?"

Bessie remained silent; Anna signalled for me to take Bessie's arm. Making soothing noises we gently helped her from her chair. All seemed to be going according to plan, when suddenly Bessie's knees gave way and her legs slid uncontrollably like those of a rag doll. Anna, moving swiftly , placed her own foot at right angles to Bessie's and in the same movement supported Bessie's knees with her own knee easing them back into the upright position. We both took a step to the bedside, moving Bessie with us. Suddenly Bessie panicked and struggled to free herself from our grip.

She managed to pull herself from my hold and with her free arm was lashing out at us shouting "Leave me alone. Who are you? I'll tell my Joe".

At that moment there was nothing I would have liked more but Bessie would have fallen. Anna meanwhile looked calm and continuing her gentle melody of soothing noises managed to get Bessie to the bed and flipped her legs onto the mattress to prevent her from sliding onto the floor. Signalling to me to remain where I was, she crossed to the other side and together we eased Bessie into the centre of the bed and safety. Once in this position we realized that her clothes and incontinence pads were soaking wet. Bessie herself was oblivious to this, and seemed exhausted. As we watched she pulled the blanket around her shoulders and entreating Joe to appear, fell into a deep sleep like a child.

Anna began to pull back the screens "We'll have to leave her in wet clothes for a while" she instructed "She is exhausted but at least she's asleep now, poor love. We'll have to try to get back to her before visitors arrive. Perhaps it will be a bit easier once she's had a rest."

I nodded in agreement. It was not ideal, but in the circumstances it seemed cruel to disturb Bessie again, besides, we still had at least 15 more patients to deal with before the early shift got back from lunch and visiting hour began.

Anna, head down and looking as if she was going into battle, grabbed our trolley and marched ahead to the next room. So, our work continued as we helped the other ladies onto their beds changing pads and clothing as necessary. The early shift arrived back just as we had pushed our trolley into the sluice, and started to clear it by sorting the dirty linen into either of two huge bags which hung from iron-framed trolleys, ready to be collected by the porters later. Into one we put wet linen, but if it was soiled it went into the one identified by a thick red stripe around its circumference.

I was just wiping down the top of the trolley when Sister appeared in the doorway. "Make sure the linen is sorted correctly" she began "We've had complaints from the laundry. The soiled linen goes into a completely different sort of wash, and if you put it in the wrong container you are putting staff at the laundry at risk." She glared at us making me feel immediately guilty of some heinous crime. "So be warned" she continued "I am organizing spot checks to ensure we comply."

Turning she swept out of the room.

"Yes Sister" Anna and I replied in unison to her retreating back.

Anna was humming gently to herself as we restored the sluice to some sort of order. I didn't dare to speak. I caught sight of my reflection in the stainless steel of the bedpan washer. My face was red and shiny and my hair stuck out in wisps under my cap, which was perched at a strange angle on my head. I had only been on this ward for an hour and yet I felt completely exhausted, and the smell which had seemed so odious when I arrived now seemed to be a part of me and was seeping from my pores.

Inside my head, sentences were forming which I dared not express; "You put the laundry staff at risk"

What about us? It's the nursing staff who put the soiled linen in the bins in the first place, what about the risk to us?

It was visiting hour and as we passed Sisters office, we noticed a lady in a purple coat with a matching hat was speaking to Sister, who looked far from pleased. Thinking no more of it we carried on filling in the fluid balance charts of the patients who had been wet when we put them to bed. Although this was an inaccurate measure, we needed to ensure that a patient's intake and output correlated. If their output fell this could indicate either they were not drinking enough or, more seriously that their kidneys were not working properly.

I looked up and saw Sister marching towards us with determined strides. She didn't look happy and my apprehension increased when she said "Nurse Meredith, Nurse Cooper. Please come to my office at once."

She turned abruptly and we followed wondering what it was all about. Once inside she shut the office door firmly, and sat down. I noticed that her cheeks were flushed as she began

"Nurse Meredith, I have just had the daughter of Mrs. Greenway make a formal complaint to me, regarding the state in which she found her mother today." Anna and I stood together shoulders touching; I felt Anna begin to tremble as Sister continued "Her mother was lying on top of her counterpane, covered by a blanket with soaking wet clothes on." She paused and realizing that she must be talking about Bessie, I waited for Anna to tell her what had happened.

"But Sister"... Anna began.

"No nurse. There are no buts. You, as the senior nurse on the ward at the time were responsible for the patients, and you should have ensured Mars Greenway was not left in wet clothes."

"Sister" again Anna started to talk. "Nurse Meredith, I don't want to listen to any excuses. It is not good enough. I do not expect to have complaints made about my ward because of lazy nurses. Do you understand?"

Sister Bells face was now a deep red and I could see a blood vessel pulsating in her temple. So vehemently had she spoken, that tiny globules of saliva had cascaded from her mouth into the air. I opened my mouth to speak, but the words died on my lips, as she stared at us. I felt simultaneously very afraid and very angry and was grateful when, with a wave of her hand, she said "Get out of my sight. Take yourselves off to tea." We left her office silently and neither of us spoke until we had left the building.

We remained silent until we were sitting in the relative safety of the dining room. I noticed Anna's hand was still shaking as she sipped her tea. I could bear no more. "What a bitch" I began "That was totally unfair. She just wouldn't listen to you".

Anna smiled grimly "Didn't anyone tell you about Sister Bell? She's useless. She'll never stick up for her staff, and then when the doctors come in she's all over them like a rash. It's gross"

"But how do you put up with being spoken to like that?"

Anna shrugged "You have to learn to I'm afraid Joy. Don't take it to heart. I think we did what was right for Bessie so she," she jerked her head in the general direction of the ward "can say what she likes."

I sat quietly considering what Anna had said; she continued "Truth Is Sister is stuck in a hard place. Theoretically she tells us we should challenge the patients when they ramble on, as they do. She was giving out the meds last week and Bessie started to ask her if she were Joe. She leant over and said into Bessie's ear "No Mrs Greenway. My name is Sister Bell. I'm in charge of this ward. Joe was your husband but he has died." I looked shocked but Anna carried on "Well that is correct. Joe died 5 years ago, but poor Bessie has no memory of that. She was distraught. She sobbed all afternoon. Sister just left her to it."

We sat in silence, it all sounded so awful. "Sisters problem is she can't cope when reality doesn't fit in with her clever theories" Anna explained quietly. I sighed. This ward was proving to be a challenge and at that moment I wasn't sure it was one I could rise to.

Doubts or not, tea-break was over. We hurried back to the ward, and tried not to cross paths with Sister Bell. We needn't have worried; she was obviously avoiding us too and spent the rest of the shift in her office. At 5pm Staff Nurse Pearson arrived back on the ward for the rest of her 'split shift'; having worked the morning she was now returning to work the evening. She certainly had the short straw as the workload was heaviest in the morning and the evening but it was wonderful to have three pairs of hands to manage 28 dependent patients; often the late shift had to cope with just two.

Our shift ended at 9.45 and I made my way to the nurse's home too tired to even speak. Lying on the bed I rested my aching legs on a pillow in an attempt to stop them throbbing. The next thing I remember I was terribly cold and it was 4am. Pulling the bedclothes over myself I tried to settle back to sleep before the alarm woke me again at 6.30am and another day on ward 5.

Meal times, in the hospital, were one of the busiest times of the day. The porters would push huge steel heated trolleys from the kitchen, and plug them in on the main corridor of the ward. This was a sacred time and no-one dared interrupt the routine. The Nurse-in-charge would officiate, standing on a stool, and serving each meal individually to each patient according to his choice from the day's menu. Nurses stood meekly in queues with kitchen maids, tray in hand ready to serve the patients. Good nutrition was an important part of patient care and a key part of recovery. By having such control the Nurse-in-charge could identify and address any problems.

However on Ward 5, the whole system was in danger of collapse. Most patients were unable choose what they would like to eat, and many couldn't feed themselves. Each nurse was usually allocated a ward housing 5 patients, and it was their task to ensure each patient had their meal. That was easier said than done, as many of the patients were very confused. Theory taught us to sit with each patient, to ensure they did not feel hurried, and feed them, describing, as you did so, what you were doing and what food they were receiving. However on ward 5 this was just another theory which failed in practice. More often a nurse would sit with a group of patients encouraging them to eat their meal and assisting those who needed feeding often offering a spoon to one, then the next and so forth, until all the patients had eaten. Sadly our attempts to 'encourage' often fell on deaf ears and it was not uncommon to have meals thrown on the floor or food spat at us. It was a very complex problem.

One dinnertime Staff-nurse approached me. "Have you been shown how to do the tube feeds Nurse Cooper?"

I shook my head. I was aware that on one of the wards all the patients had a thin plastic tube; a naso-gastric tube. This had been passed via their nose into their stomach and taped securely in place. These patients were deemed unable to eat adequately to survive and were therefore tube-fed.

"Come with me" Staff instructed "and I'll show you what to do."

Following her into the kitchen we found 4 cartons labelled 'N/G Feeds' which had been sent from the diet kitchen.

"Great these are what I was looking for. The diet kitchens send us up liquidized food hopefully, although they do sometimes forget and we have to improvise". She took 4 plastic jugs from the cupboard and emptied the cartons contents into them lifting them until they were eye-level. "They each have about 300 mls of the stuff." She said, stirring the mixture gently, then she splashed a drop onto her inner wrist saying "It needs to be tepid". Satisfied all was well she, put the jugs onto a tray and headed towards the ward.

"Basically it's simple" she explained "the food needs to be of the right consistency, with no lumps. That's important. These tubes aren't very wide and they block easily, then they're a real pain to clear. The last thing you want is to have to take the tube out and re-pass it. It's a nightmare to do."

I nodded, suddenly feeling quite anxious that I could be responsible for blocking the tube. "Obviously, the diet kitchen does monitor its consistency, but I tend to add a bit of water. Better safe than sorry don't you think?"

Not waiting for my reply, she entered the ward and made her way towards the first bed.Hilda lay in foetal position. Her head, resting on a pillow, looked out of proportion to the rest of her emaciated body. A thin clear plastic tube protruded from one of her nostrils for about 6 inches, with an incongruous bright blue spigot, acting as a bung, in its end. Her nose was hidden beneath heavy strips of white zinc oxide tape which anchored the tube into position. Staff-nurse moved to the sink to wash her hands and I followed.

"Hilda had a CVA (Cerebral Vascular Accident commonly known as a Stroke) several months ago." She explained "Every time she had any fluids, she choked, so passing an NG tube was the only way she could be fed. She's very frail now, as you can see. She's not really aware of anything. It's a hard situation, especially for her family. Her poor husband couldn't take it. He rarely visits now."

She sighed and I could feel her pain. I looked across the ward, at the other patients, all of whom were thin and frail, lying motionless in the starchy whiteness of a hospital bed. Staff-nurse followed my gaze. "That's Elsie, Gladys and Ethel" she pointed to each in turn "Each have a similar story to Hilda. These feeds are what are keeping them alive."

She shrugged, and drying her hands vigorously, said "Well we'd better get on. When you get time you can look up their notes in Sisters office. Now watch, what I'm doing. I'll explain it all. Then if you're happy, you can give Gladys her feed."

At Hilda's bedside, Staff removed the spigot from the tube and connecting a large plastic syringe, withdrew a small amount of fluid, which she squirted onto a strip of litmus paper that was in tray on Hilda's locker.

"First you aspirate some fluid to make sure the tube hasn't been misplaced. If it's gastric it will turn blue litmus paper pink." I watched, fascinated, as the strip of paper turned pink. "Great! We are aspirating gastric contents. The last thing Hilda needs is for us to pour her feed into her lungs".

She smiled, but I suddenly realised what disastrous consequences could follow such a routine job. "Right" Staff continued, "So we've checked the tube is patent and in the right place. Now all we have to do is give Hilda her lunch." She removed a plastic funnel which had some pink rubber tubing attached, from a stainless steel bowl on the locker and continued. "Make sure the connectors at the bottom fit tightly into Hilda's tube, and" she Joined the tube together, then pointed to a steel clamp-like clip, with a screw in the centre "we can regulate the flow by adjusting this gate clip."

She moved closer to the bed. "Hello Hilda" she began "its dinnertime. I hope you are feeling hungry."

Hilda didn't move or show any sign that she had understood what had been said. Staff-nurse carefully filled the funnel and tubing with some water from the jug on the locker, kinking the tubing as she did so.

"You need to expel the air first, and then flush the tube." she explained speaking as she worked. Finally she connected the feeding tube to Hilda's. She released the clamp and watched as the fluid level fell, at which point she started to pour the feed in adjusting the clamp as she did so. "It's important to give the feed slowly. We don't want to give you indigestion do we Hilda?"

Again there was no response. I watched silently for the next 15 minutes as Staff completed her task. "Right, your turn now." She said as she began to clean the equipment and leave everything ready for Hilda's next meal.

"Dinner time Gladys" I had managed to remember all the basic instructions and observed by Staff, I gave Gladys her feed via the NG tube.

"Well done "Staff said as I finished, "Are you confident enough to give Elsie her meal?" I hesitated, and then nodded, just as Anna's head appeared around the door.

"Phone-call Staff" she said "Shall I take a message?"

Staff shook her head "No I'll take it" and as she left the room continued "Just carry on Nurse Cooper. You're doing fine. I'll try not to be too long"

It was quiet in the empty ward as I continued my task. Elsie, like her neighbours did not respond to anything I did or said. As I stood next to her, watching the liquid disappear into the tube, I felt overwhelmed.

I had been so excited to master a new skill; it was another tick in my official "Record Book of Practical Procedures" and something to boast about later, yet the excitement had now vanished to be replaced by sadness as I cared for Ethel my last patient. I could imagine these ladies in their prime; as wives, mothers and grandmothers and friends each with a life to lead and a story to tell. Now the families and friends who loved them seldom visited unable to bear the pain of seeing the shell of the person they loved. Of course we fed them, moved them, washed them, changed their pads when they were soiled; yes they were alive and they were still people, but what quality of life did they have? I pushed the thoughts to the back of my mind. I am a nurse, I reminded myself. My job is to care for people, I can do no more. To survive this ward this mindset would be essential.

In reality I didn't have to try too hard to ignore my doubts as the endless physical effort required to care for the patients on ward 5 left me too tired to think. My only desires off duty were hot baths and sleep; and still I was constantly exhausted. .

After what felt like an eternity I had just a week left on ward 5 my spirit lifting with every minute. Soon I'd be back with Mary and Jane for a 6 week 'study block' at the school of nursing; regular hours; weekends off; lie-ins and a break from caring for 28 dependent patients. I could hardly wait.

It was in this mood that I arrived on the ward, the next day for a late shift. Nothing much had changed, but then again not a lot did change on this ward.

It was 'Bath' day and it was our happy job to give 6 patients their weekly bath. Anna and I emerged from the office grim-faced. "Great we're down to bath Jess, Edith and Sarah, for starters" she said "I hope you've had a good lunch you are going to need all the strength you can get."

I shrugged "You know, I don't think Sister likes us. How come we get all the heavy patients all the time?"

Anna nodded "I don't think she's ever forgotten the Bessie episode, but don't take it personally, let's just get on, thinking will only depress us."

Jess was sitting next to her bed, smiling sweetly, when we arrived with a wheelchair. She was a large lady of 85 who had been admitted after being found wandering down her local High Street, on a cold winter's morning, wearing only her nightie. Initially treated with anti-biotics for an acute urine infection she still suffered episodes of confusion. Her daughter, a slight woman with mousey brown hair, had wept for days when she realized that Jess was unsafe to be on her own at home. So Jess had remained on ward 5; her name on the waiting list for a place in a Nursing Home with little prospect of one becoming available.

Our job was to care for Jess and part of this care meant keeping her clean. Cleanliness, especially in her latter years, had not been high on Jess's agenda and subsequently washing and changing her clothes was often a battle.

"Hello Jess" Anna began brightly "We're going to give you a bath."

"Don't need one" she replied. Her blue crimplene dress was spattered with the remains of the mince she had eaten for lunch.

Anna pointed at the stains "Look" she began "You've spilt some dinner down your dress. We'll put a clean one on for you."

Looking in the locker she found a dress in a similar style, but this time it was pink. She showed it to Jess. "You'll look nice in this one. You're daughter might be coming in later. It will be good to look clean?"

Jess looked uncertain, but after staring for a while at Anna's kind face, nodded. Anna looked triumphant and together we quickly helped Jess into the wheelchair. She was one of the few patients on the wards who could weight-bear and remain upright for a couple of minutes, although walking was out of the question. I started to run a warm bath, using antiseptic soap supplied by pharmacy.

The large white, high-sided bath stood in the centre of a square room, with the inevitable clinical white tiles on the wall and a window too high to see out of. It looked far from inviting, but Jess was quite relaxed as we undressed her. Carefully placing the wheelchair at the end of the bath, we lifted her legs into the warm soapy water and, standing either side of her lifted her gently into the bath. Jess beamed at us both.

"Shall we wash your hair?" Anna asked.

Again Jess nodded. I had just finished wetting her long grey locks and was rubbing in the green medicated shampoo when there was a knock on the door and Staff's head appeared. "Sister wants to see you in her office, Nurse Cooper" I hesitated indicating my wet hands, but Staff continued "You'd better hurry; you know what she's like. I'll take over from you here"

Anxiously I hurried to her office wondering what I had done wrong. If Sister asked to see you in her office it was seldom good news. She looked up from the off-duty rota as I entered. "Nurse Cooper" she began. "We have a bit of a crisis I'm afraid. Our junior on nights has gone off sick. She can't really be spared, so I have informed the office that you will take her place." I began to object but she continued "Tomorrow you will start Nights, working until the weekend, when I understand you finish on ward 5."

With a wave of her hand she dismissed me. As I left her office I heard shouting coming from the bathroom "Help Police. Help. They're killing me" the door opened and a dishevelled Anna appeared pushing Jess, who was still shouting. Anna pulled a face "It's not fair is it Jess."

Exactly. It wasn't fair. At that moment nothing seemed fair, but I had no choice but to comply.

Nights meant working with Nurse Briggs. Initially I was apprehensive as I could not imagine how I would cope working all night but when Nurse Briggs discovered this, she took me under her wing.

"You'll be ok." she reassured me "And forget the Nurse Briggs, its Sue; it's much less formal on Nights." I soon discovered that nights was basically the same hard physical slog of changing pads, beds and making patients comfortable. Everything took longer though because it was dark and we didn't want to wake everyone up, we crept around noiselessly. As soon as we had finished one round of turning and changing everyone, it was time to start another.

We had a new patient however. Mrs Finn was 80. Leg and back injuries from World War 2 meant that she found it difficult to walk. Despite this she had managed to be fairly independent, but following the recent death of her husband, life had become much more difficult. The final straw came when she developed a urinary infection, which made her ill and confused. Her Doctor had been called by worried neighbours, and had found her sitting huddled in a wet armchair, in a cold house with no food in the cupboards. She was admitted to the ward for antibiotics for her infection and general care and assessment.

As we began the drug round, Mrs Finn was asleep, snuggled down in bed, her curly silver hair like a halo. "Mrs Finn" I gently touched her shoulder and was surprised to find myself looking into startling blue eyes. "I'm one of the night nurses" I explained "The doctors want you to take these tablets. They're antibiotics for your water infection."

She nodded and opened her mouth. I put the tablets in her mouth and gave her some water from the spouted plastic beaker on the locker. "It's important you drink lots too" I added and she obediently took a big gulp.

"I don't think she'll be any trouble" I remarked to Sue "She's a sweetie. It's good to have a co-operative patient."

We finished giving out the medications and settled everyone down for the night. Sue dimmed the lights and the ward was plunged into semi-darkness.

It was time to do some paperwork and have a quick cup of tea, before the next onslaught of turns and changing pads. One of the anomalies of our profession, I found was the high proportion of nurses who smoked. I remembered that over half of my sets hands shot up when, in PTS, the Medical Consultant had asked the question. He had looked stern saying, "You do realize do you not, that smoking causes Heart attacks, High Blood Pressure and various types of cancer to name but a few?"

There had been embarrassed nods from the guilty parties, but somehow it wasn't enough to deter them. It was the 60's; smoking was cool and helped people relax; 'Come on, do us a favour, what are you worrying about?' was the attitude.

On days, it was no problem to find somewhere to smoke. It was allowed in the Nurses home and even in the canteen. But Nights were difficult. The hours spent on the ward with just one break made smoking impossible. As I walked into the office with our tray of tea, Sue jumped and blushed. "Oh it's only you" she began "I thought it was Sister."

She opened the drawer and I was surprised to see a curl of smoke released and spiral up to the ceiling. "I was desperate for a fag" she began adding "We have to be careful on Nights, but I can't manage all night with only one ciggie." She inhaled deeply "We've got a system though." She opened the top drawer of the desk again and I saw placed in the corner was a half glass of water and a pair of scissors.

Seeing me stare, she smiled. "It's simple really. When I'm desperate I come in the here and light up, then if I hear Sister approach I open the drawer cut the tip of the cigarette and drop it into the water. We all do it. Never been caught yet; although I think they may be turning a blind eye." She jerked her thumb in the general direction of Matrons Office where Night Sister worked from "I reckon they feel sorry for us and choose to ignore it."

She was silent for a while then added as an after-thought, "If the ward had a verandah or something I'd go out there, but this one doesn't, so I have to make do." "Doesn't anyone ever notice the smell?" I asked crinkling my nose up, at which she produced a large can of air freshener from under her chair and sprayed it liberally around the office.

"No that generally sorts that out." she laughed.

A little later, Sue had finished her cigarette and we were sitting in the office sipping our tea, when a terrible scream made us jump to our feet. I felt the hairs on the back of my neck stand out as, torch in hand we rushed down the ward to find the source of the noise. As we entered the room we found Mrs. Finn sitting up, her eyes wide open in terror. She was shaking and a fine film of moisture clung to her forehead, I took her hand

"Mrs. Finn, what is it? What's the matter? Can you tell me?"

There was no reply, except for another heart-rending scream. I gently wiped the sweat from her forehead, making soft soothing sounds as I did so. Sue pulled the screens round her bed and turned on her overhead light to low mode. Gradually Mrs. Finn relaxed. When her eyes closed and she seemed asleep I uncurled her wrinkled fingers from my hand and retreated silently.

I left the ward for my meal-break just as Night sister arrived to do a round of the patients. The hour passed quickly and as I approached the ward on my way back, I heard the screaming again.

In the office Sue shrugged. "I don't know why she's screaming again" she said. "We've done her obs and they are all normal. I've sat with her and tried to calm her down but nothing seems to help. Sister made me turn her light off. She said it was disruptive for the other patients. Typical, Sister goes and the screaming starts again."

Wrapping herself in her grey cloak, she picked up her bag and headed out of the office "Sorry Joy" she began "But I must have my break. Do your best and if you're worried you'll have to bleep Sister. OK? She'll probably get the doctor to do a verbal order for some sedation. Perhaps a shot of Largactil will do the trick." She smiled as she waved goodbye.

The sound of the screaming was dreadful; I made my way to Mrs. Finn's bed and switching her light on, sat beside her, gently stroking her hands. Gradually she became quiet, and seemed to drift into sleep. I crept out, but fearing Sisters wrath, switched her light off. I hadn't even reached the office before the terrified noises began again. I rushed back, switching on the bed-light as I did so. This time I noticed that Mrs. Finn seemed to relax once the light was on, so as I left this time, I did not turn it off.

Back in the office, I started to flick through the thick wad of paper that was Mrs. Finn's notes. Several pages of Doctors scrawl seemed to date from her initial injury, during the war. Struggling to decipher the hand writing, I found to my amazement, the perfect account of how, during the blitz, she had been at home alone when her house suffered a direct hit from a German bomb. She was sheltering in an indoor Anderson shelter and was dug from the rubble after being buried for more than 8 hours. 'Could this' I wondered 'explain her terror. And could it be, as it appeared, that being in the darkness made the fear worse?'

I discussed it with Sue when she returned from her break, and she in turn with Night-Sister and it was agreed that for the time being we leave Mrs. Finns night light on. For my last few shifts on ward 5, I never had to experience that heart-breaking scream again.

Chapter 5:
Normal working hours

The pattern of our training meant that after working on the wards for 6 months, we returned to the School of Nursing for a 'Study-Block' or 'Block' as we called it. During these precious 4 weeks set 175, re-assembled in the classroom and enjoyed working 9-5, Monday to Friday, with every weekend off. Even the least academic became excited at the luxury of having evenings to ourselves and a break from the early morning alarm. We were even allowed to wear our own clothes and were only too happy to leave our uniforms to gather dust.

Protocol dictated that we studied each of the main systems of the body. Anatomy and physiology were taken by our nursing tutors and were followed up by lectures from the Consultants, covering the various diseases associated with that part of the body. For example after studying the respiratory system, a medical consultant would lecture about conditions such as Bronchitis and how it was treated. Next we could expect to learn about how to care for patients with these specific illnesses. The analogy, if it was perfect, would mean that following 'block' we would all be placed on a medical ward and so back our knowledge up with practical experience. However this idea was faulted because, although students, we were a vital part of the hospitals working force and were actually sent where we were needed. By the end of our training, however, the General Nursing Council(or GNC in its shortened form) stipulated that we needed to have worked in all the key areas of the hospital.

Despite our limited experience, it seemed the NHS was undergoing a period of change. When it was established in 1948, hospital nursing administration was governed mainly by a senior nurse known as Matron; this was still the case. Matron was all power-ful: responsible for all aspects of a nurses training, as well as the general running of the hospital wards. Nurses, ward maids, and even doctors would scurry away to avoid confrontation with Matron as she toured the wards, her watchful eye ready to pounce on anyone daring to lower their standards in any way.

Striking like a kestrel snatches a mouse from the field she would suddenly appear with comments like "Nurse, I hope that is not lipstick I can see on your mouth". The stricken nurse would stop and stand silently, staring at the ground unable to reply. "Report to my office in the morning at 9a.m. sharp".

Matron would instruct, turning abruptly, leaving her victim looking shocked. Or "Nurse your hair. It needs pulling back out of sight. Report to my office."

What actually happened in her infamous office was not often recounted but it was a rare for a nurse to repeat her 'crime.'

However, in the 60's the Minister of Health decided to set up a committee under the chairmanship of Mr. Brian Salmon 'to advise on the senior nursing staff structure in the hospital service i.e. Ward Sisters and above'. This report ultimately weakened the role of Matron. No-one was safe from the change in the air.

There were now 2 sets below us and we enjoyed having people junior to ourselves. We spent many hours discussing our careers and looking back at how far we had come. I loved being back at the main hospital and close, once again, to Mary and Jane; there didn't seem enough hours in a day to catch up on all our news. One evening as we lay on Mary's bed, sipping coffee, she suddenly said "How is it that in all hospital fiction, there are loads of romances between doctors and nurses. What are we doing wrong?"

Jane yawned "Well, I know a few in our set have a bloke, but I don't know anyone that's going out with a doctor."

I laughed "Me neither, though Barbara has so many dates I can't keep up. Perhaps they're all medics."

"No" Jane said, "No I don't think it's us. You must confess there seems a strict pecking order in the hospital. Doctors are high in the equation, the more senior they are, the more remote they seem to be to the nurses, well our level nurses anyway."

"You're right" Mary agreed. "Student nurses and medical students are right at the bottom of the pile."

Jane and I nodded, and a comfortable silence descended on the room.

Mary moved to the window. Situated on the second floor as we were, if you craned your neck you could just catch a glimpse of the sky. She opened the window and the smell of supper cooking in the kitchen drifted into the room.

"Cabbage" she stated "What a surprise. To be honest" she continued "I reckon living here puts pay to having much love-life at all."

"What do you mean?" I asked.

"Well, the first barrier to cross is the set-up downstairs. Men, it seems to me, are regarded as public enemy no.1." she smiled, warming to her subject. "For a man to collect his date the first obstacle is home-sister sitting in her cubicle like a soldier on sentry duty. Then it's 'the interrogation' to find out who he has come to visit. And finally he has to wait while she broadcasts over her tannoy "Visitor for Nurse Cooper. Visitor for Nurse Cooper"."

We laughed. She had a point.

"How many times have you seen someone nearly choke on their supper and rush out of the room? I mean you have to be keen to put up with the indignity of it all".

Jane sitting with her arms wrapped around her knees nodded vigorously. "And it's worse if it's a doctor. I saw that houseman, from my ward once come to pick –up someone. Everyone stared at him and he got pinker by the minute"

"Exactly. Case closed."

Mary glanced at the clock. "Blimey is that the time? Its Thursday isn't it" and without waiting for a reply she began gathering up her things. "Come on you lot. We don't want to miss T.O.T.P."

"TOT what? What are you talking about" I asked as I helped myself to her brush to do my hair.

Jane laughed "Its Top of the Pops on TV at 7.30, don't tell me you didn't watch it at St. P's?"

I shook my head "Well you just wait and see."

We ate a hurried supper. As Mary had predicted it was cabbage, with sausages; the sausages were pink and felt fluffy on your tongue, and the cabbage was completely limp and tasteless. At 7.28 exactly the canteen emptied as everyone made their way to the lounge, which contained the only television in the nurse's home. Home Sister sat in her cubicle looking stern as if awaiting a riot, as we all crowded into the lounge. Usually the room was deserted, but this Mary informed me, was the exception to the rule.

Around the edge of the room were low, tan coloured plastic chairs; the sort that in the hot weather sweated and stuck to any bare inch of flesh that was left exposed. Their low backs meant that your head had no support, so if you relaxed and fell asleep, you would awake with a jolt as your head slumped to one side. Tonight, however they were all taken, as was every other inch of space in the room. Mary made her way to a corner, with a limited view of the TV and we followed. For the duration of the BBC's 'Top of the Pops' all attention was fixed on the small screen.

Those who were off-duty arrived early to pick the best seats and on-duty Nurses missed their meal if they were lucky enough to get 2nd supper break from 7.30-8pm. An observer could be excused for being surprised at the scene, as those who had just been dealing with matters of life and death became teenagers, gyrating and dancing with Pans People as the Beatles song "Hello; Goodbye" drifted over the air; joining in with Simon and Garfunkel as they sang of "Mrs. Robinson" and some even shedding a tear as Bobby Goldsboro voice thick with sentimentality described his love for 'Honey' and how she had died and he missed her. At

8pm, as the show finished, the lounge emptied as if by magic, becoming soulless and barren again, its source of life gone for another week. We were the last to leave

"Blimey that was something" I remarked. "Perhaps sometimes we need to forget about all the things we do and see and just have a bit of escapism. Don't you think?" My friends nodded.

Miss Barnett, the head tutor, bustled in to classroom 1 dressed in a rather shabby suit, which accentuated her bosoms, looking every bit an intellectual. She could well have been an Oxford Don. She held up her hand for silence.

"Good morning nurses" she began "I understand that you have some catching up to do but may I remind you that study block is an important time and I am here today to give you a brief outline of what is expected of you academically, if you are to qualify as State Registered Nurses."

We looked expectantly at her. Now she had our complete attention she continued "Perhaps you were surprised that the recommended reading list for your training included 'Notes on Nursing' by Florence Nightingale." There was a buzz around the room as we acknowledged that she was right. I mean she died in 1910, wouldn't she be a bit outdated?"

"We included her for a reason." She continued "Florence Nightingale is regarded as the mother of modern nursing. She had a vocation to be a nurse and despite strong opposition from friends and family she, together with some similarly inspired ladies, travelled to Turkey to care for soldiers wounded in the Crimean

War". She paused "Perhaps you learned about her during your history lessons at school?"

A few people nodded. "If so, you will know of the terrible conditions she found in the hospitals. There was a complete lack of cleanliness and sanitation; if soldiers didn't die immediately from their wounds they often died from infections and disease caused by the conditions they were nursed in".

Again she paused and her voice faltered. Taking a deep breath she continued. "It is hard to believe but there was not even enough chloroform to anaesthetize our soldiers. Ms Nightingale found only officers were unconscious for their operations. Our brave young soldiers had legs amputated while they were still awake, and often died later from gas gangrene or Typhus." The room was silent as we imagined the suffering and pain this had caused. Miss Barnett looking at our shocked faces continued.

"Florence Nightingale and her dedicated colleagues worked in those conditions improving cleanliness, washing and caring for those young men and tending to their terrible wounds. In addition they wrote to politicians and friends at home so that people became aware of what was happening. She implemented practices of care that are still in use today. Nursing had previously been the domain of unscrupulous, uneducated women who often used a measure of gin to help them fulfil their duties. Florence Nightingale transformed nursing, into a glorious vocation. I trust as you continue with your training you too will be proud of this wonderful profession, and realize just how privileged you are, to care for people in their time of greatest need."

There was a silence in the room as she finished and the hairs on the back of my neck tingled. Miss Barnett certainly understood the psyche of her young students; she had us in the palm of her hand. At that moment I felt that, if asked, I would do anything I could to uphold the integrity of nursing.

She clapped her hands and the spell was broken. "Nurses I suggest we break for coffee, be back in 15 minutes exactly." She turned and swept from the room.

Coffee was a hurried affair. Miss Barnett's words echoed in my mind, making our normal chatter seem dull. I was once again caught up in the bigger picture; the wonder of a vocation; the fulfilment of my dreams of becoming a nurse. These feelings had almost vanished as I coped with the actual slog of working on the ward 5; but now I longed for them to continue. I wanted to fall in love with nursing again.

Back in the classroom, however the romance and rhetoric were replaced by yet more paper-work. Miss Barnett began briskly "Nursing today is governed by the General Nursing Council. Each registered nurse is directly answerable to them and must abide by the rules and regulations. Today we will give you a book in which you are to record all the procedures and conditions you come in contact with during your training. You must keep these books safe and it is your responsibility to present them to the Ward Sister at the end of each placement.

If the Sister and you agree that you are competent in any particular area she will sign and put a cross against each individual situation. These books are the evidence required to show that you have reached the required practical level to care for patients with each of these illnesses. They could even be used as evidence in court, if you were, at any time, accused of professional incompetence" Miss Barnett glared at us over her wire-framed glasses. I sighed, and watched the rain splash against the dirty window, aware that my moment of nostalgia had passed. We were back to the practicalities and humdrum of a nurse's life.

Chapter 6:
ENT

It was the last day of 'Block' and our spirits were high. Somehow the 9-5 life, complete with endless lectures, had lost its thrill. Mary leaning back in her chair said "Well I've enjoyed catching up with everyone and it was good learning more theory but" she hesitated, searching for the right words. "I miss the patients and I can't wait to get back to the wards." There was a brief moment of silence until a communal "Urgh" echoed around the canteen table.

Jane joined in "I know what you mean, but I can't believe 'blocks' over, or that we are no longer the lowest of the low. There are now 2 sets of girls junior to us. That means we now have some poor sod we can boss about."

More impossibly, or so it seemed, we were about to acquire a belt, thereby changing our title from 'no-belt' to 'white-belt'. Surely bed-pans and back rounds would be the domain of our juniors. At last, we were to be allowed to do dressings, lay-up trolleys and perhaps even assist surgeons in theatre.

At that moment a cry went out across the canteen "The change list is up". A mass scraping of chairs and exodus ensued as we rushed to the corridor where the list had been pinned, jostling like rugby players in a scrum, to find out where we had been allocated. Somehow Mary had managed to get to the front and elbowing her way out of the crowd, she took me by the arm

"I'm on 22, male surgical. I've heard horrible stories about Sister Mitch." She paused looking concerned, but I didn't feel sympathetic.

"Oh come on Mary. Where am I going? Did you see?

"Children's Ear Nose and Throat."

I snorted "Great. They don't take juniors there do they?" Mary shook her head. "Great so I'm still the junior then... can't wait"

Around me there were animated screeches as friends discovered they were working together, or were bound for a popular ward. I just felt grumpy; and was still in a grump by the evening. To me it seemed that everyone else was going to busy, up-beat wards where all the action was. Someone was even allocated to main theatres. I had no time for Mary's concerns about Sister Mitch's short temper.

"Whatever is the matter?" Mary asked eventually when she could stand my miserable face no more.

"I'm going to bloody ENT" I said sulkily "Need I say more?"

She pulled a face "Oh for goodness sake" she scalded "Why don't you just go and see it. You might even like it."

The Ear Nose and Throat hospital was an independent building, a 5 minute walk away from the main hospital. The day had become bright after earlier showers, so I decided to walk and visit the children's ward, and perhaps collect my off-duty.

The building dated from the Victorian era and was similar in lots of ways to the Nurses Home. The same black and white tiles were laid in the entrance hall, leading to a grand staircase with gleaming oak banisters, smelling of beeswax. A cranky iron lift with concertina doors was operated by Alf, a cheerful looking fellow, wearing the hospitals navy-blue porters' uniform. With his peaked cap pushed back on his head at a rakish angle, he looked like a porter at a railway station anxious for a tip.

"Where to miss?" he asked as I entered the lift.

"Children's Ward please" I smiled enjoying the anonymity of not wearing uniform. I was joined by a fraught mother, holding tightly the arm of a pale child, who was repeating "Don't want to see no doctor" and an elderly lady clutching a bag of rather squashed grapes.

Alf clanged the doors shut and the lift rose stopping almost immediately at the 1st floor "Outpatients, cafeteria and public conveniences."

The mother dragging her child behind exited, ignoring his increasingly frantic mantra. "I don't want to see no doctor"

We continued upwards. "2nd Floor. Male and female adult wards". The lady clutching her grapes left, making her way towards the male ward where a group of visitors looked expectantly towards the ward doors.

"There's 2 more minutes to wait" Alf told me in a whisper "Visiting Hour is 2-3pm. That Sister Cook won't take any nonsense. You mark my words. Those doors will open at 2pm on the dot and not a moment before." He slammed the gates shut again.

"Is it visiting on the children's ward?" I enquired as we reached the third floor.

Alf considered this for a moment then said "Yes and No miss. Cos its kiddies they have longer hours. Parents can visit anytime between 12-6pm. It's a bit more relaxed."

I felt relieved; I liked 'relaxed.' Alf pointed towards the children's ward "That way Miss. I wouldn't like you to go the wrong way because that's the operating theatres." "Fine, thank-you." I mumbled anxious to be off.

Alf paused as he closed the gates "New nurse are we Miss?" I nodded. How had he guessed? "Look forward to meeting you again then" he replied as the lift disappeared from view.

The children's ward, when I entered, reminded me of a scene from a museum. The room was square with a high ceiling and elaborate plaster cornices. If these were an architect's dream, more so was the huge marble fireplace in the centre of the inner wall from which carved cherubim tasted from bunches of swollen grapes that twisted like tentacles to the floor. The grate, enclosed behind a huge wire-mesh guard, was laid with wood and paper, in case temperatures required that a fire be lit. A semi-circle of brightly coloured children's armchairs, stood before it, reminiscent of those seen in the story books of Peter Pan or Snow White.

In stark contrast were the 12 miniature metal hospital beds which were spaced around the outer wall, each with its own small locker. At the far end of the room some brightly coloured Formica-topped tables with small wooden chairs were grouped together to make a dining area. The children, dressed in the standard striped hospital pyjamas, were busy doing jigsaws or colouring with their visitors. Only one child clung tearfully to the neck of an anxious–looking woman, I imagined being his mother. She rocked him gently making soothing noises as she did so.

"Sisters off" staff-nurse informed me, when I ventured into the office "But you are on the rota."

She handed me the off-duty book. It looked promising. I had the weekend off. I smiled relishing the thought of a lazy week-end at home.

"Looks quiet today" I remarked and immediately wished I could snatch the words back.

Staff raised her eyebrows. "That's because it's Wednesday. Most of the kids are in for T's and A's (which I later discovered was the abbreviation for adenotonsillectomy or in layman's terms the operation to remove the tonsils and adenoids). They are usually in for 5 days. Tomorrow this 'lot'", she indicated the children I had seen in the ward "are moved to the convalescent side next door and we admit another bunch to have their op on Friday"

I hadn't realized that what I was seeing was only half of the picture and another room, identical in size, but brighter and containing more pictures and toys, ran from the far end of the corridor and was used for the children as they recovered.

"You'll see it isn't the doddle you think, when you actually work here" Staff continued.

I nodded, wishing again that I hadn't been so thoughtless earlier adding "I'm really looking forward to it". Before I could put my foot in it further, I smiled gratefully and left.

On the way back to the Nurses Home I tested the subterranean passage connecting the ENT hospital to the main one, and ultimately, the nurses home. The tunnels, notorious for letting in the rain, had flooded in one section and now the only safe passage was across a carefully laid builder's plank. Coming towards me on the plank, balancing precariously, arms out-stretched was a well dressed gentleman. I smiled and waited. Unfortunately at about the same time the aforementioned gentleman lost his balance, and after a brief period of arm flapping his right foot slipped from the plank into the water to a stream of obscenities. He was forced to continue to walk one foot on the plank, one in the water; I watched trying not to laugh, as he, with a great show of dignity, ignored me, and continued his journey determined not to acknowledge the squelch his foot made as he walked and how his tailored trousers clung to his leg, as if he were a schoolboy who had been for an impulsive paddle at the seaside.

Monday arrived too soon and I felt anxious as I arrived for a late shift. The operating theatres across the landing were in full swing, and most of the little beds were now occupied with the young patients, most of them sleeping following their operation. Their pale faces in their white op. gowns were a stark contrast to the chattering, busy children I had seen on my last visit. There was no visiting on surgery day, so the nurses were kept busy comforting and acting as surrogate mothers to our young charges, as well as attending to their clinical needs.

There were three of us on a late; Staff Nurse who took overall control, a second year student nurse called Eileen and myself. As I sat at sisters big oak desk waiting for report to begin, I found myself calculating that either Eileen or myself would have to care for the entire ward of convalescing children by themselves. Surely it couldn't be me. How had I ever thought it would be a quiet ward? Sister's voice interrupted my thoughts. "Welcome to the ward, Nurse Cooper. As this is your first shift here, you will be working with Staff Nurse caring for the children undergoing surgery today".

"Yes sister, Thank-you" I replied, then quickly tried to make notes as she updated us on each of the patients.

Staff- nurse took me to one side when report had finished. "There are 6 children having their tonsils and adenoids removed today. 3 are back" she indicated the sleeping children "and one is just going."

As she spoke a trolley appeared through the ward doors pushed by a theatre porter dressed in the standard blue cotton trousers, tunic and cap known as 'Scrubs'. On his feet were white gym shoes and he smiled at us as he entered.

"Afternoon ladies" he began "The late shift I presume?"

"We are indeed, Paul. Meet Nurse Cooper, this is her first shift. It's called 'being flung in at the deep end' eh? Anyway, gal you'd better take this one" she said turning to me "Rule one of surgery is never keep theatre waiting." She spoke quickly, her short clipped sentences sounded quite curt. I hesitated "You alright taking a patient to theatre?" and when I didn't reply she continued "There's really nothing to it. Paul will show you the ropes, won't you Paul?" she nodded vaguely at the porter.

I had never actually taken anyone to theatre, let alone a child, but Paul reassured me as he put his arm across my shoulder. "No problems pet. Just do what I say." He handed me the slip of paper he was carrying. It contained the name and the number of the next child on the list.

"He's in there" Staff pointed to the bed in the corner hidden behind blue striped screens. I entered quietly. Simon was sleeping; the name on my slip of paper corresponded to his hospital bracelet. Paul moved forward and lifted him gently onto the trolley, wrapping him in a green cotton blanket as he did so. We exited the ward, crossing the landing to the operating theatres. Simon remained asleep.

The ante-room to theatres was called the anaesthetic room, and as we entered we were greeted with a casual "Hi there" with a definite Australian accent.

I smiled and Paul replied "Hi there Karl" winking at me he whispered "Did you know that half of our anaesthetists come from down under?" I didn't have time to reply as Karl was checking Simon's details. Satisfied that all was well, he applied a tourniquet to Simons forearm and began to tap it gently with his finger to bring the small veins to the surface. Next he picked up a syringe containing the anaesthetic and connecting a light blue plastic needle to it said "Little scratch coming young man" and proceeded to insert the needle into a vein and slowly deliver the drug. Still the child slept, the only difference was a change to his breathing which became deeper and noisier as the anaesthetic took effect. Karl placed a black rubber mask over the child's face and began to manoeuvre the trolley towards the swing doors of the operating theatre, dismissing us as he did so. "Thank you Nurse. He's all ours now".

As I turned to leave, the theatres door swung open to reveal a masked, gowned figure looking almost ethereal as she pushed a trolley before her. The unconscious child was lifted onto the theatre trolley and whisked inside, the doors swishing closed on a world of ultra cleanliness, stainless steel instruments and equipment whose use could only be imagined by the layman. It was intriguing, but this was not the time to wonder, Paul was holding the door open for me.

Staff was taking the pulse of one of the post-op children who had been operated on earlier. She called me to her side "When a child comes back from theatre we start by doing the obs every 15 minutes and record them on the chart. She indicated a page of graph paper which had been subdivided into 3 areas, lying on the bed table. If they remain stable after an hour we reduce it to every 30 minutes for a further 2 hours, then if all is well we check it hourly and that continues overnight". Pointing to the adjacent bed in which another pale child slept she said "That's Billy; another T's and A's. His obs are due now. Do those then Susie's" she pointed to yet another child "will be due too so you can do them"

As I turned to Billy she said "You'll get very good at doing obs here. It's a continual task." She moved closer and asked "How would you know if a child had started to bleed? That is a complication following a Tonsillectomy. That's what we are checking for."

"Their pulse would rise and their blood pressure drop", I hesitated before continuing, "They could become distressed and restless. Perhaps sweaty?"

"Well done, that's right" she was about to continue when the phone rang. She grabbed it "OK" was her short reply. "That was theatre. Simon's done. I'll collect him. You carry on with the obs."

At the end of the shift I was amazed I had thought ENT was a doddle? As well as all the obs, we had to deal with 6 poorly children, who not only had very sore throats and the effects of the anaesthetic to deal with, but more notably wanted their Mummy's'. I seemed to be endlessly making soothing noises and cuddling the children as I washed the blood from their pale faces and changed them back into their pyjamas. Worse, however, was trying to get the children to drink, because although they were thirsty, swallowing anything was very painful. Somehow we did all that was required and as I left the ward that day it gave me a feeling of pride to see "my" children, sleeping quietly; pale but recovering.

The next morning, I was surprised to see the same children up and dressed in pyjamas. The Night staff told us all was well and there was no evidence of any abnormal bleeding or other complications. All had been given soluble Paracetamol to reduce their sore throats. After report our first job was to organize breakfast. Still pale and tearful I wondered how the children would cope with eating. On the formica tables at the end of the ward, stood a pile of blue and red bordered cereal bowls, a huge jug of milk, and several large catering packs of Cornflakes and Rice Krispies.

I pulled a face. "Wouldn't something softer be better?" I asked, only to be told that it was important that the children start to eat again to prevent scar tissue forming in the throat, and cereal was ideal for this purpose. Their analgesia should now be effective, so what was I waiting for?

Jumping into action I called "Come on Simon. Come on Billy, it's time for breakfast" They followed me warily to the table. "Can I have sugar on my cornflakes?" asked Simon.

I nodded "You even get to choose your own bowl."

He selected a blue one and I put a spoonful of cereal in it, which he topped with a large spoonful of sugar and flooded the dish with milk. I was surprised that he didn't object more. It was obvious that his throat hurt when he swallowed, but he managed quite a few spoons before stopping. Staff sat next to Billy and a blonde haired little girl called Victoria, encouraging them to eat a little. She smiled at me "Well done, as long as they have a small portion that's fine. Little and often, that's what is needed."

The rest of the day was punctuated by regular stops for drinks and snacks. At elevenses the children were pleased to be offered a little dish of ice-cream with their drink and if they managed some lunch, jelly and cream was their reward. For the first day Paracetamol was given regularly as a matter of course.

By the end of the morning the children were becoming fractious. Tired of endless puzzles and colouring, I was watching the time and wishing it was visiting hour when the doors flew open to admit a tall vaguely familiar gentleman, well attired in a dark tailored suit and shoes so shiny they could be used as a mirror. Following him was a younger man whose clothes were hidden beneath a knee-length white coat.

The door to the ward once again opened, and in rushed Dr. Jimmy Davis, our houseman and popular junior doctor. He wore a short white coat and his stethoscope was slung casually around his neck, ready for action. At this point, Staff- Nurse looking hot and flustered came bustling across the ward, pushing the notes trolley. She nodded to acknowledge the well dressed gentleman I learned was Mr. Fry, the ENT Consultant and his registrar, muttering

"Sorry to be a bit late Sir".

Mr. Fry stared at the clock for a moment, and then made his way to the first bed. Dr Jimmy, his blonde hair flopping into his eyes, opened the buff coloured folder he was carrying and coughing nervously to clear his throat began.

"This is Victoria Bell." He smiled kindly at the girl then continued "She is 7 years old and had a 3 year history of recurring tonsillitis, usually having 5-6 attacks each year. On examination, her tonsils were scarred and necrotic. She had an adenotonsillectomy yesterday and to date her recovery has been uneventful." Mr. Fry, who had been listening intently, turned to the child.

"Why hello Victoria" The child, suddenly overcome by the attention lowered her head and did not reply. The ward became unexpectedly quiet, as even the children seemed to sense the tension.

Staff-nurse, face a deepening crimson moved to Victoria's side "Are you going to talk to the nice doctors?" she asked.

There was no reply. The silence hung, almost visibly, in the air. Mr. Fry looking far from pleased turned to his houseman. "Dr. Davis" he began "have you examined this child post-operatively?" Jimmy nodded. "Are you happy with her?"

Again Jimmy nodded adding "She seems to be healing well."

Mr. Fry shrugged and said "I think we will just trust our houseman's word and move on.

The group proceeded to the next bed, Simons, which I suddenly realised was empty; I hadn't noticed him slip to the toilet. Staffs eye bore into mine, willing me to act. I hurried to the toilet, but not before I heard the now exasperated Consultant explode. "How can I possibly conduct a ward-round when my patients are either not available or just ignore me? Staff Nurse this is just not good enough."

The atmosphere became increasingly tense as Mr. Fry stood with arms folded waiting for Simon to appear. I suddenly realised why he was familiar; he was the 'plank- casualty' from the sub terrain passage. Staff-nurse trying hard to remain professional, apologized again.

As Simon exited from the toilets I grabbed his hand "The doctors are here to see you" I began and Simon, who liked an audience, returned to his bed quickly, happy to show the site where until yesterday his tonsils had been, to anyone who was interested. The atmosphere in the ward improved; the storm seemed to have blown itself out, yet when I saw Staff's unhappy face I wished she too had witnessed Mr Fry's experience in the watery tunnel. Perhaps then she would have laughed and realized that all the pomp and ceremony was a bit of a farce, and the doctors, were not Gods, but human like us.

The ward seemed quiet when the doctors left but, not for long, as Staff opened the door to let in the visitors, eager to see their off-spring. Beckoning to me we headed to the ward kitchen for a cup of tea When Maria returned with the remnants of the children's tea on her trolley, she handed us 2 little iced fairy cakes "Here Nursey, I give you these. That doctor he was, how you say? Horide?"

We laughed taking the treat "Yes Maria. He was definitely horide today"

I was just licking the pink icing, when once again the door opened. "Caught you." We both jumped as Jimmy, our Houseman, entered. "That scared you didn't it?" he began then in a gentler voice said "Just thought I'd come back to make sure my favourite Staff-nurse was alright. Our dear Mr. Fry was certainly having a bad day."

Staff smiled, and I realized that she was really pretty. "That's nice of you Jimmy. Thanks for coming. But we're ok." She turned to me and I nodded in agreement. "Anyway, I think you deserve one of these cakes, for being so kind."

She picked one from the plate and threw it towards him. Jimmy caught it and in a single move thrust the whole cake into his mouth. He turned to go, spluttering as a shower of crumbs cascaded down his jacket "Thanks. Must go. See you soon" and, he disappeared into the corridor.

"What a kind bloke." I observed, struggling to believe that a doctor came back to apologize for his Consultant. Staff nodded unaware that I was searching her face for signs that it was more than just kindness. Did he fancy her? There seemed no way of knowing. "Besides" I reprimanded myself "what a cynic I was becoming, can't anyone be kind without there being an ulterior motive anymore?" Later, I recounted the story to Mary, as we drank tea and finished the last of the custard creams. "Don't you think Jimmy sounds nice?" I asked her.

She nodded, eyes narrowing as she replied "Yes, very nice." There was a pause before she added "and I'm wondering if someone, not too far from here, has taken a fancy to him."

I had been on the ward for 6 weeks when Sister called me into her office. "I have heard from the Allocations Office" she began "Apparently one of the students allocated to work in ENT theatres, is off sick. She has had an appendectomy, so is off sick for at least a month. Theatres are short-staffed and we thought it would be good experience for you to work there for a month." I must have looked apprehensive because she continued "It would give you an excellent all-round experience of ENT and of course could serve as your theatre experience for your finals."

I smiled, willing my face to show enthusiasm but secretly I was terrified. Theatres? It seemed a completely alien world to me. How would I cope? Jimmy had just finished examining one of our new patients when I left Sisters office. I was about to walk past when he stopped me, catching my arm.

"Hey Joy. You ok? You look as if you've seen a ghost."

I smiled weakly. "It's not a ghost. It's worse." I began and was pleased to his look of concern, "I've got to go to ENT Theatres."

He relaxed "Oh is that all, you'll be fine." He smiled "and besides, there are a lot of pro's. Just think I'll be there."

It was 8am on the dreaded day. Taking deep breaths I knocked on the door labelled 'Theatre Sister'. It was opened almost immediately by a slim, dark-haired woman, whose theatre 'Scrubs', shapeless as they were, looked like a Christian Dior garment on her.

She smiled "Nurse Cooper?" and signalled me into her office. "I'm Sister Thorn. I'm afraid you are being flung in at the deep end," she began, making my heart sink even further. "We have 12 ops on the list today and we've just heard there might be an emergency from Cas.- severe epitaxis, that's a nose bleed you know" she added helpfully "Anyway it might need cauterizing. I'm sorry we haven't time for a tour. Sister Beale had kindly lent you to us for a month, so I'm sure that eventually we will have time for a proper introduction." She paused and led me out of the office adding, under her breath, "That is if we all survive today."

We had entered a narrow windowless room, with a row of wooden benches down one side opposite 20 grubby looking lockers. In the corner was a neat pile of the familiar, green cotton 'Scrubs.' Sister pointed at the pile. "Help yourself to a locker and change into some scrubs." She looked at my legs "You'll need to take your stockings off, they create static which is dangerous in theatres and there are shoes in the corner but you'll have to hunt for your size. Wait here and I will send someone in to collect you."

She turned and left. Again I took a deep breath, trying to take in my surroundings and remember her instructions, silently cursing that no-one had told me I would need to bare my unshaven legs. I undressed hurriedly into scrubs and was searching through the stack of white leather clogs when the door opened again.

"Ready yet?" This time a different figure stood in front of me. She smiled "I'm Staff-nurse Jennings, but please call me Carol. We try to be less formal in theatres. She looked me up and down. "Good you look fine. You'll just need these." She handed me a green cotton cap and a white face mask. I had begun to pull them on when she continued "No hair at all may be visible and your nose and mouth must be covered by the mask when you are in theatre."

She gave me one final inspection then led me to an inner door, she paused. "There are three main rules 1) do not leave my side. 2) do not touch anything and 3) do not speak unless spoken to.

Opening the door she entered and I followed meekly, grateful that my mask hid my pink face. If I thought I would look conspicuous, I was wrong; no-one took any notice of our arrival.

The theatre was rectangular with high ceilings. Two arched windows at the far end of the room had lost their previous splendour and were now obscured with thick coats of white paint and nailed shut so no light or air could penetrate. Shining white tiles covered the walls and a black rubber anti-static floor covering added to the general starkness. In the centre, a vast oval light shed its beam on the operating table and around it the gowned surgeon and his aides worked on the patient, unrecognizable under swathes of green cotton sheeting, with their shiny stainless steel instruments.

A strange mixture of odours hung in the air making it feel oppressive. The sharpness of the antiseptics used to clean all the surfaces blended with the sweetness of the anaesthetic gases and the organic stench of infected tissue and blood. For a moment there was silence, broken only by the hiss of the anaesthetic machine and the gory slurping as the sucker cleared the blood from the patient's throat. Suddenly it was over. With a sigh the surgeon stood and turning to the anaesthetist said "He's all yours" before wandering to the sink in the corner where he unceremoniously stripped his gown and gloves off and pouring soap over his hands and forearms began to prepare for the next case.

Surgeons and their assistants had to go through the "scrub-up" procedure before each op. This entailed washing the hands and forearms, with soap, a brush and hot running water for at least three minutes. The area is then dried with sterile towels, and the person is assisted into a sterile gown and gloves. If at any stage during this procedure the person touches something unsterile, they instantly become unsterile and must start the whole procedure again. It was not uncommon for newcomers to theatre to have to repeat the process several times, at the end of a day their hands could be very red and sore.

Sister, who had been assisting the surgeon as 'Scrub Nurse', began to dismantle her trolley, putting the instruments aside for washing and re-sterilizing. At her side was a nurse; a 'Runner'; the theatre term for general dogs body who was always at hand to provide the required instruments. She was busy counting the number of blood-soaked swabs which hung over the side of a stainless steel bowl where they had been thrown during the op. Each swab was counted, as it was used and when it was disposed of, to ensure none were left behind in the patient. If the swab count did not tally the patient could not be released.

Today all was in order and Paul, the theatre Porter, arrived with a trolley and, assisted by the anaesthetist, lifted the unconscious patient onto it. Carol handed me a bowl containing a pink liquid

"This is chlorhexidine. It's the antiseptic we use to clean" she explained, handing me a pile of paper towels, and with a wave of her hand indicated the area that needed cleaning.

Obediently I set to work, wiping every available surface, glad that there was something I could do. By the end of that shift I suspected that my next month would be spent endlessly cleaning. How right I was. The role of junior nurse in theatre was very basic and involved lots of cleaning. Cleanliness in theatre is, of course, essential.

It was the week-end and Carol and I were on-duty together. Theatre although closed for routine surgery, had to be staffed in case of emergency. Three weeks had passed since I started in theatre and I was in my final week. We sat sipping our coffee on the Saturday morning, a luxury reserved for the week-end. Carol stretched and pulled a folder containing what looked like a long list from the shelf. "Sorry to say" she began "Weekend means more cleaning" I sighed and looked resigned, brightening when she said "But it's also a very good time to get to know all the instruments; what they're used for, and what their name is."

Since my arrival I had been amazed by the instruments laid out in glass-fronted cabinets along the walls. There were so many, yet the permanent theatre nurses named each one as if they were childhood friends. It was their responsibility to keep them in good working order, packing them as needed for each operation, into huge plastic trays; these were then wrapped in green cotton theatre towels, labelled and sent for sterilizing in the main hospital. They were returned the next day, ready for use.

We spent the morning cleaning, washing down the walls, and scrubbing the bowls and receivers which were then put into theatre's own autoclave. We sterilized small articles like the tubing from the suction machines, after we had hammered them with a wooden mallet to loosen all the dried blood and secretions inside. Theatre life I discovered was not very glamorous.

At lunch Carol said "This is your last week in theatre isn't it Joy?" I nodded. "Well" she continued "No theatre experience is complete without the nurse acting as 'Scrub Nurse' at least once. What do you think?"

I gulped "What me? Scrub? Oh Carol I don't think I know enough".

Being a 'Scrub nurse' meant you were 'assistant' to the surgeon passing him everything he needed to do the operation. To do this you had to 'scrub-up' just like him and dress in gown, gloves and mask. It sounded terrifying.

Carol smiled kindly "I bet you've heard some horror stories?" I nodded and she said "Come on then; tell me what you've heard."

"Well," I began "Last week one of my set was in Mains, scrubbing for Mr. Jordan who was performing an appendicectomy. She told us that suddenly he just stopped, folded his arms and stared at her. She didn't know what she had done wrong and when she asked him what he wanted, he just ignored her. The whole theatre came to a standstill and everyone just looked at her."

I paused to take a bite of my sandwich and pictured the nurse concerned, Barbara. She was so humiliated she cried when she recounted it to us. Poor Barbara. We had all sympathized, and if Mary had her way, we would have marched to Main Theatre and lynched the man.

"So what happened?" Carol asked.

"Apparently Sister Buchan, she's the senior Theatre Sister, I think?" Carol nodded. "Well" I continued "she was passing and intervened when she saw what was happening.

Barbara told us that when Sister asked Mr. Jordan what the problem was, he put on a silly voice and said 'I notice you've once again asked a student nurse to scrub for me. I thought I made it clear it's not what I expect.'

Carol pulled a face "I wish I'd been a fly on the wall. Sister Buchan is not very tall but when she gets cross she lets everyone, and I mean everyone, no matter what their rank, know."

I smiled "Yes that's just what she did. Apparently she said "Mr. Jordan, as I explained previously, the allocation of scrub nurses is my domain. Now I think Nurse Smith is doing very well in the circumstances. However, if you are unable to cope with a simple appendicectomy without a more senior Scrub Nurse, I shall quite happily scrub and assist.'

Carol laughed "I guess he declined her offer?" I nodded. "Great." Carol replied "She's a diamond. She won't let anyone bully her nurses."

As we cleared away the coffee cups Carol said "Main theatre is much more stressful than here though, Joy, so I still think you must scrub sometime next week. Anyway, our ENT surgeons are usually ok and we will look after you, you know." She looked at the Operation List "Oh its Mr. Wills on Monday and he's got several T's and A's. Great. That's sorted."

She wrote my name in the 'scrub nurse' column. It was official. I sighed. Mr. Wills, I remembered, wore green operating wellies on which someone had drawn the outline of his toes with flowers entwined around them; On one boot was written "Thy kingdom come" and on the other "Thy will be done." He must have a bit of a sense of humour, or no-one would have dared to do it, I reasoned. I felt a bit re-assured.

For the rest of the weekend, every opportunity I had I laid and re-laid the tonsillectomy and adenoidectomy trolley, learning, as I did so the names of the instruments and the order Mr. Wills would use them, so I could hand them to him without being asked. This was the ambition of every scrub nurse.

I hardly slept on Sunday night as I repeatedly recited the names of the instruments to myself. I worried especially about the St. Clare Thompson adenoid curette because it had a special guard which was not always used, so I needed to know how to remove it if Mr. Wills did not want it or how to release the guard if he did use it and it needed to be cleared. When I eventually slept, I dreamt of the forceps flicking the guard on and off independently.

Morning came. Carol stood with me as I scrubbed up thoroughly and put on my latex gloves without contaminating them. Mr. Wills in his personalized wellies, took his place at the head of the table and, trembling, I stood at his side as the operation began.

All was going well and I began to relax. Mr. Wills removed the adenoids and handed the instrument to me so that I could remove the debris collected beneath it. I flicked down the guard as I had practiced so many times, but to my horror saw the bloody piece of tissue somersault into the air, as if in slow motion, and land on the surgeons lap. Every eye had followed its flight. Even the walls held their breath.

Mr. Wills, recovering first, gave me a wink and shouted "Bulls eye."

The tension was broken and everyone burst into laughter. The operation continued uneventfully with everyone turning a blind eye to the bloody mess on Mr. Will's gown. I knew I would never forget my one and only experience of being a scrub-nurse, and Jimmy, our houseman, who had seen the whole incident made sure all my colleagues on the ward knew about it and teased me relentlessly.

With my time on ENT almost over I felt very sad when the following week, I said goodbye to all my colleagues. My greatest sorrow though had to be bidding Jimmy good-bye. He was a good doctor, but more than that he was the first doctor to treat me like an equal and for that I was truly grateful. Besides, setting work aside, he was a gorgeous and Mary had been right all along. I fancied him.

Chapter 7:
Night Duty

If there was one placement everybody dreaded it was 'Night Duty; Bank'. Nights on the wards were usually covered by a system called 'internal rotation'. This meant that in every 4 weeks every student nurse (except for those in the first 6 months of their training) could expect to work 3 weeks of day duty followed by 1 week of nights. This meant that the ward was covered by nurses familiar with its needs and practices. Although fair, it was exhausting; the shift pattern being 7 nights on: each night being from 09.30pm until 08.30am, followed by 3 nights off and you returned to the ward on day-duty.

Night duty/Bank, however, was a different story. It meant you could be allocated to work anywhere in the hospital for 4 weeks to cover sickness or any crisis that happened to arise. It was exhausting. Worse; there wasn't the usual security of knowing the ward and how it was run. On 'bank' you could end up in a completely new area every night of the week and still be expected to provide the same professional care.

I was sitting in the canteen devouring fish and chips, my favourite. I was enjoying my placement on a male medical ward where I had been for about 4 weeks and wasn't expecting to move. I didn't notice the expression on Mary's face as she approached. "Joy, have you seen you're on the change list? You're on nights. Bank." She patted my shoulder sympathetically.

"You can't be serious?" I groaned but one look at her face and realised it was no joke. My social life would have to be cancelled; on night bank you did little but work, eat and sleep. If the stories I had heard were true even nights off were spent trying to catch up with sleep.

I was right to be afraid; nothing had prepared me for it. My first shift was on a men's surgical ward. Nurse Clarke, or Liz, as I was allowed to call her, was in charge of me and the ward of 28 patients. Tall and slim, her sleek brown hair folded into a French plait under her cap. She had 6 months more experience than me, the striped belt she wore displayed this. Liz had already worked for 3 nights on the ward and appeared to know everything. She quickly took me under her wing,

"Right Joy, let's get going" she instructed as she emptied the contents of the drug cupboard. "We'll get the drugs done quickly. We've got 6 drips to look after tonight and I want to get everyone settled before Mooney does her rounds, or there'll be hell to pay"

Mooney, although just a name to me then, was the night sister responsible for the 4 wards on our floor. She could be summoned by a bleep in case of problems, but also did regular rounds of the wards and occasional spot checks.

The first couple of hours flew past in a haze of giving out drugs, drinks and injections, smoothing pillows and emptying catheter bags. The list was endless. Chaos reigned until suddenly, unexpectedly an air of calm descended and everyone appeared to settle. We dimmed the main lights; night had begun.

Liz smiled "Well done; that was great. We might even manage a cuppa before Mooney arrives. Rule no. 1 of nights is, don't let Sister catch you drinking, eating...." Her voice fizzled out as striding purposely down the ward in a navy-blue polka dot dress was a women I assumed was Mooney. Liz seemed to shrink as she approached.

"Nurse Clarke" she began, ignoring me completely "There is the small matter of our Founders picture. It is still open. What are you thinking?"

"Sorry Sister" Liz mumbled looking at her feet, adding by way of explanation "Its Nurse Coopers first night... Bank.... I'll make sure it doesn't happen again."

With that Mooney, turned and marched briskly down the ward, the doors making a sound like the closing of a book as they closed behind her.

Before I could speak Liz instructed "Bed 1's drip is due through soon keep an eye on it." And with that she disappeared through the swing doors, only to re-appear a few moments later. "Right, I'll sort out the drip, you get us a cuppa" she instructed.

"What was all that about?" I asked as we sat sipping tea, huddled around the nurse's desk. The desk lamp was on, creating an oasis of light in the darkened ward.

Joy shrugged "Oh, it's crazy" she began "Did you notice that picture in the frame with shutters as you came in tonight?" I nodded. I remembered noticing the severe gaze of the gentleman, a founder member of the hospital.

"Well rumour has it that if you leave the shutters open at night, he walks...." she gestured eerily and whispering continued "they say he comes through the ward in his surgeon's gown and someone on that ward always dies that night."

I shivered, and glanced over my shoulder involuntarily. Joy took a gulp of her tea and stood up. "It's the junior's job to close the shutters as soon as they come on duty. Sorry, forgot to tell you." With that she disappeared into the utility room, the hiss of steam as she filled the steriliser sounded like a train passing through the station.

It wasn't long before I discovered firsthand the witching hour dreaded by every junior nurse in the hospital. Most of the patients were sleeping peacefully; Mooney had done her ward-round and Liz wrapped herself in her heavy grey cloak with scarlet lining rather like a child hugs his security blanket after a bad dream. She glanced at the clock "Blimey. Is that the time? I'm off to lunch."

Lunch at midnight? It sounded strange, but then everything did that night. I didn't think I would be able to eat anything at this hour; but I had a lot to learn. As she got up to leave Liz noticed the anxiety in my eyes.

"You'll be ok," she whispered "None of the drips are due through yet. Just keep an eye on Len in cubicle 6. He's had bad news today.....He was restless when we passed him with Mooney. I thought she might stop and have a word with him, but no. I should have known, she's not renowned for her compassion." She turned to leave adding "If you get any problems just bleep the bitch."

The ward seemed terrifyingly empty with Liz gone. I sat at the desk nervously adding up the columns on the patients Fluid Balance Charts, recorded to ensure their input correlated with their output. When people have had surgery or are very ill it is essential to ensure that the kidneys are functioning efficiently to ensure the patient's heart is not put under undue strain.

My heart was pounding. I had only been on the ward for four hours; I knew nothing, yet here I was in what seemed like sole charge of 28 ill patients. What if....I dared not entertain such thoughts so I stood, picking up the heavy black rubber torch, an essential piece of the night staffs equipment, and began to do my first official ward round. I crept past the patients shining the torch into each of their faces willing them not to stir, and leaving only when the rhythmic movement of their chest assured me all was well.

Cubicle 6 was at the very end of the ward. I could see the light was on inside and the pale drawn face of its occupant was obvious as I opened the door. He was sitting upright on the edge of the bed; the mask from his oxygen cylinder had slipped from his face and was hissing ineffectively into his pyjama jacket. I bent over to reposition it. Opening his eyes he seemed to notice me for the first time. "Put it back on if you want Nurse" he began. "It ain't doing much good though."

I smiled searching for the right words to say. "The Doctor thinks you should keep it on Len" I explained

"Doctors, doctors what do they know". He paused, his breath coming in short painful bursts. I waited awkwardly until he continued. "They've told me there's nothing more they can do. I'm done for."

I knelt down by his side and took his thin hand in mine. I wanted to say something that would help; be positive: give him some hope, but the words would not form on my lips. It seemed an eternity that we sat there and I watched sadly as he struggled to breathe, his expression revealing the inner turmoil he faced. I felt impotent and stupid. Words meant nothing. What could I say?

A bell broke the silence. It buzzed intermittently like an angry hornet. He shrugged as I got to my feet awkwardly. A grateful smile flitted across his blue-tinged lips "It's OK love. Mustn't hold you up. You've got enough to do without listening to silly old buggers like me." Allowing me to replace his mask, I left his room to answer the bell. When Liz returned I tried to hide my tear-stained face.

No patient should be woken before 6am. That was the rule. So, as soon as the hands on the ward clock reached 6 the ward lights were switched on and once again it buzzed with activity. Mr Jones in bed 2 had, before he retired, worked on a market stall selling fruit and veg. He was used to rising early and had been a willing volunteer to be our 'tea-boy' when Liz had asked him the previous evening. Long days standing at his stall had exacerbated his varicose veins and he was currently recovering from surgery to remove the offending blood vessels. To aid recovery, exercise, although painful was very important, and Liz had told him sternly that a brisk walk up the ward giving out a welcome first cup of tea of the day could be part of his rehabilitation.

He hobbled up the ward to meet me as I pushed the tea-trolley in; the bandages on his legs had slipped a little and one was hanging below the hem of his striped pyjamas. He pulled the cord of his dressing gown around his rotund stomach and smiled.

"Thank you so much Mr. Jones" I said "it's very good of you to help us like this. Beds 4, 5 and 6 are still not drinking, so they won't need a cup and bed 10 mustn't have sugar, otherwise everyone else can have what they want." As I hurried away I added "I don't know how we'd manage without you.

Grateful the tea round was in progress I rushed to the ward sink where another trolley loaded with stacks of bright plastic bowls and tooth mugs lay waiting for me to give patients who were unable to get up. I was helping my 5th patient to sit up and retrieve soap and towel from his locker when Liz appeared. "How are you getting on?" she enquired.

"5 down and 5 to go" I explained.

She pulled a face. "Joy, we've still got the drugs to do. We'll never finish. I'm not getting at you it's just there really isn't time for us to do 10 washes in the morning and they all get a proper bed-bath when the day-staff come on. Have a quick look round and leave any that are asleep, or Fisher will go mad when she comes on."

I shrugged; about to object but Liz had already gone and was hurrying towards the drug cupboard pulling the obligatory large bunch of keys from her pocket. I glanced again at the plastic bowls waiting, and then pushed the trolley decisively into a corner. It was almost 7am; the list of jobs to complete before the day staff arrived at 7.30 seemed never ending. Giving out the medicines was surely more important than washing your face and besides, Liz was right, a quick scan of patients listed to receive a bowl revealed most of them were still asleep, oblivious to the activity around them.

I joined Liz as she locked the drug cupboard and pushed the trolley towards bed 1. "You OK" she asked.

I wanted to say 'no, I wasn't ok. I was tired and my feet hurt. I had been walking up and down this ward for the last 10 hours and right now I just wanted to be in bed.' Instead I nodded meekly "Fine thanks"; with that we began another round of the patients, this time giving each the medications they needed.

The next 30 minutes passed quickly as my tired brain struggled to check each prescription chart; I fumbled as I unscrewed bottles and decanted tablets into plastic pots, repeating the drugs name and the dose to Liz, as I did so. Our patients were well rehearsed with this procedure and some of them had memorised their hospital number and recited it to me as I approached them, their hand outstretched to receive their tablets. Last night I thought how strange this had seemed, but this morning it was absolutely wonderful to have our job made so much simpler in this way. How much longer it was when I had to find the number on the patient's wristband, recite it to Liz, pour a drink from the jug and help the patient to take each pill; trying always to be kind and professional, when inside I was screaming "Please hurry up." At last we finished. The drugs were locked away and the bed-table restored to its usual position.

Liz seemed agitated as she looked anxiously at the clock then at the ward doors as they flew open to reveal the arrival of the day staff.

"Check the sluice" she urged me "Just make sure its tidy or there will be hell to pay." She disappeared towards the ward desk, collecting the chart-boards from the ends of the beds as she did so. As I hurried to collect the plastic bowls and tidy up the sluice I saw Liz frantically scribbling in the patient's report-folder.

Mr. Jones, our 'tea-boy' stopped me as I clattered past his bed pushing my trolley. "It's all done Nurse" he said winking conspiratorially. "I've washed the cups and the kitchen looks as good as new." I was about to thank him when he clutched my arm. "Best hurry up... it's almost time for her" he gesticulated towards the door "she likes everything to be just so..." I smiled and continued towards the sluice not fully comprehending his meaning.

I was just rinsing the final bowl and stacking it onto the shelf above the bedpan washer when Sister Fisher swept in. "Nurse" she began in icy tone. "I am aware you are not a regular member of my team, so perhaps I can excuse you a little, but really this is not acceptable." Her eyes scanned the sluice, eagle-like, and stopped when they reached the sink which contained the tooth-mugs I had been about to wash. "I expect the sluice of my ward to be impeccable when I come on duty, not in a state of chaos like this." I opened my mouth to speak but her glare silenced me. "Follow me" she commanded, marching briskly to the patient's toilet as I followed miserably behind. She entered each cubicle, tutting and sighing as she did so. "The toilet rolls nurse, have you never been told there must be precisely 2 sheets unrolled." She adjusted each roll appropriately. "Whatever do they teach you in the School of Nursing these days?"

Head held high; back erect she swept back onto the ward to receive the night report from Liz who stood as if on a military parade, by the desk. I hid in the sluice, to finish my task and avoid further confrontation, cross that I had been treated like a naughty school-girl, rather than a nurse who had worked relentlessly for the past 11 hours.

Report over, Liz came to collect me and we made our way off the ward towards breakfast and rest. I was aware of numerous pairs of eyes staring at us with silent sympathy; the patients understood the injustice and were on our side. Their understanding soothed me and melted the unspoken anger in my heart giving way to an all consuming tiredness.

"How is it" I wondered for the twentieth time since getting into bed that morning 'that I am utterly exhausted but can't get to sleep?" Pulling the pillow over my head I waited for sleep to come. It wasn't to be. It was lunch-time for the real world and life continued busily and noisily. My room, although on the fourth floor of the Nurses Home was directly above the staff kitchen and the aroma of baked fish and over-cooked cabbage wafted relentlessly upward, combining with the clanging of the huge cooking pots as the kitchen porters stacked them into a hazardous tower for the weary washer-uppers. Fragments of shouted instructions invaded my room "We need more fish..." "Don't put that there".

Suddenly I could bear no more, and flinging the pillow onto the floor I marched furiously to the window and slammed it shut. Falling back into bed I pulled the sheet over my head and drifted into a fitful sleep disturbed by dreams of fish; scores of them swarmed into my unconsciousness in a kaleidoscope of colours, brushing my face with their fins, chanting the mantra "Don't put that there... don't put that there..."

I woke again and sat up wearily needing the bathroom; apparently my body didn't think it was time to sleep either. Returning to my room the heat felt overwhelming. Unthinking I flung open the window only remembering when I heard the cry "Any more fish?" why I had closed them in the first place. I glanced at the clock. One o'clock; it was no good. I would have to cope on four hours sleep.

I dressed slowly and wandered downstairs to the lounge. A couple of friends on a late lunch-break from the wards were sipping tea from plastic beakers. "Hi Joy; you look rough" they greeted me. "What's up?"

I replied monosyllabically "On nights. Can't sleep."

Their eyes filled with sympathy "Tough" they commiserated patting me on the back as they passed. "Hope you're not on Ward 3. Briggs says its chaos."

"Great" was the only reply I could manage.

They disappeared and the lounge was empty again as I sank wearily into a low regulatory easy-chair. It was plastic and seemed designed specifically to be hot and uncomfortable. I was aware of an old black and white film showing on the TV then the next thing I knew I could hear, once again, the voices of my friends.

"You still here Joy?"

It was almost five o'clock. I nodded slowly. One of the pair stopped at my side. "How many nights have you got left?" she asked.

"Three" tears filled my eyes and began to trickle down my cheeks. My friends were concerned.

"You'll make it" they soothed "The first set is always the worst. Have a chat with your senior tonight. She'll sort something out for you."

When the time came to go back on duty, I entered the ward filled with dread. I was so tired an eleven hour shift seemed impossible. Yet somehow I found myself standing next to Liz, giving out the night-time medications. Mr Bloomfield in bed One, who was recovering from surgery to repair an inguinal hernia, started the banter. "Here are our lovely night-nurses. You ok?" Liz and I nodded simultaneously and basic training jumped in. We had been taught that nurses do not admit to emotions; get tired or sad, or angry for that matter, and if they do they push the emotion inside and only allow it to surface when they are off-duty. Well that was the theory, but at that moment his kindness was just too much and once again my eyes welled with tears. Mr Bloomfield missed nothing; he had 4 daughters of his own and boasted to friends that there was nothing about women he did not know. His voice softened "Hey, what's this? Someone's boyfriend been giving her a hard time?"

I scrubbed my eyes impatiently and forced myself to smile, albeit weakly.

"Get rid of him, Nurse" he continued "He's not worth it if he can't be nice to you."

I wasn't sure how to answer and felt myself blushing. Mr Bloomfield reached over and began to rummage in his locker, emerging triumphantly with an assortment of foil-wrapped chocolates in his hand.

"Here you are my lovelies. These will make you feel better. Chocolate; the way to a woman's heart".

As I moved to his bedside to put his sleeping tablets into his hand, he stuffed the chocolates into my hand and whispered "You send him to me if he gives you anymore trouble. I'll sort him out." I smiled gratefully, feeling my composure return "Thank-you Mr Bloomfield. I'll do that and we'll enjoy these chocs with our cup of tea later."

We moved on to the next bed and were once again treated with warmth and kindness. I realised that several patients had noticed my tears and in their own way were trying to make me feel better. By the end of the drug round we had collected quite a pile of chocolates and fruit. Liz deposited them on the ward desk to enjoy later when the lights were out and everyone was settled.

Before Liz disappeared into the utility room to put the steriliser on she said "Just check the drips are ok Joy. Then we can have our tea."

I took the torch and did as she asked, but when I reached the third bed, I realised, with dismay, that the infusion was not running; in fact the lower chamber of the drip set was completely empty, as was the entire bottle of fluid. Looking carefully I saw the fluid was in the tubing and disappearing rapidly towards the patients bandaged arm. Although unsure what needed to be done, I knew enough to realise it was important to stop the flow as quickly as I could, so I turned the regulatory valve off.

I rushed to find Liz in the utility room. She stood in a cloud of steam as she lifted a bowl from the steriliser with a large pair of forceps.

"Liz" I began trying to sound calm "Bed 6's drip has run through."

"Bugger" she replied. "Just what I needed". She closed the steriliser asking. "Have you turned it off?" I nodded. "Good. Well done. It's only a little early. It shouldn't be a problem. Come with me and we'll sort it out." I followed her across the dark ward, and when we reached bed 6 she checked his prescription chart. "He's written up for another 1000 ml of Normal Saline over 8 hours. Can you get another bottle?"

When I returned with the fluid Liz was applying her personal Spencer Wells forceps to the tubing just below the closed clamp. "We'll get you some of these forceps to keep in your pocket." She said. "They are essential treatment when dealing with drips."

As I watched Liz hung the new bottle of fluid up on the stand and attached the empty tubing to it. She turned to face me. "Basically we should have caught this drip before it went so far." She explained "If we put a full bottle up without dispelling the air in the tubing, it would be extremely dangerous, as it would force air into the circulation and could cause an air embolus."

I must have looked horrified because Liz smiled and touched my arm "It's ok. The drip is stopped by the valve and my forceps. There is no danger now. Watch carefully."

She squeezed the lower chamber of the giving set until it was half full. Taking her pen from her pocket she wound the tubing, above the forceps, tightly around it; squashing the air upwards as she did so. Gradually the tubing filled with fluid as the air bubbled back into the bottle. When the tubing was full, she began tapping it gently with her pen. She laughed. "It doesn't look very clinical but believe me its effective. It gets rid of all the tiny bubbles. We're almost there."

Satisfied that the air had dispelled, she stopped tapping and released the forceps and valve, watching carefully as the fluid started to drip again. Finally, looking at her watch, she adjusted the valve until there were about 16 drips per minute. She smiled "That's about the right rate. We'll keep an eye on it but it should be fine. Thank goodness you caught it when you did."

She glanced at the clock. "Oh go and make a cuppa. I'm parched." I hurried to the kitchen returning with 2 mugs of steaming tea. We sat huddled in the pool of light by the desk. I cradled my mug to my chest; its warmth was comforting. Liz had found a toffee and was chewing relentlessly.

She glanced at me and frowned "What was all that about with Mr Bloomfield? Didn't know you had a boyfriend. Are you alright?"

I sighed, unsure of what to say. "Sorry" I began "everything just got to me..... It's just." once again I felt my eyes fill with tears, but I plodded on "It's just that I am so tired, I don't know what to do with myself."

Liz looked concerned "You sleeping?" she asked. I shook my head. Liz reached into her bag which lay at her feet.

"You should have said" she reprimanded. "Its common, especially on your first set of nights. Look" she placed a buff envelope, into my hand and continuing in a whisper said "Try a couple of these. They're sleeping tablets Mogadons. We give them to the patients, don't we? And they usually help don't they?"

"Yes but..." I was really surprised. Take tablets prescribed for the patients? My face gave away my concerns.

Liz continued "Look, if you went to the doc and told her you couldn't sleep, this is what she'd give you, but then you have to go first to that nosey Home Sister to make a doctor's appointment and she makes a real fuss. Anyone would think she personally paid the bloody doctor. Besides, her surgery doesn't start till midday you'll waste the whole morning when you could have been asleep. So we usually dispense ourselves a few tablets from the trolley. What's the worry? You're doing them a favour anyway because you can't manage without sleep and you would have to go off sick. Take one and I bet tomorrow night you'll be fine." She thrust the envelope into the bottom of my bag before continuing "Just don't broadcast it, that's all..." with a shrug of her shoulders she finished her tea and disappeared into the Utility room to empty the steriliser. I felt relieved, perhaps after all, I might manage my span of Night Duty.

After breakfast, I undressed hurriedly and opened the precious package. Placing the two round, white tablets in my mouth I swallowed them, washing them down with a gulp of nasty, luke-warm water from my chipped tooth mug. I was so excited I could have been drinking the finest champagne. I settled back, nestling as much as I could into the thin regulation pillows and the starched sheets reminding me of the ward. I lay starring at the ceiling longing for sleep to overwhelm me. Then nothing until the shrill ringing of my alarm-clock woke me after what seemed only a matter of minutes. It was 7.30. I felt incredulous. I had slept for almost 11 hours. Outside it was dark. The Mogadon had succeeded. Worried that there may be unpleasant side-effects from taking sleeping pills I dressed tentatively but the only effect was one of overwhelming relief. I felt normal again.

Bank nurses had to report to Night Sister every night, who would then send them to the appointed ward. I had been on ward 3 for the last 4 nights and imagined I would remain there. I was looking forward to seeing Liz again and thanking her for her advice.

Sister Parnell was on-duty that evening. I ambled over to the table, where she sat studying a large folder of foolscap paper. Only a tiny strip of dark hair, severely parted in the middle, was visible under her frilly spotted organza cap.

"Nurse Cooper" I began.

Without raising her eyes she ran her finger down her list until she reached my name. "Casualty" she instructed.

I hesitated thinking I had misheard her "Sorry?" I began.

This time she raised her eyes and stared at me intently. I felt my face become hot as she did so. "Did you not hear me nurse?" she spoke quietly emphasising each word "I said you are needed on Casualty tonight."

I stood mesmerised. Casualty? I had never even set foot in the place. I had heard stories of busy nights there; and casualty nurses were always put on a pedestal as they recounted the gory details of accidents they had encountered, but I was terrified.

I began to protest "But sister, I've been on ward 3 for the past few nights…"

"Nurse Cooper" her icy voice cut through my objections. "I don't care where you have been. I am telling you that tonight you are needed in Casualty. So please stop wasting my time and go."

Defeated, I turned to leave but not before I heard Sister "Tutting" loudly and exclaim to no-one in particular "insolent girl". My heart sank. Perhaps casualty wouldn't be that bad.

The hospital had been built in the Victorian era and, although architecturally pleasing, it struggled to meet the demands of modern day medical emergencies. Casualty was situated in the basement, below street level, which meant that arriving ambulances were forced to transport patients on trolleys, in various degrees of distress, at breakneck speed down a steep slope. To complicate things further the beds in the ambulance then were fixed, so the ambulance crews' first job was to collect a trolley for their patient.

I learnt later that a longstanding arrangement meant that if patients were very ill the crew would keep sounding the sirens and it was the job of the most junior nurse to grab a trolley and rush it up the slope to them.

When I arrived, that day, it was chaos. A road traffic accident had left all the permanent staff and senior doctors dashing between three of the cubicles, dealing with the victims. I stood still feeling conspicuous and frightened, unable to imagine what good I would be in this terrifying place. In the corner huddled a group of the accident- survivors who although uninjured were visibly shaken. I tried to avoid their eyes because I knew I wouldn't be able to answer any of their questions.

A rather dishevelled staff-nurse with flushed face and startling red curly hair cascading from her cap like a chestnut horse's mane, appeared at my side. She took my arm enquiring. "You Bank?"

I nodded miserably and was about to add that this was the first time I had set foot in the place when she continued "Great" and started to propel me towards what looked like a small clinical room.

In the corridor outside a group of rather inebriated young men were holding a heated conversation overlooked, by two uniformed policemen. By way of explanation my guide, whose name badge informed me was called Staff Nurse Briggs pushed me past the crowd and into the room. On the door was a chipped enamelled sign: 'Minor Ops.' I tried again to explain that I really wouldn't be much help, but Staff Nurse gave me a quick smile and said "No worries. It's simple. The good doctor over there will take care of you." And with that she left.

The room looked shabby and unloved with tired, white clinical tiles and a stifling smell of antiseptic and alcohol. The only furniture was a black metal examination couch covered by a sheet currently spattered with a mixture of blood and iodine. On the couch, looking pale and scared was a guy of about 18 called Dave. The smell of cheap beer attacked my senses as I noticed the doctor, who was in the final stages of suturing a deep laceration across the back of the boy's hand. He tied the final knot, sighed, and then noticed me.

"Hi" he began. "You drawn the short straw?" I nodded and he smiled. "Well tonight seems to be fight night at the station. This lad and his mates outside had a few drinks, then there was an argument, and this" he gestured outside to the crowd "is the result. The police are here because several of the lads have been arrested, but it's our job to stitch them up and check them over before they are taken to the police-station." Suturing complete, he straightened his back and began to peel off his gloves. "So then" he continued "That all seems ok. Let's get this lad on the move and the next one in."

I dressed Dave's hand with clean gauze, securing it with a large strip of plaster. I just needed to check his

Neuro obs to ensure there were no problems. Usually it was a quick job, but not today. Taking Dave's pulse and blood pressure was no problem but when I took his hand and asked him to squeeze mine, he obviously thought I had a different agenda. He was staring intently at my chest and following his gaze I realised he was trying to focus on my name badge.

"J," he began "Now what does that stand for I wonder?"

I smiled briefly trying hard to look professional but he was not deterred "Julie ... that's it isn't it Nurse? I had a girlfriend called Julie, but she wasn't as pretty as you."

To my annoyance I felt myself blush, but aware of the queue of people waiting for our attention I spoke briskly "No Dave, it isn't Julie and right now I need to finish these obs so you can leave. Please be a good chap and help me."

He became quiet and I thought my rebuke had worked. I leaned forward to shine my pen torch into his eyes to check that his pupils were equal and reacting to light. All was well with the left eye but when I moved towards the right he suddenly lurched towards me, his lips pursed as if to kiss me. I jumped backwards into the arms of Dr Blake, or Simon, I later learned, who had noticed what was happening and come to rescue me. "I'll finish off here" he said "Go and get yourself a quick cup of coffee before we tackle the rest of the queue."

He pointed to a cubicle where I could see the tell-tale electric kettle and tray of mugs. I disappeared towards it but not before I heard Simon say "Now then young man let's just check your eyes then you can go off with the nice policeman outside." Dave did not think much of the plan and for the next ten minutes the whole department heard him lamenting "No not you. Where's that lovely Julie. I love her ... I really do."

Fortified by the coffee and feeling more confident by the minute, I assisted Simon to suture all the lads who had been involved in the fight. Generally speaking as the alcohol took effect they became much quieter and needed less local anaesthetic. The next couple of hours passed quickly.

With one more lad needing sutures Simon summoned him into the room while I prepared my final trolley. As he staggered through the door, I noticed the livid red wound on his forearm but was surprised to see that his arm was still hand cuffed to the burly, uniformed officer who accompanied him, his helmet under his arm.

"Any chance of losing the cuffs constable?" Simon asked pleasantly.

The policeman coughed "No can do I'm afraid doc. This lad was the ringleader and what's more he's got form. It would be more than my life was worth if he did a runner. No I'm afraid the cuffs stay. Where he goes; I go too."

Simon shrugged as the policeman proceeded to settle his ample frame on a nearby stool. Simon began inspecting the boys wound "Right, this looks as if it needs a fair bit of attention. I'm just going to numb the area." Picking up a syringe full of local he started to inject around the wounds, when there was a sudden thud and the hand- cuffed arm jerked violently.

We turned to see the policeman; face a ghastly white had slid from the stool and was now lying in a heap on the floor, his helmet rolling around next to him, like a skittle at a funfair.

"Nurse" Simon began "It looks as if our policeman has fainted could you just check him out?"

I knelt beside that policeman speaking quietly "Constable, are you ok?"

His eyes flickered as I spoke and some colour returned to his cheeks "Where am I?" He muttered looking around the room slowly.

"You've fainted. You're ok." I said checking his pulse as I did so. He struggled as if to get to his feet. I put an arm on his shoulder

"Don't move. Just keep still. I think I can hear one of your colleagues outside. I'll get help." He started to protest, then sank back as if too weary to care. In the corridor a sergeant was taking notes from a witness. "Can I have a word Sergeant?" I interrupted, explaining what had happened "Can you help" I continued. "Our patient needs quite a few stitches and it's hardly ideal for doctor trying to suture when your colleague is passed out next to him."

The Sergeant groaned "Leave it with me." He vanished into the room and reappeared after a few curt words and the sound of opening handcuffs. Finally the constable exited, helmet restored to its position under his arm.

"Sorry about that lass" he whispered as he passed "Serge has made me promise to talk to someone about my needle phobia before I cuff anyone else in hospital again." He disappeared down the corridor and as soon as he was out of earshot came the sound of laughter from his colleagues. I suspected he would never live it down.

4am and Casualty had at last emptied. All patients had either been admitted to the wards or sent home. It had been a busy night and although the department was in dire need of re-organizing and cleaning, everyone was tired and desperate for a break. Staff-nurse, who was looking even more dishevelled now, called us

"Well it appears we have a lull, so let's make the most of it." she began, "The canteen is closed now, so I'm afraid toast is the only food I can offer, but let's get something to eat and then we can start to clear up...."

She stopped talking as the familiar sound of the ambulance sirens were heard outside. A low-pitched groan echoed around the room.

"Well it looks as if that plan is off" she shrugged. "Sorry everyone". As I searched for an available trolley, an ambulance driver burst into the department, carrying a large steaming pie. His smile said it all "Heard you were busy and this was going begging at the station, so thought you might fancy a bit of apple pie."

Apple Pie had never tasted so good.

My final night saw me sitting next to Liz listening to the report on ward 3. The day staff were getting ready to leave, checking the obs. were done; the fluid balance charts were up-to date and finally removing the dirty cups from the patient's lockers and stacking them in the kitchen. Expectancy filled the air as the day staff looked forward to some rest, a bath and a good night's sleep. It must be catching as despite facing an 11 hour shift I felt exultant. I had survived. I was back on duty with Liz, the ward did not look too busy and tomorrow was almost here.

Then instead of the usual routine of breakfast followed by a hasty retreat to bed I would make my way to Euston Square Station, from where a district line train would take approximately 60 minutes to take me home. There, Mum would be waiting and together we'd have cups of tea, from the worn brown earthenware pot and hot buttered toast cut from real bread, not the mass-produced stuff used at the hospital chosen, like every item, with economy in mind. I forced my thoughts to return to work, not daring to anticipate the bliss of falling into my own bed, with a soft mattress and sheets which were soft and fragrant having been dried in the sunshine and buffeted by gentle breezes.....

"And finally Mr. Brown; Bed 28 is having surgery tomorrow to repair a right inguinal hernia. He's first on the list. Consent is signed. Pre-med is written up. So he'll need to be Nil by Mouth from midnight."

I jumped as I realized that I had day dreamed through most of the report and Liz was staring at me. Staff-nurse yawned and the rest of the day shift appeared, as if by magic. "Have a good night" they called over their shoulders as they retreated from the ward.

Liz was still staring at me "You look happy" she said.

"I'm great" I replied and unable to keep the sound of victory from my voice continued, "Last night tonight. I've survived. Thanks to you."

She laughed and said "Don't know about that. We've still got tonight to get through. Let's get to work."

And we did. And time flew. The routine, which had seemed so taxing a week ago, was comfortable and supportive. The patients who had been operated on at the beginning of the week were recovering. There was a sense of fun and humour in the air as we gave out the evening's medicines and helped our patients settle for the night.

"Is this your last night?" asked Mr. Jones, our faithful tea-boy. "I'm off home tomorrow too, so they'll be looking for a new recruit for the morning cuppas won't they?" He smirked "Well it won't be our problem, eh nurses?"

Liz nodded "You're right. This time tomorrow Nurse Cooper and myself won't be worrying about things like that I can assure you."

Mr. Carter in the next bed joined in the banter "I bet you won't." He winked and opening his locker, pulled out a box of chocolate which he handed to us. "My wife bought you these we wanted to say thank you" he explained. "I'd been dreading coming in here. You hear such stories. But you've all been so kind. I won't say it's been a holiday, but it's been o.k.

And so it was, that at the end of that night, as I tidied the sluice and adjusted the toilet rolls in readiness for Sister's final inspection, I was suddenly overwhelmed to find that I loved this job. It was hard and we all had bad times but, although it sounded corny I felt it was a real privilege to meet these people who were our patients and make a difference to them.

I tried to explain this to Liz as we made our exit from the ward. "Oh kid." she groaned "It's the tired-ness talking. It makes us go soppy. Give it a break." But I glanced at her as she waved a final goodbye to Mr. Jones and I swear I saw a tear in her eye. Despite what she said, I think she felt as I did.

Chapter 8:
Living out

All student nurses had to live in the Nurses Home for the first 2 years training. No exceptions. So passing the 2 year deadline was a significant moment. Professionally we exchanged our white belts for striped belts and that one transaction found ourselves overnight, senior student nurses; now deemed able to be responsible for running a ward in the absence of any trained staff.

With that first flush of confidence came a longing, for many of us to be free from the ties and restrictions of living-in. We had changed gear; progressed and two years of being subservient and following, what seemed to us, archaic house rules was enough. We wanted freedom. Simple things like having a private telephone conversation with a friend or entertaining or socializing normally with men were important. We'd missed them.

Mary, Jane and I clutched the inevitable mugs of coffee as we discussed the options "So we want to move out" Mary began. "What do we do? Where do we go? Can we afford it?"

Jane was better informed "Jenny and Barbara are moving out. I heard them talking about it at lunch."

"Right. Plan of action. Point 1; Talk to them" Mary began to scribble her list on a huge pad of paper.

At supper we saw Barbara drinking coffee in the lounge. She grinned when she heard our questions.

"Yeah. Sandy, Nicky, Karen and I are all moving in together. Tufnell Park. Can't wait. There's a Mrs Barnsley. She owns lots of flats in the area. Likes letting to nurses apparently." She thrust her hand into her dress pocket and produced a slip of paper, which she handed to Mary. "Here this is her number. Give her a ring." Gulping her coffee she turned to make her way back to the ward. "Good luck" she called over her shoulder "It'll be nice to get out of this dump."

The flat, Mrs Barnsley showed us the next day, was hardly palatial but it had three bedrooms and looked clean. It was situated on the upper floors of a three storey Victorian terrace on the main road through Tufnell Park. In total, the house had been sub-divided into 3 self-contained units. A basement apartment; a ground floor flat; and finally our upper maisonette, as it was grandly called.

Our new landlady- to be, rather breathless after climbing the steep staircase, told us proudly "It's all newly decorated as you can see and" she paused to emphasise what she was about to say "It has a new kitchen and bathroom."

Looking round the kitchen door we nodded, aware that the sink did look fairly new, as did the fixtures in the bathroom. The only other furniture in the kitchen, however, was a strange green cabinet with a pull-down flap that served as a work surface, an ancient fridge and a rather grubby looking table with 4 chairs, so it was hardly a cooks' paradise.

"It's on the main bus-route to the hospital, so no travelling problems" Mrs B. continued. We held our breath as she slowly came to the most important fact for us; what was the rent? "The rent is 69 guineas a month" she announced adding sternly. "And I'll have no funny business or late rent. My sons will be round to collect it the first Monday of every month."

I watched mesmerized as one of her many chins wobbled as she spoke. Mary smiled. We had been warned about Mrs.B and her use of guineas. It was a sneaky way of maximizing the rent. 69 guineas sounded almost the same as £69, but as a guinea equalled £1 plus 1 shilling, those extra shillings soon added up. It would not be too many years until with decimalization of the pound, guineas became extinct.

We had previously calculated that we could afford £13-£14 each for rent, and I was desperately trying to do the necessary sums when Mary spoke. "Thank-you for showing us around,. We are very interested. Could you hold the flat for us for 24 hours? We could get back to you by tomorrow." Mrs B drew her breath in so sharply her dentures wobbled, but did agree to hold it until the next day.

We smiled politely and made our way back to the hospital, finding to our delight the journey on the bus only took 20 minutes. The general consensus was that the flat was just what we needed; all that was required was to find two more people to share it with us.

Jane took the initiative "I think Anna and Helen might be interested." These were two friends in our set, who I did not know very well, but Jane had worked with them and she was a good judge of character, so Mary and I left Jane to contact them as soon as possible.

Later that evening as we were once again working out our finances in Mary's room, Jane appeared with

Helen and Anna in tow. "They've said yes" she screeched jumping up and down in excitement.

Mary, standing, gave them both a hug "Are you sure it's ok?" she asked "Has Jane explained about costs etc.?" Of course Jane had; so arrangements were made for us all to meet with Mrs.B the next day and confirm we wanted the flat. At last we were moving out. It had all seemed so easy, it didn't seem possible.

Our parents, however, were a bit more difficult to convince, believing that we would either starve to death, or be kidnapped and sold in the white slave trade they had reputedly read about in the press. We, on the other hand were full of bravado reassuring them we could afford the monthly rent. Our answers were a little less confident when questioned about the heating system. Later, we would discover for ourselves the reality of living in a flat, in which the sole means of heating was a 2 bar electric fire in the lounge and hot water came from an immersion heater funded by a pay as you go meter, which gobbled shillings down like a child could devour chips.

The flat, when we moved in, seemed like heaven. It was summer and we enjoyed the novelty of showering and changing out of our uniforms in the locker rooms at the hospital when we came off-duty. (It was unthinkable to wear your uniform outside the hospital.) We took turns to cook, shop and clean and we all seemed to just enjoy the freedom it gave us. In the balmy summer evenings we walked to nearby Parliament Hill Fields and watched as the sun set over the city. If we felt too tired or lazy to go out, we'd listen to our favourite LP's on our portable record player. Songs from Bob Dylan, the Beatles and the show everyone was talking about, "Hair", echoed around the room.

Of course, our late night sessions where, with mugs of cocoa in hand, we discussed patients, men and colleagues continued.

It was on one of these occasions that Helen suddenly said "We've been here for over a month now, and I think we should have a party."

Mary looked uncertain "I'm not all that much of a party person" she explained "Are you serious?"

Helen was upbeat "Oow come on.. Everyone has a party these days. It'll make the place seem more like home. And we've got loads of friends living nearby... they'd all come." There was a silence in the room, but Helen, undeterred continued, "Just think Joy, you could invite that Jimmy Wassesname? You know the one from ENT that you're always going on about."

I felt my cheeks turning red as she continued "It would give us the chance to give him the once over."

"Helen please" I begged "I don't keep going on about him. Besides I haven't seen him since I left ENT."

She looked victorious "Precisely.... If we have a party you get to see him again."

We knew it; she'd won. We picked a Saturday 2 weeks away, when we were all off-duty. Mary, organized as ever, stuck a sheet of foolscap paper on the kitchen wall labelled; "Ideas re Party" the list grew steadily, until suddenly the day arrived. Helen burst into the kitchen singing "Tonight, tonight"...

Mary laughed "Yes Helen, message understood. Let's get the list down"

By 8pm that evening the flat looked ready for a party. We had pushed the furniture back to the walls to create a feeling of space and replaced the 60 watt light bulbs with red ones which bathed the room in a crimson haze. Despite Helen's protests, Mary had cut little squares of cheese which she combined with a chunk of tinned pineapple onto cocktail sticks. These she stuck artistically into a halved orange so it resembled a hedgehog that had had an encounter with a compost heap.

Helen was indignant "Mary I'm not saying there anything wrong with them, but people aren't interested in food, they only come to parties for the music and the alcohol."

I was tempted to add "and the sex and the Pot." I had heard reports of a couple of "Parties" that had been over-run with gatecrashers and descended into a bit of an orgy, and I was feeling nervous.

Mary however was unperturbed. "Well Helen" she argued "my friends will definitely be interested in the food." and she continued to fill the cereal bowls with salted peanuts and crisps.

One battle remained. The lounge was quite small and Helen felt our large bedroom upstairs would make an ideal second area for people to "chill".

This time Jane spoke "Well I'm happy to give up my room on one condition. I'm working a late tomorrow so I need sleep. At 1 am whatever is happening in my room stops and it becomes my bedroom again."

Mary nodded her consent and Helen, outnumbered, agreed. Within minutes our beds were stripped and covered with a counterpane to improvise as seating. We made the bedding into individual packs, like those used for patients returning from theatre, and stacked them in the wardrobe.

At 9 pm just as we were beginning to think that no-one was coming, there was a tap on the door. Two girls of a similar age to us stood there, wearing flowing flowery dresses in a kaleidoscope of colours. Their long hair was pulled back from their faces and one of them had weaved a weary-looking daisy chain through her blonde curls. "Hi remember us?" They asked. I nodded trying my best to look as if I did as I ushered them in. "Its Chloe and Laura. From the basement flat." they explained "Helen told us you were having a party and we thought it would be cool to come Are we the first?"

For a moment it was awkward, but as I opened the cider the girls had bought and Mary showed them where to find "the nibbles", Helen, who had been "Creating a party atmosphere upstairs", appeared. We were surprised to see her dressed in a long turquoise kaftan, embroidered with an intricate feather design, and round her neck she had woven a long string of coloured beads interlaced with tiny mirrors. She looked stunning and greeted the new arrivals enthusiastically, hugging them and saying "Chloe, Laura I'm so glad you could come."

Wriggling free, Laura produced a small packet from her tiny linen bag and said "I've bought you a present, I saw it at the market last week and thought of you" Helen looking as excited as a small child on Christmas morning, tore off the wrapping paper to find a round enamel badge bearing the words " Ban the Bomb." Once again she clung to Laura saying "Thank you so much" and carefully pinned the badge to her kaftan.

All at once the guests began to arrive. The party, it seemed had begun. For the next hour a steady stream of people entered the flat, some known; some not. There seemed to be two distinct groups. Group 1 we categorized as the Hippy crew. Their long hair flowing past their shoulders, girls in flowery long dresses, blokes in worn jeans with flowery shirts, or tee shirts with livid slogans; 'ban the bomb;' and 'Make love; Not war'. They clutched small paper –wrapped packets and bottles of cheap cider, and after doing a quick requie of the flat, disappeared upstairs. Burst of songs by Jimi Hendrix or Bob Dylan drifted downstairs, together with the sickly, sweet smell of incense. Helen, it seemed was at home in that group. She appeared downstairs occasionally to collect more drinks from the kitchen, looking ecstatic. "Everything ok Helen?" Mary enquired.

"It's cool, it's just so cool" she replied as she disappeared upstairs again to the source of such coolness.

Group 2's dress code comprised of mini-skirts and a smart little polyester top for the girls and jeans and a casual shirt for the blokes. There was the odd exception. Barbara, one of our set, quite out of character, went for the big entrance. Making her way to the centre of the lounge, she clapped her hands to get our attention and when she was sure we were all looking, pulled off her coat, and then did a big twirl saying "What do you think?"

She was a tall willowy girl and her long black hair, usually concealed in a neat bun at the back of her neck, today fell loosely over her shoulders. The main focus of the room, however, seemed to be her slender legs, which looked about half a mile long as she appeared to be wearing red satin shorts, with a co-ordinating figure hugging red and white top. For a moment no-one spoke, so she repeated the twirl. Mary began cautiously "You look nice. Shorts are really you."

Barbara snorted "These are not shorts Mary. They are Hot-pants. The latest from Carnaby Street." She paused to let the information sink in "They cost a bomb, but I needed cheering up so I thought; What the Heck."

After such a speech what could we do? There was a burst of applause and comments like "Well done Babs. You look great." restored her flagging confidence and she strode into the kitchen to get a drink. One of our other guests, Henry, a friend of Helens and a chartered accountant, seemed to be paying particular attention to the Hot-Pants. We saw him too enter the kitchen, and before long they had found a quiet corner of the lounge and were giggling together.

Everyone soon settled into party mode; chatting in small groups and as Mary had predicted enjoying the "nibbles". In the background, our scant collection of LP's played on our faithful old Bush record-player. The Beatles 'Hard Day's Night' competed with Donovan 'Trying to Catch the Wind', but eventually Mike Jagger asking everyone to 'Get off Of His Cloud' had a few of us up on our feet, dancing. As usual there were more women than men but undeterred we danced in groups with the few couples smooching on the edge of the room.

Just when it had seemed everyone had arrived, Jimmy was at the door, carrying a bowl containing what seemed to be a mixture of fruit floating in a pale straw-coloured fluid. He was accompanied by another guy who, although shorter, looked almost as gorgeous as Jimmy. "Sorry we're late" Jimmy began, speaking loudly to make himself heard above the music. "I'm second on call and it took a while to get away." He paused and gave me a smile that made my knees turn to water. "I might have to dash off too, I'm afraid." he continued "and I gave your number as my contact for tonight. Hope that's ok?"

I nodded. Of course it was ok. Anything to have him here, with me now, in the room was more than ok. My spirits soared. He handed me the bowl he was carrying and said "I've bought some punch" and as I took it he added "Oh and meet John" His companion smiled.

"Hello John" I mouthed clutching the bowl to my chest. "Come and get yourselves a drink."

We made our way to the kitchen and I rinsed some glasses and ladled some punch into them. Mary arrived, anxious to meet this Jimmy she had heard so much about. Introductions completed, I poured a drink saying "Jimmy's bought some punch Mary. Fancy a glass?"

She nodded politely, but when Jimmy wasn't looking she beckoned me into the hallway. Once out of earshot she began to whisper "He's lovely pet but"... her face clouded.

"What's the matter Mary? It's not like you to be lost for words" I asked.

At first she hesitated, and then still whispering replied "It's just the punch. Do you think it is ok? Maggie from Cas told me last week that she'd been to a party with some Med Students and she can't even remember what happened. The punch had been doctored with Ethyl alcohol. Everyone ended up unconscious."

I thought for a moment then replied "Two things Mary. A) Jimmy is a Houseman not a Med. Student and I don't think he'd do anything that stupid. B) He's on-call tonight, so he's unlikely to want to be rendered unconscious."

Still she looked hesitant, but sipped the drink gingerly. At that moment Jimmy arrived in the hall. "You ok ladies?" he asked "I hope the punch is not a disappointment; it's very low in alcohol I'm afraid. It's mainly fruit juice and a bit of white wine." He paused and when we didn't reply continued "If I get called in, it wouldn't look very good if I turned up drunk, so I guessed it would be safer if I bought my own drink. At least that way I know what's in it."

He smiled and once again I remembered why I liked him, but the question was did he think similarly of me or was he just an all-out nice guy who made everyone feel special?

The rest of the evening rushed past and the lights got dimmer and the music softer. A few people seemed to be dividing into couples, but there was still a large group of us who were happy just to enjoy the music, drink and have the occasional dance if the mood was right. Jimmy was part of this group and was probably every party's dream guest, making sure everyone was included and telling countless funny stories. I looked enviously at Barbara who was wrapped in Henry's arms, looking blissfully happy as they swayed to the music.

I had disappeared into the kitchen to wash some glasses, when I was vaguely aware of our phone ringing and a few minutes later Jimmy appeared by my side, putting his jacket on. "Fraid that was the hospital. I'm needed in cas. Got to go. Thanks for a good time."

I tried not to show my disappointment and said. "Thanks for coming Jimmy. It's been great." I handed him the, now empty, punch bowl and as I did so our fingers touched briefly. It was as if an electric shock passed through my body. "Here take this"

I stammered aware that my cheeks were beginning to glow. Drawing near, Jimmy leaned forward and kissed me gently on the cheek, then with a wave of his hand, exited. I stood very still staring at the spot where he had just been. My hand went to my cheek. Jimmy had kissed me. Nothing else mattered, except the delicious memory of the softness of his lips on my face.

Jane broke the spell as she burst into the kitchen. "I can't believe its 2 am" she began "I'm knackered. Have you seen Helen lately?"

I shook my head. No I hadn't seen her for ages. What's more I hadn't heard anything from our "upstairs group" either.

"Well" Jane continued "It's an hour past our agreed deadline and I'm sorry but I have got to go to work tomorrow, sorry I meant today. There's nothing else for it. We'll have to find Helen."

The downstairs room was rapidly emptying as our guests, many of whom were working later, made their way back home to bed. We found Mary and together we crept upstairs. The room, when we entered was very quiet and our eyes took a while to adjust to the darkness. The only light was provided by a few, almost burnt out, candles placed on saucers around the perimeter of the room. A sweet cloying perfume, which I didn't recognize hung in the air, like the scent of flowers in the garden on a hot summers evening. Through the haze, we began to recognize groups of bodies huddled together, as if asleep. Overflowing ash-trays were littered around the room and sporadic bursts of strange bell-like music came from the record –player in the corner.

Mary found Helen sitting cross-legged on the floor, inhaling deeply on what looked like a home-made cigarette. She smiled dreamily as we approached. "Hello you lot" she began "isn't this wonderful. I could stay here forever."

Jane hesitated for a moment then, looking more assertive, said "Yes it is wonderful Helen, but do you think we could have our room back? It's after 2am and we could do with some sleep. You can go downstairs. Most people have gone."

It took Helen a little while to process the request, but smiling ethereally, she struggled to her feet and eventually with the promise of more drinks persuaded everyone downstairs.

The room once empty looked like a rubbish dump, with cans and empty cigarette packets littering the floor. Several bottles containing thin sticks of incense and melted wax from the candles formed mini-landscapes on the chipped saucers on which they stood. Mary opened the window wide, and retrieving the packs of bedding from the cupboard we had put them in earlier, our beds were soon ready for us to fall into, Downstairs the party continued, but for us our only agenda was sleep.

It was after 10am when we stirred, woken by the banging of doors and the smell of bacon. Downstairs Helen greeted us "Hi you lot. They've all just gone. I made them all bacon sandwiches. Wasn't it wonderful?"

Mary and I glanced at each other. We had slept but my eyes felt very heavy and a rock band was thudding in my head. The smell of the bacon, mixed with the odours of unwashed bodies, cigarette smoke, incense and cheap booze. I took a deep breath to try to get rid of the feeling of nausea that was rising in my throat and sank into the nearest chair. Mary opened the window and surveyed the trashed room and prescribed tea before we could fully assess the damage.

Several cups of tea later I felt almost human, ready to tackle the huge pile of washing up while Mary and Jane tried to restore some resemblance of order to the flat. For Helen, however, it was all too much and in a croaky voice she reminded us that she was on Nights that night. She disappeared into her room and all we heard from her was the occasional snore or grunt from under the bedclothes.

Somehow, Jane got to her late shift, leaving Mary and I to restore some order to the flat. By tea-time, although tired, we felt more positive.

As we brewed yet another pot of tea Mary said "It's gone 6. Shall we take Helen in a cup of tea? She'll need to eat before work."

I nodded and took the tea into her placing it by her side. I shook her gently "Helen it's after six. I've bought you some tea." A grunt was the only reply. For the next 30 minutes we called her at 10 minute intervals, but she still did not move. By 7 o'clock we were concerned and felt action was called for, so entering the room together we pulled off the bedclothes and shook her until we got some response, although it was only a flickering of her eyelids. We persisted "Helen you need to get up. It's gone 7 and you need to catch the bus by 8pm or you'll be late."

There was a groan. "Drink your tea Helen" said Mary placing a fresh one on her bedside table. Slowly her eyes opened. "Drink it." Mary commanded watching as Helen slowly rose up supported by an elbow and sipped the liquid tentatively. "Do you want anything to eat?" Mary asked "Toast? Boiled egg?" Another groan was the only response.

Mary and I decided we could do no more but as we sat in the lounge, munching on our toast, we heard the promising sound of drawers being opened and the banging of the bathroom door announced that, at last, Helen was up. "Damn." the word echoed around the room, coming as it did from the bathroom and suddenly a half-dressed Helen appeared, in her hand a strange black bundle which seemed to be dripping water onto the floor.

"Look at these" she said. "They're my only tights. I washed them yesterday. Someone must have drenched them. Now what am I going to do?"

Mary and I shrugged "Sorry Helen. Ours wouldn't fit you." The absence of any heating in the flat made drying clothes a nightmare.

Mary glanced at the clock "You've got half an hour. You could put them in the oven. It might dry them". This seemed the only option, so Helen lit the oven and turned it to low, placing her tights on one of the shelves. Just 25 minutes later, however, another volley of "Damns" hit our ears. Once again Helen appeared in the lounge holding her tights which now appeared to have several huge holes in them.

"They've melted" she wailed, pulling them on to show us the extent of the damage. The area below her knees had 2 large holes on each leg making her look like the victim of an accident. Poor Helen. It was all too much. Just a few hours ago it had been so 'Cool' and life had seemed so good. A big tear welled up in her eye and spilled down her cheek.

Mary came to the rescue and emerged from the kitchen carrying a tube of 'paint-on black shoe polish'. "Here try this" she said. Kneeling down she began to fill the holes on Helens leg with the shoe polish. When she had finished it was difficult to see where the holes ended and the tights began. "Just make sure you don't change your tights before you come home in the morning or everyone will wonder why you've got spotted legs." we warned Helen, who despite everything, managed a watery smile. It seemed the party was well and truly over.

Chapter 9:
P.P.W.

Opposite the red brick main Hospital was a more modern utility type of building, known to the staff as PPW. At first glance it looked more like a hotel; its uniformed doorman standing, like a sentinel, at its revolving glass doors. On the arrival of an expensive looking car he would bustle forward to assist the occupants and their luggage into the building. This building was the prestigious Private Patients Wing, where Consultants bought their paying customers who needed in-patient treatment.

For these people the hurley-burley of an NHS hospital ward was unthinkable. They were accommodated in the single wards on the first 3 floors of the building with an independent Operating Theatre occupying the top floor. The consultants were frequent visitors to the building, caring for their patients personally. This was not the workplace of junior doctors and it was hard, as student nurses, not to feel intimidated in such a powerful place.

The reasons patients paid what seemed to us, exorbitant prices, for this kind of care were varied; for many the attraction was the privacy of the single rooms, each equipped with their own bathroom and telephone. Others enjoyed the personal attention of a Consultant;

and some requiring cosmetic surgery were only able to access this privately. The largest groups of patients however, were businessmen whose firms provided private health care in an effort to ensure sick leave was taken at a time convenient to the firm, not the hospital.

It was here that second year student nurses often found themselves working. Although the majority of the trained nurses were supplied by an agency, it was argued that students could gain valuable experience of medical and surgical conditions in this situation. It was, on the whole, not a popular place to work; patients were known to be very demanding, treating nurses as their servants. The only plus point was the fact that the staff; patient ratio was much higher than in the main hospital and it was therefore much less busy.

One cold winter's morning, with sinking heart, I navigated the revolving doors and made my way to PPW3, ruled over by the intrepid Sister Cowley. Mary's words over breakfast still made me bristle "For goodness sake" she had snapped "Be positive. I know you've just got your striped belt and are longing to get into a surgical ward and boss the juniors about, but that will come." She paused long enough to see my face crumble and my eyes become shiny with unshed tears. "At least PPW's quiet. You can get some studying done." were her final words as I stumbled from the dining room.

I was pleased to hear a buzz of conversation as I entered Sister's office, and began to relax. Glancing around the room I identified at least 6 different uniforms as each agency had its own; generally a basic fitted cotton-polyester dress, in white, blue or, surprisingly, pink. The nurse's plain white disposable paper caps looked positively dull compared to my frilly one, but their white soft shoes looked cool and continental, and as I listened in to their conversation I realized that these girls were well travelled in their nursing careers. Fiona, a slim dark-haired girl smiled at me. "Hello. You new?"

I nodded recognizing her lilting Irish accent. I was about to continue when silence descended on the room as Sister swept in. I felt my face go red as she scanned the room, then me, taking in every detail.

"Nurse Cooper?" she asked. "Yes Sister" I replied trying to sound more confident than I felt. Behind her dark-rimmed glasses her eyes narrowed momentarily, than as if the sun had come out on a dull day she smiled saying "Welcome to PPW. I know first days can be daunting but I'm sure you'll find your time here rewarding".

She nodded and as suddenly as it had come out, the sun disappeared, and I was again aware of the power she held in that place.

I was pleased to discover that I was to work with Fiona. She took my arm as we left the office. "Lucky me" she began "I get to show you around instead of giving out breakfasts. Follow me." At the end of what seemed like a mile of corridor, she stopped. "We get to look after the folks in these 6 rooms today,"

I nodded, looking at the heavy wooden doors and trying to remember what we had been told about the patients inside. It felt strange to be walking on thick plush carpet rather than the lino of the wards and I was amazed how quiet it was. Fiona pointed out the Nurses Station. It consisted of a recess in the corridor, the walls of which had been furnished with some rather cheap-looking cupboards. An expanse of dark laminate served as a desk-top, under which stood two revolving stainless steel office chairs with black plastic cushions.

Behind the desk was a large board on which all the rooms were outlined and numbered. When the patient rang their bell; the room lit up. Fiona stopped beside them "Take note of these" she began. "Patients expect their needs to be met immediately and they can get very rattled if you don't answer quickly."

I pulled a face. "That's hard isn't it? What if you're dealing with someone else?"

Fiona nodded "Couldn't agree more, but these are private patients, and because they are in single wards, they don't see that other people may have more urgent needs that their own." She paused watching my face as I took in what she had said. "As far as the patients are concerned," she continued quietly "they have paid to be looked after when they need it, and it's us who do the looking after. You'll learn a few skills in diplomacy here, if nothing else."

At that moment there was a flash from the board and room no 316 buzzer began, sounding like an angry bee. "Right on cue" Fiona muttered "That's one of ours. Mr. Thompson. Let's see what he wants."

Mr Thompson was sitting on the edge of his bed looking very distressed. He was wearing a pair of maroon striped pyjamas. A matching silk dressing gown with an embroidered coat of arms on its chest pocket was draped over the bed. Peeking out from under the bed just visible were a pair of brown leather slippers. He looked up as we entered and I noticed that his lips looked blue; a strange hissing noise came from behind the mini-mountain that was his pillows. "Hurry up girls" he began "Got to get to the office; can't seem to find my shoes."

Reaching over Fiona recovered the clear plastic oxygen mask from its hiding place behind the pillows, and pulled the elastic over his ears. "Mr Thompson, I think you'll feel better if you put your oxygen mask back on." She chided gently. "You're not going to your office today. You're in hospital. Remember?"

He didn't reply, but allowed himself to be settled back onto his pillows. And we watched as his lips lost their blue- tinge. "Breakfast is coming in a minute" Fiona began "Would you like some porridge?" He nodded and we organised his breakfast and left him watching the news on the television whilst he ate. "We'll be back later to help you wash" Fiona promised.

Once outside again she gave me a brief history. "Poor old boy" she began, "He was a MD of a big business. Engineering, I think. He had a couple of big heart attacks and that together with the fact that he was a 50 fags a day man, has weakened his heart. He's in to try to get him established on a routine of medication, to help his heart cope, but as you saw, he has only to take his oxygen off for a moment and he gets confused. It doesn't look good. I think he's going to need 24 hour care. I don't know whether the family will be able to cope with help at home or if he'll have to go in somewhere. We'll have to wait and see."

In the next room was Madame Duples, an elegant French lady, in her mid-sixties who had come to England for a face lift as a patient of Mr. Mark, a plastic surgeon, Fiona showed me the pre-operative photo of what seemed to me a perfectly ordinary lady, whose face, although not entirely unaged, was rather stunning. Obviously Madame, did not agree and she now regarded us through the slits of her two swollen, bruised eyes.

Her hair, in the photo brunette and neatly folded into a perfect French pleat, was hidden from view under a swathe of stained bandages. Today was her ninth post-operative day and Mr. Mark was to visit to remove her sutures. On the general wards, sutures were usually removed by nurses, but here, this task was the prerogative of the famous surgeon himself.

Fiona seemed very anxious as I followed her into the treatment room and watched as she cleaned the larger of the two trolleys. She sighed and picking up a card-board box began to rummage through its contents, muttering to herself. "You ok?" I asked.

She shrugged "Suppose so, but I hate this. Mr. Mark is so fussy. We've got a list of his peculiar ways somewhere in our 'fad box." She pulled a white card from the box before studying it intently. Next she filled her trolley with a huge variety of dressings, tapes, cleansers and bandages, checking the card as she did so.

"Wow that's a lot of stuff" I began.

"Exactly" she interrupted "that's why I hate it. He is notorious for being sickly sweet to his private patients and a complete bugger to everyone else." She paused "They say that he'll do a quick scan of your trolley and then always ask for what's not on it. He has you running about like a headless chicken. Awful Man." She surveyed her handiwork "Well I've got everything I can think of on here. Let's just see what happens."

At exactly 10.30 Mr. Mark arrived on the ward and made his way straight to Madame's room. Fiona, face flushed, scurried in after him. I followed meekly. Madame positively oozed with delight as Mr. Mark addressed her initially in French. "I need to take those sutures out today and examine you very thoroughly."

He smiled profusely at Madame, but to Fiona only said "Trolley Staff Nurse."

She disappeared and I watched as he began to undo the extensive bandages, to reveal his patients swollen, discoloured face. Fiona arrived with her trolley just as the last bandage was removed. Mr. Mark sighed loudly and, glaring at Fiona said "I'll need a bag for these, Nurse or did you envisage I'd stuff them in my pocket?"

She flinched and said "There are bags on the trolley Sir," pointing at the clinical waste bag clipped to the end of her trolley.

Another sigh came from the surgeon as he continued "Well perhaps you could find the energy to take the soiled bandage and put it in the bag".

He thrust the debris carelessly at her before turning to his patient and saying "I'll just wash my hands, and then I'll have a good look at my handiwork." Smiling he left the room, to return moments later, dripping hands held at shoulder height.

Fiona offered him a sterile towel and he snatched it, and, ignoring us completely, addressed Madame. "How are you finding being a patient in England Madame?"

Sighing she replied faintly "I am coping.... Just" She hesitated "The food... C'est terrible."

He took her hand before continuing "I am so sorry my dear. I can only imagine your distress. Alas I have no authority concerning domestic arrangements."

Lowering his voice and glaring at us as he whispered "It is so hard to get decent staff mon Cherie."

Fiona and I stood upright as if to deflect his attack. Decent staff? What a nerve? As for the food, why PPW was renowned for its excellent cuisine. Mr. Mark continued "Have you considered having your food delivered privately? I understand Harrods or Fortnum and Mason provide an excellent service." His attention returned to more medical things and he began to examine Madame's sutures. Satisfied he smiled "They look wonderful, my dear. I will get on with the task of removing them. I will be gentle, but Madame you must be very brave."

He pulled on some sterile gloves and opened the lids of the gallipot and dressing bowl. Fiona retrieved a bottle of Chlorhexidine solution from the bottom of the trolley Mr. Mark tutted. "Nurse, how many times must I express my dislike of chlorhexidine. Get me some 0.9% Sodium Chloride"

Again Fiona scanned the bottom shelf of the trolley and this time found two ampoules of Sodium Chloride. "In the bowl Nurse" hissed the doctor "Where else would I want it." He watched carefully as Fiona snapped open the glass files and poured their contents into a gallipot.

Working with fine stainless steel forceps, he lifted the knot of the first suture and cut the black silk underneath with suture scissors, easing the thread from the wound with the forceps. Madame sat very still, hardly daring to breathe. Standing at the side of the bed in case my assistance was required, I initially felt superfluous, but suddenly Madame grabbed my hand and squeezed it violently, digging her perfectly painted scarlet fingernails into my hand until I almost cried out.

Fiona, on the other hand was sent from the room by the increasingly irate surgeon. He decided the gauze for the final dressing was the wrong size and when she returned with the stuff he had asked for, he decided that the tape she had supplied was too wide. Fiona returned with a narrower one, but that apparently was too narrow. Once again Fiona exited. While she was gone, Mr. Mark removed the final suture and cleaned the dried blood and debris from Madame's face. He stood back admiring his handiwork. "Beautiful. My dear you look beautiful."

I struggled to keep my face in neutral as I looked at the patient's bruised face with livid red tracks indicating the extent of her surgery. Beautiful was not the adjective I would have used, especially now her dirty hair, highlighted with streaks of the pre-operative iodine and clots of dried blood, hung tangled about her face.

Undeterred Mr. Mark took her brush and began to gently tease the unruly hair. Satisfied he picked up the hand mirror which was lying on the trolleys lower shelf and with a hand on Madame's shoulder said "Allow me."

I watched anxiously. Would she scream? Mr. Mark's eloquent voice continued softly. "Don't look at the bruising or the scars, my dear. They are temporary; they will go. I ask that you look at the firmness of your profile and the smoothness of your cheeks. Surely Madame you must acknowledge that now you will be truly beautiful." Madame nodded and wiped a tear from the corner of her eye "Merci Monsieur," she whispered "Merci…"

Mr. Mark inclined his head slightly and taking her hand kissed it gently. "Tomorrow nurse will assist you shower and wash your hair. But today, my dear you must rest; recover." He turned to leave "Au reviour Madame. I will call again tomorrow."

At that moment, Fiona, several reels of tape in her hand arrived in the room "I'm afraid these are the only tapes we have in stock Mr. Mark."

He glanced first at them, then at Fiona and continued his exit. "I've decided a further dressing is unnecessary nurse" slamming the door as he left.

Fiona began to clear away the trolley making a lot of noise as she did so. I fluffed up Madame's pillows and, at her request, helped her out of her white silk bed-jacket which had a tiny splash of blood on. She rested back in bad and closed her eyes. "Would you like a tea or coffee?" I asked.

"Non, no I must rest" she began in a small voice "You may leave me." As I moved to do so she whispered "I have one last Job for you Nurse. I need the phone number of the shop Mr. Mark recommended. Fortnum and Mason? Is that the one?"

Fiona was furiously piling the stainless steel bowls into the sink, muttering under her breath, when I entered the utility room. "Stupid bloody man. Who does he think I am? His servant?"

I didn't speak and started to unpack the equipment from the bottom of the trolley. Eventually Fiona ran out of names to call the man. She glared at me. "Sorry".

I shrugged. "He was awful. We shouldn't have to put up with it."

Fiona laughed "Well that's how you get treated when you care for private patients. Anyway" she continued "Enough of him. Why should he spoil our day? Let's just get Madame her blessed phone number then I think it's time for coffee. Believe me I could do with one."

It took almost two weeks to feel at home on PPW. It was hard after working on the main wards and caring for so many patients who, although ill, treated nurses with respect. One day after a particularly trying shift I could hardly wait to get back to the flat and unload all my angst on anyone who would be prepared to listen.

The honeymoon period of living out had begun to fade. Summer days shortened and the leaves had begun to turn brown and fall from the trees. Like a mini whirlwind they mixed with the litter and swirled around my feet as I waited for the bus. It was dark and there was a distinct chill in the air. The late shift on PPW didn't finish until 10pm and was usually followed by an early, which started at 7.30am. Today the bus was late, making me feel even more miserable. It would be almost 11pm by the time I got home. When it eventually arrived I sat staring through the grubby windows at the gloomy streets of N.W. London wondering how this journey had seemed so glamorous and exciting once.

I wearily climbed the 3 flights of stairs to our flat, willing the lights to remain on. Our landlady, mindful of her electricity bill, had installed a time switch on the light on the stairs. If you lingered too long on the way up, or your bags were too heavy for you to hurry, with an audible click the lights would go out and you would be plunged into complete darkness. Then, fearing for your safety you were forced to climb the last steps clutching the wall and on reaching the front door try to unlock the door and let yourself in. Today, I made it inside before the lights failed.

Jane's face appeared around the lounge door. "Great you're back" she began. "I was getting worried."

"Late off." I explained with a shrug.

"Oh you poor thing, you look done in. Fancy a cuppa?" I nodded and sank into the nearest armchair.

Returning minutes later with a steaming mug of tea, Jane looked anxiously at me. "Good day?" she asked.

I shook my head, annoyed that I felt ready to cry. "Oh Jane" I began "Don't be kind. I can't take it. I feel really fed- up."

She was quiet for a moment then said "Is it work? It might help to talk about it." I nodded, she was probably right, she usually was.

"I don't think I like working on PPW." I began "I feel like a glorified maid. All I get to do is answer bells, take flowers out of rooms, or worse arrange ones that have been delivered. Then I have to act like a waitress taking meals into the patient's rooms. Do you know today, this is typical; one of my patients is a bloke in his twenties. He's had an op on his knee, I think he hurt it playing football; his firm has paid for him to get it done privately. No NHS for him; he thinks he's above it. Well when we got his menu, he had ordered steak and in big letters had written 'Medium Rare'. OK, I can see his point, but just because steak is on the menu doesn't mean the chef is grilling each to order. It's cooked then sent by lift to each floor. The likelihood of him getting his steak medium rare, is very rare (Excuse the pun)".

Suddenly it all seemed very funny and we laughed so much I couldn't continue. Wiping her eyes, Jane asked "What happened then?"

I took a deep breath "Well no-one wanted to be the one to take him his meal and explain the situation to him, because he had been a real so and so all day, so we drew lots and of course, I drew the short straw."

"Did he complain?" Jane asked.

"No. I just smiled sweetly, plonked his tray on his table and got out of that room as quickly as I could. I was sure he'd ring his bell yet again."

"Did he?" Jane asked.

"Actually he didn't and what's more he ate the steak. Perhaps it was medium rare, who could say, but that's not why I became a nurse is it?"

Jane waited for me to continue. "I guess it just made me think about the whole private patient thing. For example, today I took a patient to X-ray. Well in the main hospital that was a porter's Job, but in PPW the nurses do it. What's more PPW doesn't have its own X-ray department, it uses the main hospitals one, so we were surrounded by loads of ordinary patients, some looking quite ill, and then we were whisked to the front of the queue just because we came from PPW. I ask you, how fair is that?"

Fair or not, next morning I was back in PPW. I was half way through my 12 week placement. During report Sister told us that the young girl in room 12 was to go to theatre for a tonsillectomy. Whilst the surgery was simple enough, the patient was not.

Omar was 14 years old and was a princess from Egypt. Her large room was home to herself, her mother, 2 ladies in waiting and several surly well-built Egyptian men who guarded the entrance with ferocity. When the porters arrived with the trolley to take her to theatre a minor skirmish broke out, as the guards first refused to allow the porters to enter the room: a compromise was found when it was pointed out that the princess was able to move herself onto the trolley and the porters did not then actually have to lift her. Next, it was who would take her to theatre. This was mine and the porter's job, but as this was not acceptable a frantic burst of activity ensued as the ladies–in-waiting begged to be permitted to accompany their charge. Eventually, the princess was taken to theatre by me, one body-guard and one lady- in-waiting on the understanding that the non-medical personnel could not be admitted to theatres or the anaesthetic room.

All went to plan until, operation successfully completed, the princess was released from theatre and it was my job with a porter to escort her back to the ward. As the lift arrived at the ward revealing myself, the princess and the porter to her entourage, the pantomime began. The bodyguards, who had been guarding the lift, stared in disbelief as we wheeled their unconscious charge back to her room. They surrounded the trolley, eyes sweeping the corridor to identify any would-be attackers, and screeching hysterically to each other in their own tongue. As we couldn't understand what was being said we tried to continue into the room.

Once inside the tirade increased, as the bodyguards were joined by the ladies-in waiting, who seeing the princess's pale, unconscious face with remnants of blood clinging to her mouth, began to wail and with much pushing and shoving each tried to take the child's hand. Her mother, just exiting from the bathroom, as we entered ran weeping to her daughter's side. We stopped next to the bed, to lift the patient from the trolley to her bed, but such was the melee we found we could not move at all.

Suddenly a voice rose above the chaos. "Silence." Immediately, there was calm and I saw, to my relief, Sister Cowley stride into the room. Even the bodyguard's aggression faltered as she addressed them. "The princess needs quietness. She has had her operation and all is well, but you must allow us to look after her." Pointing to the door, she commanded "You must leave." With a shrug of their shoulders, they nodded and retreated to stand outside the door.

The next to be dismissed were the ladies-in-waiting, who looking surly, released the princess from their grasp and drifted reluctantly, following Sister's outstretched hand, to the sofa. Here perched on the edge, like a pair of blackbirds watching their young, they starred silently as we lifted the girls' slight form from the trolley onto her bed. Sister and I unfolded the bedding and made the princess comfortable, whilst the porter left to return the trolley to theatre. Sister smiled at the princess's anxious Mother, as I checked the girls pulse and blood pressure, for the first of what would become half-hourly observations.

Sister, now confirmed in my mind as a complete hero said, "You know what to do Nurse. Half-hourly obs. Let me know if you are concerned, or if she wakes and is uncomfortable. We can give her something for pain."

She left the room and I was surprised to find everything remained quiet, although the ladies–in waiting whispered from the sofa, and the bodyguards glared at me each time I passed. The princess recovered well and by the morning was sitting up in bed eating ice-cream, but the incident made me realize that actually Sister was in control, and for that reason, she earned my respect.

However all the respect in the world could not convince me that it was right for student Nurses to work on PPW. It seemed to me we were cheap labour and I was glad when my 12 week placement came to an end. As it so often seemed my final shift on the ward was a critical one. One of the agency staff did not arrive, so we were working with one nurse less. Several of my patients were quite poorly and I had spent some time listening to the wife of a patient with terminal Lung Cancer, tell me how they had met 50 years previously.

He was everything to her and my heart sank as she said "Please God, he won't take my Cliff away from me. I can't manage without him."

Cliff lay, semi-conscious, hardly aware of our presence and I knew that her prayer was unlikely to be answered.

In the next room, Mr. Watts, a business man had just had surgery to repair his "detached retina". Following this operation it was essential that the patient's movement was minimal, so he was nursed flat in bed, eyes bandaged and sand bags placed at each side of his head. This meant that the patient was completely dependent; it took three nurses just to move him to ensure that his head was supported at all times. Getting three of us in the same place at the same time was more than problematic. Two staff-nurses and I had just started the procedure when we were aware of a bell ringing.

Staff shrugged "We're all busy at the moment. It'll have to wait."

Mr. Watts wriggled uncomfortably. He was used to being independent and giving orders and he was finding his new submissive role very difficult. "It's ok. Mr. Watts" I tried to re-assure him "Just do what we say. There is no rush. Just relax."

It took 5 minutes to re-position him, leaving me free to answer the bell.

As I entered the room, reaching out to switch-off the persistent ringing, I could sense the tension in the air. The patient, a girl in her mid-twenties whose inflamed appendix had been removed a week previously was lying on the bed.

She didn't move as I approached. I began "Sorry it's taken a while to...." she lifted her head, glaring at me angrily. "Why should I put up with this?" she interrupted. "When I ring my bell I expect you to answer. I am a private patient and I do not expect to be kept waiting."

I hesitated trying to think of an appropriate response but all I could think of was the unfairness and before I could stop them, the words tumbled from my mouth indignantly. "As I said, I'm sorry for the delay, but I was doing something important and although you are a private patient, I'm afraid I come with the NHS and I answer bells when I can."

The silence hung in the room like smoke. I renewed the water in her jug, as she requested and nodding an acknowledgement exited. Somehow the episode epitomized the last 12 weeks for me, and it was with relief, I left PPW for the last time that day.

Chapter 10:
Senior on Surgical

I had been nursing for two years. It scarcely seemed possible, but it was true. A striped belt now circled my waist and sometimes, not always, junior nurses would stand back to let me pass through a door. I loved my career and my self-confidence had blossomed. For the next few weeks, I was to be on Ward 16 to practice my newly acquired skills. I could hardly wait.

Ward 16 was a busy, male surgical ward, run like clockwork by Sister Jones, who had a reputation for being efficient but fair. The surgical team was headed by an experienced and competent surgeon called Professor Franks. Junior doctors fought to be part of his team, realizing that the experience they obtained there would be second to none. So it was with great excitement that I pushed open the heavy wooden swing door on my first day of duty there.

The ward itself was unremarkable, arranged in the old-fashioned 'Nightingale' style; a cross-shaped room with beds spaced around its walls. I loved working on these wards, although later they were outlawed for "the lack of privacy for patients", and re-designed with the beds housed in bays. For nurses, however their benefits were numerous, not least the real sense of camaraderie which they encouraged as patients shared their experiences.

It was also easy to see, at a glance, what was happening and this made patients safer. No-one seemed to collapse and remain undetected on Nightingale wards. The senior nurse sat in the centre at the huge oak desk overseeing the patients with a careful efficiency. The only exceptions were beds 1 and 28; two single cubicles at the top end of the ward, used if the patient's condition meant he needed to be nursed in more isolation.

It was 7:30am. Val, a girl from my own set had been on Nights. "Hi Joy" she called, beckoning me to her side. "Is it your first day?"

I nodded enthusiastically. "Let me give you a tip" she continued "Staff and Sister are due on at 8am. If I were you I'd let the juniors give out breakfasts while you start organizing today's ops. There are 8 on the list and it starts at 8.30 so you are going to be frantic." She handed me the operating list saying "They're all quite with it, so shouldn't be any trouble. They know not to eat or drink and we've put the 'Nil by Mouth' signs on the bed".

At that moment Night Sister entered the ward, looking weary. Val hissed "I've got to go and give the first pre-med with Sister". As she bustled off she pointed to a frail gentleman whispering "He's next on the list. You'd better organize him."

Smiling and clutching my list, I approached my patient. It only took a moment to gather up his toilet things and direct him to the bathroom. I started to run the bath as he undressed. "Now Mr. Stephens" I began "The Professor likes you to bathe before you have your op and when you have finished, just put this on, and lie on your bed. When it's time we'll give you an injection to make you feel sleepy. I handed him the statutory white op. gown explaining as I did so that the ties did up down the back, and then, confident that he understood what to do, left him.

At 8 am Sister arrived with her two staff-nurses. They swept into the ward, laughing, like old friends, the scarlet lining of their thick woollen cloaks flashing like poppies in a field of corn as they made their way through the ward to Sisters' Office. Moments later they re-appeared, and headed for the desk, where the night staff were hurriedly completing the report for the night. They listened carefully as Val updated them and I was pleased to see that she was allowed to sit down. A considerate Sister: now that was something worth having.

Then the day staff had report. Sister stood as I approached and took my hand. "Good morning Nurse Cooper. Welcome to ward 16. I hope you enjoy your time with us and learn a lot. This morning I have put you to work with Staff, doing the drugs and dressings."

I smiled, grateful to be welcomed in this way but also delighted to, at last be released from the endless rounds of washes and bedpans. I was at last a senior nurse.

Staff and I tackled the drug round together. We flew round, and finished after only 15 minutes. "Wow that was quick" I remarked.

Staff smiled "Well drug rounds are usually quicker on surgical wards than medical. Our patients are generally younger and fitter and don't have such complex needs as those on Medical wards." She noticed me smiling. "Wait until you're running around hairless giving injections for pain after the ops. You won't be smiling then."

It was just after 9am. "We're to go to first coffee" Staff instructed. I pulled a face. I had not long had breakfast and I was looking forward to doing the dressings. "Sorry" Staff explained "But it's to prevent cross-infection. The orderlies have just finished cleaning and we need to let the dust settle before we begin to take dressings down and expose the wounds."

"Of course, sorry." I muttered annoyed at myself for not thinking. To say the ward was run like a 'tight ship' was an understatement. Each person from the kitchen maid to the most senior consultant was part of the team whose mission was to provide the best possible care for our patients. If it meant taking an early break, fine.

Staff was already studying the small red book listing the dressings required that day, when I returned from my break. On the immaculate worktop the night staff had arranged successive piles of sterile lidded stainless steel bowls in which were sterile gauze, cotton–wool balls, a white paper dressing towel, 2 pairs of forceps and a pair of surgical scissors. A smaller version of the bowl stood next to each bowl.

Staff sprayed the entire trolley with surgical spirit and dried it with clean paper towels before putting the bowls on the top shelf and a large bottle of chlorhexidine and a roll of zinc oxide plaster on the lower shelf. A white paper bag was clipped to the side to act as a waste bag. Finally we put on paper face masks that covered our mouths and noses; "a tool to prevent infection" she explained.

"Right" Staff turned to me "First I need to check your scrubbing-up technique."

Together we washed our hands and forearms thoroughly under a running hot tap for 3 minutes, taking care to include every area of our hands and nails and then dried them carefully with a clean paper towel. "That's fine" said Staff "But don't forget once your hands are clean you mustn't touch anything unsterile, or you'll have to wash them again."

I nodded trying to look confident. She grasped her hands together as if in prayer and held them in front of her face. I followed her, pushing the trolley and watching as she parted the screen by the first patient's bed, using her elbows.

I must have looked doubtful because she laughed and said "Don't worry. You'll get the hang of it. It looks worse than it is."

I nodded, then wondering just how many times that day I would be washing my hands said "Don't your hands get sore with all that washing?"

She nodded "Of course. It can be a real problem but it makes you more careful not to touch anything unsterile."

Our first patient was Jimmy whose sutures were due to be removed. "We always start with 'clean cases' first." Staff explained as we drew next to his bed. Jimmy, looked nervously at us, his pale face a stark contrast to his mop of ginger hair. The week before, Jimmy, a police constable, had developed abdominal pain whilst directing the traffic on Tottenham Court Road. At first it was merely a niggle and he blamed the pie he had eaten earlier, but as the day progressed the niggle became a serious pain. When he was very sick at the police station later, a kind duty sergeant had arranged for him to be brought to Casualty. Later that evening, he had been operated on to remove his inflamed appendix.

Staff manoeuvred her trolley through the screens. "Hello Jimmy" she began "I'm going to look at your sutures today and hopefully they can come out."

Jimmy looked terrified and slithered down his pillows as if trying to hide. "Will it hurt Nurse?" he asked and when Staff shook her head added "Sorry to be such a coward".

I patted his hand "You'll feel a pulling sensation, that's all."

Folding back his bedclothes I continued "Let's just ease your trousers down so that we can get to it"

The dressing was just below his umbilicus. I peeled off the plaster and gently removed the dressing discarding it into the waste bag. Revealed on his pale, shaved belly was a livid red scar about 4inches long and 12 black silk sutures each individually tied lay across its length.

Staff inspected the wound gently stretching the suture-line to ensure the sides did not gape. "That looks good Jimmy" she explained. "I'll take out alternate sutures then re-assess." Her smile was hidden beneath her mask, but Jimmy seemed to relax as she spoke. She placed the sterile dressing towel beneath the wound, then took the forceps in one hand and the scissors in the other and carefully lifted the knot of the first stitch. Keeping the scissors as near to the skin as possible, she cut the black silk and swinging the exposed suture 180 degrees, using the blade of the scissors as a lever, pulled the suture out. I watched Jimmy's face which registered no discomfort at all.

Staff continued until every other suture was removed. "That's half of them out Jimmy" she said and it was good to see him smile broadly. "I'm just going to give it a bit of a tug" she continued, looking carefully at the scar-line and noting that it did not gape, "That looks good ; I'll take the rest of them out now."

She removed the remaining sutures, then cleaned the dried blood and debris from the scar with the chlorhexidine, and covered the area with a dry dressing. "It only needs a bit of a dressing to protect it for the next day or so Jimmy, but all the sutures are now out and it all looks good. I expect you'll be on your way home soon."

Jimmy smiled "Thanks Staff that didn't hurt at all." She left me to re-organise Jimmy. In the utility room she placed the used equipment in the sink. "One down; nine to go" she said with a sigh.

The morning continued as we had expected. Staff took sutures out of 3 other patients and they all were well-healed. I was becoming restless, longing to remove sutures myself but the last 2 patients on the list weren't as straightforward.

Henry Barnes had been a patient for several weeks. As we approached his bed I saw a look of apprehension flit across his face, Staff bent to speak into his ear, as he was a bit deaf. "Hello Henry" He smiled in his gentlemanly way. "Why hello my dear. What can I do for you today?"

"Nurse Cooper and I want to re-dress your toes. Is that ok?" Staff asked.

He hesitated but only for a second. "Of course. Do whatever you want".

Staff moved to the bottom of the bed and lifted back the bedclothes which were draped over a large metal cage, a bed-cradle, because the weight of the bedclothes on Henry's feet would have been intolerable for him. Henry had been diabetic requiring regular insulin injections for the past 30 years and the high levels of sugar in his blood had damaged the blood vessels in his lower legs and his foot was now almost gangrenous. The plan was to allow him to rest whilst we monitored the condition of his foot. The surgeons had been hoping that it would not be necessary to amputate, but as I began to remove the dressing I was shocked to see that the whole foot was a dusky bluish black and foul smelling pusey fluid was leaking from the area around his nail. I tried hard to not let my face register my concern. Staff examined the foot gently. I could see by her face that the area had deteriorated. She smiled kindly at Henry, who despite trying hard not to, looked as if he were in pain.

"I think I'd like to get the doctors to see your foot today". She said gently "They'll be doing the ward round soon with Sister. What I'll do is leave the dressing off and wrap your foot in one of these towels to keep it clean." She carried on talking as she did this finally asking "Is that comfortable Henry?"

"Yes thank you dear" he replied adding "I hope the doctors are pleased with it though. I am hoping to go home soon. It's my Ethel's birthday next week-end and I like to give her a bit of a treat. Breakfast in bed, you know the full works. I don't want to be in here do I?

Staff smiled kindly "Of course not Henry. Let's just wait and see what the doctors think shall we? Your Ethel just wants you to be well I think. That would be her best birthday treat ever."

Henry smiled "Of course. One step at a time... Ethel's visiting later so I can tell her what the doctors say." His smile lit up his face.

Back in the privacy of the utility room, Staff shook her head. "That foot looks dreadful. I'm sure the doctors will have to amputate. I can't even begin to imagine how Henry and his Ethel will manage after that."

She left for a few moments to update Sister who was already accompanying the Prof. on his ward round. A little later Sister stuck her head round the door saying. "You were right. Henry has to go to theatre later."

Poor Henry, we began to lay the next trolley in silence as we imagined the consequences for Ethel and him.

Staff took a deep breath. "I'm afraid our last patient is terribly sad." she began. "Terry is 22. He went to the doctor about 3 months ago because he was tired all the time and he had lost some weight. His GP did lots of tests but nothing seemed to be abnormal. Last week the Prof. decided to do an exploratory op, expecting to find some kind of tumour." She paused shaking her head sadly "When they opened him up they found he was riddled with cancer. It was hopeless; inoperable; so they stitched him up and prepared to tell the family the grim news" She took a deep breath. "Unfortunately the wound failed to heal and broke down so every day we have to re-dress it and basically hold his whole abdomen together using a many-tailed bandage."

We made our way to the cubicle. I had only heard of the many-tailed bandage, but never actually used one. On further inspection it consisted of a large rectangle composed of 4 inch gauze bandages machined together at the back to form a pad, and the free strips of bandage, when in position, were interwoven alternatively to form a sort of plait, which acted as a corset.

Terry was only vaguely aware of our presence. He needed regular injections of Diamorphine to control his pain and sedate him. Staff and I worked together, speaking in soft voices we explained our actions as we worked but I doubted that he actually heard us. "Well done Terry." Staff said. We had rolled him onto his side to remove the old bandage and insert the new one. The terrible cavity that was his abdomen was packed with gauze soaked in Normal Saline, and a large wound pad was taped above it. Gently turning him onto his other side we manoeuvred the bandage into position and Staff deftly flipped its tails, interlacing them across his abdomen and taped them securely. "All finished Terry "she said "let's just moisten your lips a little they look so dry."

She pointed at the mouth-tray on his locker containing swabs and Gallipots in which were some weak mouthwash, some bicarbonate of soda and finally some glycerine. I gently cleaned and moistened his mouth, finishing by smearing some glycerine onto his lips. Terry remained unresponsive, but looked peaceful. We left the cubicle and returned to the utility room with heavy hearts. His youth accentuated the frailty of life; none of us knew what was around the corner. For a moment we stood silently, acknowledging the full horror of what we had just seen.

Staff began to clear away the dressing trolley and announced in a loud voice "And that is the end of our dressing round." Our time of reflection was over. We had to move on. On the ward I heard the sound of the arrival of the lunch trolley.

"Thanks Staff" I began "I'll go and help with dinner."

As life on the ward settled into a routine I relaxed into it; preparing the patients for theatre and caring for them afterwards. Yet the image of Terry, dying slowly in the side-room haunted my sleep and disturbed my thoughts in the day. It was heart-breaking to witness his mother's daily vigil by his side, as she watched her only son lose his battle to live. His Father, unable to bear the pain, had stopped visiting, saying that he'd rather remember his son as he was before this cruel illness had destroyed him. His only way to cope with his grief was to hide within the security of his daily routine, working in an accounts office.

Three days later I arrived on an early shift to an eerie quiet. Screens surrounded the entrance to Terry's cubicle and Liz, the striped belt on nights hurried to meet us. Ushering us into the linen cupboard, her red eyes betraying the fact that she had been crying, she announced that Terry had died at 5am, "Sister rang his mother; she's collecting his things and the certificate later. The porters have taken him to the mortuary, and we've done all the paperwork. All that needs doing is the bed needs to be stripped and remade".

We nodded sympathetically "Thanks Liz, you must have had an awful night."

She smiled weakly "You could say that..." her voice quivered but she shrugged and continued "The men seem to be finding it hard. They are really quiet. Anyhow I must dash, I haven't finished report yet." She disappeared back onto the ward.

The silence was tangible as we gave out the breakfasts. It was not an operating day so we had time to chat. Although no-one had told the other patients what had happened, they understood and as we continued, to hand them their cereal they made their thoughts known, each in his own was way. "That lad's died hasn't he? Bleeding unfair. That's what I say" from one.

And another "That poor lass on nights…She cried her eyes out. She tried to not let us see, but who can blame her." We nodded and tried to smile, but were just running on automatic pilot. Somehow the morning passed. The others patients, hardly rang their bells and many of them seemed really concerned about us. "You alright Ducks? It's a rum do, it really is." said one patient sadly shaking his head. We tried to remain professional and mask our feelings and in the afternoon a new patient was admitted into Terry's bed. Life continued relentlessly.

That day I went off duty and cried until there were no tears left to cry; I think every nurse felt similarly. We knew death was an inevitable part of our work, but to lose a young man in such a cruel way was heart-breaking. Even our professionalism was not an adequate defence.

It was at times like this I missed the naivety of my childhood faith. I had believed that everything would be alright if I trusted God. Now the fact that terrible things really did happen to people was harder to deny. I longed for answers to my doubts but had no-one to turn to. I briefly contemplated consulting the hospital chaplain but the memory of him, carrying his portable altar into the ward early morning, and getting cross if the poor overworked night nurse had not 'prepared' his particular patient for Holy Communion meant I soon dismissed it as an option.

One thing marking my progression from junior to senior was more contact with the medical staff. Doctors no longer seemed so intimidating, they were colleagues, and I began to enjoy treating them as such. An important part of the wards routine was the twice weekly ward round, when Professor Franks, with his entire team of doctors and a few associated medical students would visit each of his patients on the ward. It was a time of teaching and decision making and had its own protocol. Tradition dictated that the senior nurse on duty accompanied 'The Round' and afterwards the doctors stayed for tea in Sister's office.

I was on a late shift and during report Sister said "It's Prof.'s round this afternoon, Nurse Cooper, I think it would be good experience for you to accompany me."

I smiled gratefully and listened while the other nurses had their work allocated to them. If there was time in an afternoon, Sister or Staff would lead a teaching session for the student nurses. Today I would miss this, but I felt sure I would learn more on the Professors round. The Professor and his entourage arrived on the ward at exactly 2pm. The patients, sensing the grandeur of the occasion were lying quietly waiting. Everything looked neat and clean. As the doctors stood at the ward entrance I noticed some of the patients start to fidget anxiously. The Prof. wore a long white coat which covered a tailored grey suit; although the shortest in height, he had the obvious authority of a leader. I had heard that theatre nurses trembled when he operated; if the slightest thing did not go his way he would shout like a hormonal teenager, until theatre sister arrived and reprimanded him.

Today his underdogs were a surgical and a research Registrar. Both wore long coats and carried stethoscopes peeking out of their pockets. Next came the doctors who were best known to us and did most of the ward work, the Senior House Officer (SHO), and House Officer (HO) and their equivalents who worked on our sister ward "Women's Surgical". The junior doctors wore short white coats and their stethoscopes, which were in constant use, were slung around their necks like a scarf. Finally, heading up the rear, were three medical students, looking fresh-faced and wearing short white coats that barely covered their trendy clothes. Prof Franks tossed his curly hair back from his face and smiled as we approached. "Good afternoon Sister" and leading his colleagues onto the ward continued "Shall we begin?" I hovered behind Sister as we approached the first patient.

Etiquette stated that the Houseman (HO) would 'present the patients,' outlining their medical history, the treatment they had received and their progress. If there was a teaching opportunity, the Prof. would explain to the medical students why that particular treatment had been used. The patients were fairly routine and on the whole enjoyed their brief spell in the limelight, as the Prof addressed each individually and shook their hands as he left.

Half-way down the ward was Henry Barnes, one of my favourite patients whose foot Staff had been so concerned about on my first day on the ward. Having subsequently had his foot and leg below the knee amputated Henry had been very unwell. It seemed increasingly unlikely that he would be able to return to his Ethel. Ethel herself was quite frail and had previously been cared for by Henry.

Today, the Prof looked concerned as the HO updated him, explaining that Henry was a little confused and the wound was not healing very well. "Was the circulation adequate?" he wondered. To check this it was necessary for the Prof. to feel the Femoral pulse, situated in the groin. Sister pulled the screens and the whole entourage huddled into the space around Henry's bed. I stood opposite the Prof. and began to pull back the bedclothes and lift Henry's gown, explaining as I did so what was happening. All was quiet as the Prof. tried to find the all-important pulse in Henry's groin.

Suddenly Henry's eyes opened wide and in a loud voice he shouted "He's touching me privates."

I leaned close to Henry to reassure him, but he was in no mood to be placated. "The scoundrel. Get him off me." he continued, his voice becoming louder and louder. The silence in the ward was palpable. Stepping back as if he was being attacked, the Prof. withdrew his hand and his face turned a delicate pink. He tried to address Henry, but was stopped by cries of "Don't you touch me. Call yourself a gentleman." He stared at me before continuing "I wouldn't mind if it was her. But you...."

Words failed him, and he sat, arms folded, his eyes throwing silent daggers at the Prof.

The Professor, pushing a stray curl back into place cleared his throat and addressed his Houseman. "We need to keep a good eye on that wound. Check the femoral pulse daily. Hopefully we won't need to remove any more of his leg."

The poor houseman nodded trying not to look at the Professor and struggling hard not to notice that the registrar and the medical students were backing out from the curtains as quietly as they could, trying hard not to laugh out loud. If the Prof. noticed, he kept it well hidden and instead continued "We'd better do some bloods too. U+E's, FBC's and Creatinine. Let's see if there 's a reason for that confusion." The HO scribbled the instructions in his notebook, and I smiled reassuringly at Henry and drew back the screens, only too aware that every patient was watching us, most with a grin; enjoying the entertainment. The Prof. still ignoring Henry's black looks, managed to maintain his dignity, and continuing as if the episode had never happened, finished the round.

For the first time, I was to be admitted to the inner sanctuary of afternoon tea with the doctors. The medical students left quickly, probably anxious to recount the 'Henry episode' to their peers. This left the medical staff, Sister and me, to squeeze into her tiny office.

Polly, the ward orderly who had worked on ward 16 for 10 years was responsible for tea. Somehow the concept of dainty little sandwiches that could be eaten with discretion were not in Polly's mindset; sandwiches to her meant "doorsteps". Great wedges of food fit to feed her hungry husband working at the docks. It was a battle in which Sister had accepted defeat long ago.

Born in Camden Town, Polly was a Londoner through and through. Nothing or no-one bothered her. Although petite in stature she had the inner strength of a terrier dog. Once Polly got an idea into her head, it just had to be so; if you let her do things her own way, she was a friend forever. Try and insist she conform to your ideas, however, and she would become public enemy no.1.

Sister, it seemed, had learnt this over the years they had worked together and they had forged an unlikely partnership. Polly, for her part would, it seemed, willingly die for Sister and ward 16. She ruled over the over the kitchen and ward maids like a chief butler in some stately home of the past. In return, the ward sparkled and shone, down to its last piece of cutlery. Meal times and the patients drink trolleys were run with a military precision and Polly was a popular figure with patients and staff alike.

With a great clattering she carried her loaded tray into the office. Sister began unloading the white cups and stainless steel teapot from the tray, as Polly returned laden with two plates of sandwiches. As she left, the Professor flashed a rare smile at her "Thanks Polly. It looks lovely, as usual."

Sister began to pour out the tea, while I passed the plates around. The sandwiches were next and seeing me check their contents the Prof said "I think its banana or egg Nurse, Polly's speciality. That's right isn't it Sister?"

Sister smiled "Are there ever any other?" Then for my benefit continued "Polly does the tea every week. It's always the same. She uses eggs that are hard-boiled and left-over from breakfast"

She indicated the sandwiches; fresh sliced white bread, medium cut with a thick covering of what looked like the cheap margarine used on the ward and inside were large chunks of glistening hard-boiled egg. "And banana" she continued "Which she pays for and brings in herself." The second plate looked identical to the first, except thick slices of banana replaced the egg.

By now everyone was eating, stopping every now and then to retrieve a lump of egg or banana which inevitably escaped when the sandwich was bitten. The Prof, wiping banana from his chin, was deep in conversation with his registrar about a new surgical technique. The registrar, not yet practiced in the art of eating Polly's sandwiches, seemed to be spending more time retrieving blobs of egg from his tie, looking distinctly out of his comfort zone. I smiled, having one of those moments, when I remembered the journey which had bought me to this day. Here I was, three quarters through my training, and in that cramped room that day, life felt wonderful.

Chapter 11:
Obstetrics

The new change list was up. Delighted, I saw I was assigned to Obstetrics. The General Nursing Council stipulated that our training must include experience in either gynaecology or obstetrics. I had no doubt which I would prefer. Mary was eating lunch. I hurried to her table, throwing my coat over the back of a chair and instructing her to save me a seat whilst I grabbed some food. Two minutes later I returned, my plate piled high with Shepherd's pie.

"Guess what" I began as I sprinkled salt on my plate.

Mary smiled "You've won on your Premium Bonds? Either that or you've seen Jimmy; don't tell me he's asked you out."

Momentarily I was distracted by this thought before my excitement returned "No, but it is good news, I'm going to Obs. All those babies!"

Mary laughed "Lucky you, although it might put you off having kids for life. Have you thought of that?"

I pulled a face "Don't be a spoil sport, it's better than gynae. All those D+C's."

Mary tutted. She was working on the gynae ward in the main hospital and only yesterday had complained that her work seemed to consist solely of taking women to theatre for a D+C, (or Dilatation and Curettage, commonly called a "scrape"). It was a very common procedure and nurses could be forgiven for thinking it was the panacea for most gynae problems.

"That's right rub it in" she moaned "There were 10 on the list this morning. It's more like a conveyor belt than a ward. Anyway, when do you start?" "Next Monday" I said still grinning, "I can't wait."

The obstetric hospital was housed in a building opposite the main hospital. Its foyer was light and airy, with large glass doors like those found in an Oxford Street department store. My excitement remained when on the following Monday I stood waiting for the lift to take me to the 3rd floor; Ward 2.I was early, so waited quietly in the wards office while a large Jamaican midwife finished writing the night-report, quietly humming to herself. I smiled, this was going to be a good placement; I could hardly wait to cuddle all those babies. I was surprised to find, listening to her report later, so many words with which I was unfamiliar. There were 28 patients and it seemed that most of them had slept well. That was a surprise in itself, new mothers, I had been led to believe suffered from extreme sleep deprivation.

Report over, Sister turned to me "Nurse Cooper?" I nodded and she continued "Welcome to obstetrics. It might take some adjustment after working on the general wards. On the whole our ladies aren't ill; childbirth is a natural process. Mums usually stay with us for up to 10 days after they have given birth, to ensure they get the rest they need to recover fully and cope with their baby when they get home.

She gave me a quick tour of the ward. Divided into 2 distinct parts, the first was a large Nightingale style room containing 12 beds for post-natal mothers and their babies. A long corridor separated them from the other side where ladies with ante-natal problems were nursed. 4 single rooms led from the corridor. They were for the use of patients who for various reasons needed to be cared for in isolation.

The atmosphere on the two wards couldn't have been more different. The first was usually a happy place, where the product of nine long months of waiting was usually greeted with utter joy and relief. Of course there were exceptions to the rule. Not every mother relished the thought of having a child to care for and even in the case of longed for babies; the emotional roller-coaster which follows birth was hard to cope with for many.

On 2B however, women fearful that their unborn child was at risk, became sensitive and anxious. For them their stay often consisted of endless days of waiting and worrying.

We passed the kitchen, just as a lady, in a white fitted uniform dress I didn't recognize, emerged, carrying a tray of steaming toast. Sister grabbed her "Sharon, just the person..." Standing back she continued "We have a new student nurse with us for 6 weeks. Meet Nurse Cooper."

Sharon smiled and I relaxed. Sister continued "Sharon is our nursery nurse. This morning stick to her like glue. She'll look after you; there is nothing she doesn't know. I'm afraid I have a meeting" and she hurried off in the direction of her office.

"Follow me" Sharon instructed and as I trailed behind her she added "You'd better tell me your first name. I can't stick to Nurse Cooper, it's much too formal."

That sounded promising. "It's Joy" I said as we entered the ward.

At the far end of the room, a dozen ladies dressed in an array of glamorous nighties, were eating cereal or sipping tea from thick white mugs. It looked like a scene from some fashion magazine, because although pale and tired, most women were dressed well. Transparent nightdresses seemed to be the order of the day; made from yards of vivid coloured nylon they came in shocking pink, sapphire blue and even livid green with plunging necklines, perfect for a romantic liaison, but not so good at covering up the enlarged, leaky breasts of the new mothers. Less glamourous were the foam rings which many sat on and when they moved, their faces screwed up in pain. Sharon's eyes followed my gaze and she said just one word "stitches."

The ladies were ready for us. "Hot toast? Lovely"; "Jam and butter please" or "Have you got any marmalade? I just have to have Marmalade in the morning." The questions flitted around the table like a butterfly and the sound of frantic spreading was followed by quiet as each munched their way through their breakfast.

Sharon broke the silence "New nurse today ladies. Nurse Cooper" I nodded a greeting, as their "hellos" spread around the table. "I'll take her to meet the babies, if that's ok." No reply. "Did you all have good nights?" Sharon asked. Another murmur began to form, punctuated by the nodding of heads. It appeared they had slept well. Only one mum said "The night nurse said Robbie had cried but I didn't hear him". "Plenty of time for hearing it when you get him home love" said one of the older mums. "You mark my words. You need all the rest you can get." Another murmur of assent floated up to the ceiling.

I followed Sharon back along the ward. At the foot of each bed was a Perspex cot mounted on wheels with a steel metal drawer underneath. Inside each, wrapped entirely in a cream flannelette sheet, so only the head was visible, were the babies. Their little sleeping pink faces looked identical to me, as I passed from cot to cot. The only discerning difference was the gingham cover, which was pink for the girls and blue for the boys. Most cots held a brand new soft toy, a 'welcome to our world present' from adoring relatives. I felt a strange warm glow inside, surrounded, as I was by all the bundles of new life, sleeping peacefully, oblivious to everything. How long would they remain silent I wondered?

There were few student nurses on obstetrics as it was usually dominated by student midwives. These were state registered nurses who were now studying for Part 1 midwifery; a 6 month course held in the Obstetric Hospital. To become fully qualified, they had to complete Part 2 of the Midwifery course which took another 6 months and was mainly based in the community. This meant once again I was 'junior nurse'; a role I knew very well. Sharon was a good mentor. After breakfast she led me to the sterile domain of the 'milk kitchen'.

She began enthusiastically "This is our first Job. You don't have to worry about washes etc., the ladies on the ward at the moment can all cope with washing themselves. Later we'll have to help a couple of them bath their babies but our priority is to prepare the feeds for the hungry little beggars."

She handed me a green gown and a packet of sterile gloves. Pointing to a small stainless steel hand basin in the corner of the room she said "First we have to scrub up; we might not be operating but the last thing these babes need is an infection because of our poor feed-making technique".

That done, I joined her as she scanned a huge chart on the kitchen wall, which outlined the babies' feeding regimes. "The midwifes talk to the Mums about how they want to feed their babies, then write up the regime for those who are to be bottle-fed. How much food they need depends on their weight and what strength the food is."

I scanned the chart quickly. I felt puzzled. "Is that usual? It looks like out of 12 mums only 2 are breast feeding" I asked.

Sharon shrugged. "That's about right. We do try to encourage breastfeeding, but to be honest not many persevere. They find it difficult or they get tired and they just give up. It's easy to just give the baby a bottle especially if you live with relatives who are all willing to feed the baby. I perhaps shouldn't say this but it seems to me that breast-feeding has gone out of fashion. Who knows perhaps it will become popular again sometime."

I watched as she placed the clean bottles and rubber teats into 2 pressure cookers which were soon hissing loudly on the kitchens oven-top. "This is how we sterilize the bottles" she explained shouting to make herself heard above the noise. "At home, if they're good, I think they use a sterilizing solution but who's to know?" Next Sharon filled the blackened kettle explaining "We make the feeds with formula and boiling water."

After 5 minutes the cookers were taken from the stove, the weights removed and the whole thing was held under running cold water, to reduce the pressure. The bottles were removed and I watched as she first consulted the chart, and then scooped up the required amount of milk powder, levelling it with the back of the blade of a knife and repeating this until the required number was reached. The now cool, boiled water was then added to make the correct strength of feed and finally the sterile rubber teats with their covers were put onto each bottle. Each baby had enough feeds made to last for 24 hours and the bottles were labelled and stored in the 'milk fridge' until needed. By the time the days supply of bottles had been prepared, over an hour had past.

Sharon glanced at the clock "It's almost 10 o'clock. The next feed is due. They'll be waiting."

As we came out of the kitchen, we heard the crying and saw a number of the mums looking anxiously at the clock. At the first bed a mum with her screaming child over her shoulder was rubbing his back frantically.

She rocked rhythmically, making soothing noises as she did so. "Thank goodness you've come." she began "He's been screaming for at least a quarter of an hour. I just don't know what to do with him.

Sharon smiled calmly "Well it is just 4 hours since his last feed, it's important to establish a routine. A baby will soon learn." As she continued down the ward she had to repeat the 'routine mantra' to several other Mums, some of whom looked far from convinced. One by one the crying was replaced by the sound of sucking as each child began his bottle.

As the last baby began to feed and peace resumed, the ward door swung open to reveal Sister helping a porter push a trolley. On it laid a woman, her deathly pale skin contrasting sharply with dark strands of her hair which were stuck to her forehead like seaweed clinging to a rock. From its stand, swaying rhythmically as the party progressed up the ward was a bottle of Normal Saline, dripping unseen into the woman's heavily bandaged arm. "We'll need some help here Nurse" Sister called and I rushed to join her.

Together we managed to help the exhausted woman from the trolley into bed. "We'll need to do Obs, Nurse Cooper" Sister instructed, as she adjusted the pillows and spoke soothingly to our patient. "Check her pulse, resps, and blood pressure, and then come to find me in my office".

The lady was barely aware of me as I inflated the cuff of the sphygmomanometer and put the stethoscope in place on her inner arm. I listened intently trying to hear the change of tone in the brachial artery when the systolic pressure became diastolic. It was quiet and I realized that everyone's attention was focused on the drama that was unfolding before their eyes. I wrote the BP recording on the hem of my apron and took her wrist to record her pulse rate. Finally I noted that her respiratory rate was slightly raised and I counted 28 shallow breaths over the course of a minute.

Sister had a chart on the table as I entered the office. She looked concerned "How were they?" she asked.

I pulled a face "Not great. Her BP is low 90/60 and her pulse is a bit weak and thready. Its 100 beats per minute. Her resps are not too bad".

She handed me the chart and as I recorded my readings she said "It's not surprising. Poor thing. Her name is Jane Adams; she is 36. This was her 4th delivery; all was going well; she had a little girl; Normal Delivery, but she had a sudden, massive post–partum haemorrhage. The labour suite looks like a war zone" She paused before continuing "They had to literally run across the road to the main hospital to get blood from the blood bank for an emergency transfusion. She had 6 units of whole blood. It's just as well she was in hospital. She would never have survived at home."

She stood up saying, "I'll come with you Nurse Cooper. We have to keep a good eye on her BP. We'll do it half-hourly I think. We must make sure she's not losing any more blood."

Arriving at the screened bed on the ward, I took up position next to Jane and began to check her BP again. Sister was opposite me. This time Jane moaned.

Sister, kneeling at her side leant over "Jane, Jane. Can you hear me?" her eyes opened slowly and she looked around herself as if trying to understand what was happening.

Sister took her hand "You're on the ward Jane, Its OK"

A flicker of a frown crossed her pale face, and then suddenly she cried out "My baby. My baby."

Her eyes opened wide as she searched Sisters face for an answer. "It's alright". Sister began "You've had a little girl. She's fine. It's you we have been worried about. You had a bit of a bleed, but it's stopped now. I just need to look at your tummy." Sister's hand rotated over Jane's belly and I could see that she was smiling,

"Good, that looks better."

She took my hand, placing it next to hers and said "The uterus is contracting down as it should. It should feel rounded and firm. Like a grapefruit. Can you feel it?"

I nodded adding "Her BP is better too. Its 110/80 and her pulse is 90."

Sister smiled at her patient. "Everything seems to be doing what it should. Have a little rest and we'll go and organize things so when you wake up your baby will be here."

Jane sighed as if the effort of keeping her eyes open was too much, and she drifted back to sleep. Sister and I left "Check her BP again in 30 minutes" she instructed. "Let me know if there are any concerns." She made her way down to the Labour suite.

There were no more problems and when Jane woke, Sister, true to her word, was pushing a cot with a pink gingham quilt to her bedside. Later, my toes curled as the eager families entered the ward for visiting hour, I saw Jane's husband, rush into the ward clutching a bunch of flowers. His face broke into the biggest smile when he saw his wife. In tow were their other 3 children, who leaned over the cot to admire their new sibling.

Jane, although still weak, looked radiant, as she sat clutching her husband's hand. "We're going to call her Grace" she told me as I once again checked her pulse and BP. "Oh, That's lovely" I replied trying my best to look professional and detached when inside I just wanted to shout "Thank you" to the ceiling realizing that, so easily, this little family could have been without a mother.

On the far side of the ward, Marie, was busy emptying the contents of her locker, into an overnight bag. She had delivered a beautiful baby girl 10 days previously and today was the day she and Jean, her husband, had been longing for; they were taking Fleur home. The bed was surrounded by huge bunches of flowers, some of which Marie was bundling up. "I'm taking some of these home with us Jean; they are just so beautiful."

Jean didn't reply. He was bending over the cot, mesmerized by his new daughter. Her tiny fingers had grasped his index finger and he was transfixed.

"Just look at him." Marie said to her neighbour. "He's completely besotted."

There was a pause as the girl replied "But he's French. It's to be expected."

Marie looked indignant "French or not, we've got to get home, preferably sometime today."

Realising he was the subject of the conversation Jean straightened–up. "When's the taxi coming sweetheart?" Marie asked.

Jean glanced at his watch before saying "It comes at 3pm, my angel. There is no rush!"

With that he resumed his position over the cot smiling at his daughter. Marie shrugged and turned again to her neighbour "Can't do a thing with him. Men. I ask you." She bent to adjust her clothing before continuing "I told him to bring me in a dress to go home in. Look what he brought." She lifted her jumper to reveal that the waistband of her skirt was stretched to its limit over her enlarged tummy. "This skirt was too small for me before I was pregnant" she groaned.

Her neighbour laughed "It's awful. Everyone seems to think you ping back into shape after having a baby as if you were made of elastic. If only…" she tapped her own belly and pulled a face.

Just then Sister hurried in to give them all the essential letters for the doctor and midwife. It was 2.45. "Better make a move then" Marie began. "Thank-you

Sister. Thank you and your staff for everything. You have all been wonderful."

She looked close to tears as Sister gave her a quick hug.

Waving me over, Sister explained "Hospital policy dictates that on discharge a member of staff carries the child for you until you are safely off the premises." Picking the child up out of her cot she handed her to me. "Nurse Cooper will do the honours today."

I smiled to reassure them. Jean gathered up their belongings, as Marie took a short tour of the ward to say her goodbyes, and we were off. The taxi arrived almost immediately and with due ceremony I handed the child to her father. The, now familiar, look of adoration on his face, Jean starred at his new daughter, his wife and finally me. With tears shining in his eyes he began "Thank-you, thank-you so much…. How can we ever repay you?"

Marie took over and somehow the door was closed and the taxi pulled off. I waved as they left. It was only as I turned to go back to the ward that I noticed their entire luggage lying in the centre of the pavement where Jean had left it.

I made my way back to the ward, carrying the bags, expecting a ticking off. Initially Sister looked surprised, but as I explained a slow smile spread across her face, developing into a gentle bubbling laugh. "That baby is going to be spoilt rotten." she began "I wish I could be a fly on the wall when they realize they've lost their luggage." She continued chuckling to herself as she labelled the bag and later as I passed the office, she called out "They've rung. They're picking it up tomorrow." She was still smiling.

On a placement in Obstetrics it was expected that we would be present at the birth of a baby. Surprisingly, this was often difficult as many people had a similar goal. The student midwives all needed to deliver their quota of babies to gain their qualification, and medical students needed to log up a specific number of births. A student nurse could be released from the ward if it wasn't too busy.

One afternoon, after I had been on the ward for about 2 weeks, Sister appeared saying "A delivery is imminent, Nurse Cooper. I've told the labour suite to expect you in 5 minutes." The patients, who were inevitably interested in babies being born, overheard, and a whisper spread around the ward.

Their encouragement followed me as I left "Enjoy yourself." "Don't faint." and "give the poor girl our love."

Patients in the early stages of labour were cared for in quiet, comfortable rooms until, when the cervix was opened to almost 10 cms, they were declared 'Fully dilated' and moved into the labour suite. As I entered the suite I was handed a gown, hat and mask and pointed towards a sink with the instructions "Wash there."

A few minutes later suitably washed and gowned, I was allowed into the clinical-looking room which felt hot and claustrophobic. The white walls were bare, lacking any signs of homeliness. A white worktop stretched the length of one wall and on this were stainless steel trays containing an assortment of gleaming surgical instruments. There were no windows, but fluorescent lights and a huge spotlight which stood on a wheeled stand, lit up the room as if it were a football stadium.

In the centre of the beam of light, on a high narrow trolley was the object of our attention; a girl, Sandra, wearing a gown which covered only her chest. She was no more than 16 years old, and looked like a vulnerable scared child as she lay flat on her back with her legs hoisted into the air, at right angles to her body. Her ankles were strapped into stirrups which hung from 2 metal poles, one at each side of the trolley. I discovered later that this was regarded by the experts as the optimum position for giving birth, although in later years it was outlawed as more focus was given to the mothers comfort and needs.

As I watched from the edge of the room, the midwife and girl looked as if they were taking part in some strange drama. The midwife, at the bottom of the trolley between the girl's legs, issued instructions to her patient. "I can see the top of the head Sandra; with the next contraction I want you to give a big push."

Sandra, looking exhausted, did not reply but clung desperately to the black rubber mask of the gas and air machine at her side. Next to her on the far side of the trolley, was the dad-to-be, Tony; a slight, figure wearing the statutory mask and gown he leant over and wiped her damp forehead with a piece of gauze.

"Not long now Sandy. You're doing great girl." Tony whispered. He too looked young and scared, as if he would be more at home riding a motorbike than sitting in this room. I was surprised that he had chosen to support his partner, many men didn't. Sandra glared at him. "It's alright for you" she began, but her sentence was cut short as she grabbed the mask and frantically began to breathe into it.

The midwife looked up and placed her hand on Sandra's huge belly. "Another contraction? Good. That's great.... Now remember what I said Sandra... Push down into your bottom." Sandra dropped the mask and a strange animal-like groan echoed around the room.

Next to her, Tony leaned forward adding his voice to the melee. "That's right Girl. Push... push... You can do it."

Gradually the groan diminished until it sounded more like a whimper and Sandra's eyes closed and her head slumped to one side. The midwife leaned forward, checking the births progress. "Good girl Sandra. We'll have a few more pushes like that."

Sandra lay still looking utterly exhausted. Tony leaned forward to comfort her but she pushed his hand away. "Get orf me. Let me tell you, you are never, ever coming near me again. I am never..."

Again the sentence was cut short and was replaced by a roar of pain. The midwife leapt forwards issuing instructions "Push Sandra, Push... One more push."

I felt overcome with the drama and emotion in the room and straining forward was just in time to see the baby's head appear, accompanied by a shrill scream from Sandra and Tony's constant incantation "Keep going Girl. You can do it."

For a moment the earth stood still and I held my breath as the midwife wiped the blood and mucous from the child's head situated macabrely between Sandra's thighs. With a great screech and one more push, the child's body slid out into the midwifes waiting hands and I watched in wonder as the baby turned from blue to pink, its cry silencing the parents, who were clinging to each other, staring at the midwife.

"It's a girl. A beautiful girl" the midwife declared as she wrapped the child in a blanket and handed it to her mother.

Sandra gazed at her baby in disbelief. She turned to Tony "We've got a little girl Tony, A beautiful little girl."

Tony could not reply, tears streamed down his cheeks and his whole body shook with deep sobs. Sandra, noticing, pulled his hand to her mouth and kissed it tenderly.

I stood watching, feeling like an intruder but also completely overwhelmed by the wonder of a new life. For a moment the world seemed a very different place and I too felt like crying. Taking a deep breath I thanked the midwife, who was delivering the placenta. I had intended to speak to Sandra and Tony, perhaps ask the child's name, but they were both in another place, clinging to each other, and staring in wonder at their daughter. I took off my gown and exited trying to look more professional than I felt.

As I returned to the ward one of the women caught my eye, "Was it alright?" she asked.

I nodded, hoping she would not notice the unshed tears in my eyes and said "Yes it was fine. A normal delivery. A little girl."

One of the other mum's was listening and said "Are you ok Nurse? You look very red."

Without thinking I replied "Yes I'm fine thanks, but I've been pushing."

The laughter started as a ripple but its volume grew as my comments were whispered from bed to bed. Soon everyone was laughing and looking at the novice nurse, who too, had pushed in labour; it would take some time for me to live it down.

The next two days saw me caught up in a bubble of joy. Mary and Jane teased me mercilessly. "Seen any good births lately?" they would ask whenever our paths crossed, then they would begin to chuckle and walk away shaking their heads as I could only innately grin.

On the third day, arriving in the canteen for an early coffee, I saw Sharon, sitting clutching a lukewarm cup of tea to her chest. She looked tired.

"You OK?" I asked.

"I'm on nights and I'm exhausted" she began "bloody exhausted."

I must have looked surprised and to be honest, I was. I thought that nights on Obstetrics was a bit of a doddle. Most of the mothers were fairly independent, so surely it was just a case of sorting out a few babies feeds; I mean how hard can that be?

I tried to look sympathetic. "Was there a problem? Did you have an emergency?" I asked innocently.

Sharon gave me a knowing look and sighed "Well looking after 12 screaming newborn babies for 11 hours, did keep me quite busy."

I hesitated "Don't the mums feed their own babies?"

Sharon smiled "Oh. I see" she began "You think all we do on nights is cuddle the odd crying baby. Wrong. Let me explain; the reasoning is that the mums need their rest to recover before they go home, so muggings here" She pointed to her chest "feeds their little darlings for them. If anyone breast feeds I, of course can't oblige and so I take the child to their mummy, changed and clean mind you. At the moment no-one is breast feeding so not only do I have to feed every baby, and work my way through the list of jobs the day staff leave me, I have to convince the mums in the morning that their little darling only woke for a quick feed and was as good as gold."

I must have looked sad because she laughed "Oh Joy, sorry to spoil your little dream, Babies don't feed and sleep to order, its bloody hard work being a Mum." She stood wearily, scraping her chair as she did so adding "and being a nursery nurse on nights for that matter." She waved briskly saying "I'm off to bed, sorry to be such a misery; See you." and she left, leaving me to readjust my rose-tinted spectacles.

Reality kicked in the next day as I moved to the other side of the ward, where ante-natal mothers were nursed. The atmosphere here was charged with tension as the ladies struggled with the complications of their pregnancy and battled to keep their unborn child. Many of them had experienced an episode of bleeding and the only treatment available to save the pregnancy was to remain on bed rest until the foetus was deemed able to survive independently (usually at about 30 weeks), then a Caesarian Section was performed to deliver the child. Ladies in this situation were usually anxious and bored, and if they had previously miscarried were absolutely desperate to deliver their baby safely.

The first patient I meet was Frances. She was in her late twenties and strictly confined to bed. This was her third attempt to have a baby and she was now 20 weeks pregnant. The previous two pregnancies had ended when she had miscarried the child at 18 weeks. I arrived at her bedside carrying a bowl of hot water. "Hello Frances" I began "I'm Nurse Cooper. This is my first day on this ward, and I've been sent to help you wash because I understand you are confined to bed."

She nodded and stretched as a yawn spread across her pale face. "Oh excuse me nurse. You must think me rude. It's those blooming sleeping tablets they keep giving me. I just can't wake up."

I laughed "Don't worry. I'm not that good in the morning, so I know how it feels. Here let me help you get set up." She leaned forward, while I pulled the metal back-rest out and re-arranged the pillows so she could sit-up. I moved the bedside table with the bowl on it as she swung her slim legs over the side of the bed. "There" I handed her toilet bag to her with her towels from the side of the locker asking "do you need a clean nightie?" The pale pink one she was wearing looked clean although it was crumpled.

"Oh God yes" she replied "Sitting in this blasted bed all day makes me feel so hot and sticky. My Eddie always takes my nightie home to wash and brings me in a clean one".

Again a coy smile lit up her face. "Is Eddie your husband?" She nodded.

"Well its sounds as if you've got him well-trained."

"My Eddie is wonderful" she beamed, as she handed me the crumpled nightie and began to rub soap onto the flannel. "He can cook, clean, iron... In fact he more or less runs our house." I smiled, turning to leave, but Frances carried on speaking "He's had to be good you see Nurse." She patted her swollen belly. "It's these babies. They just don't seem to want to grow in me."

A shadow crossed her face. "This is our third try, you know. I lost the others when I was 18 weeks gone. Poor Eddie, he was so upset; cried like a little boy he did..." her voice tailed off and she rubbed her body vigorously with her flannel. I stood feeling awkward, not quite sure what to say and aware that I had other ladies waiting for a wash, I should really get on. I had just decided to leave, when Frances spoke again. "Still" she began brightly "the doctors have said that if I stay in bed for the duration, it gives the baby a better chance." Again she patted her belly. "So here I am and here I'll stay." she laughed "That's what my Eddie says. He says I'll do the work, you look after our little baby." Again she giggled. "Men, they're so soft. Eddie would like a football team, well that's what he said at first, but I think he'd settle for just one now." She bent her head down towards her bump. "Hear that little one. You stay there and grow. That's all you've got to do. We're going to do it this time aren't we babe?"

There were no words to say but I reached out and took her hand and squeezed it gently. I felt so useless; trying to cover up the emotion I was feeling I said "Finish your wash, sweet heart. I'll be back in a minute". I fled.

Staff was in the sluice when I entered to find the list of washes. "Sorry I've taken so long" I began "I got caught up with Frances. She just kept talking..."

Staff smiled "I know. Don't worry about it. You'll find on this ward listening is something we do a lot of."

She looked so kind, the words tumbled out of my mouth before I could stop them. I so wanted it all to be alright for Frances and Eddie. "That girl," I began "Frances... she's so desperate for a baby. She's 23 weeks now. That's good isn't it? Do you think she will be alright?"

Staff shrugged "Honestly I can't say. No-one can. We just have to wait and see." I nodded and took a deep breath. "Right, now who needs a wash?"

Consulting the list, I grabbed a bowl and headed for the next patient, trying desperately to kick start my professional aura. The day continued as many 'first' days. I felt slow and awkward, everything seemed to take forever and I was sure Staff would get sick of me asking "Where's this?" or "how do I do that?" but she didn't seem to mind.

Sitting drinking tea and eating dry Madeira cake later, in the canteen, I was glad the shift had finished. Mary arrived too and lowered herself heavily into a chair next to me. "Good day?" She asked.

I shrugged "OK I suppose, I missed the babies though." She looked sympathetic. "And you?" I enquired "how was your day?"

She pulled a face. "No need to ask. Non-stop D+C's with a few hysterectomies thrown in." She looked miserable, which was unusual for Mary, then said "You know I shall be glad to finish on gynae. I'm sick of women's bits."

I patted her hand "Hang in there gal. It won't be long before you're back with your men's chests."

As I entered the ward for a late shift the next day, an aura of pain and tension hung in the air. The screens were drawn around Frances bed and I felt a deepening sense of gloom. Sister hurried into the office as we waited for report. She looked upset and rushed through the rest of the patients details, updating us as she did so.

She came to Frances, and paused, taking a deep breath before continuing.

"Frances went into premature labour this morning at 11.30. You recall she was only 23 weeks pregnant, so the child was not viable." Again she paused "Frances is naturally very upset. I have given her some sedation and she is currently asleep. We have phoned Eddie and he is aware of the situation and on his way in. Please look out for him. Medically speaking the doctors have decided it would be beneficial if she goes to theatre for an ERPC." Looking directly at me she added "That is an Evacuation of retained products of conception. Its standard procedure to ensure nothing is left in the uterus as that would be a huge infection risk. She will probably go up to theatre this evening, so she is nil by mouth."

I felt the loss almost physically and I could see my colleagues too were upset. Poor Frances, poor Eddie.

Report over Sister approached me "Come with me" she instructed. "There is something I would like you to see."

I followed her apprehensively into a small clinical room; she closed the door behind me. Lying on the worktop was a stainless steel receiver covered with a green cotton dressing towel. She removed the cloth to reveal a tiny, yet beautiful, lifeless baby girl. Every detail of the child seemed perfect, from her tiny fingernails to her fair curly eyelashes. She had just been born too soon to live. I stared, feeling my eyes fill with tears.

Sister put her hand on my shoulder "I'm sorry. I know it's terrible and I am not doing this to shock you. I just feel strongly that it is important for you to know what a 23 week foetus looks like." She hesitated "You have heard, I'm sure, that abortion has recently been legalized up to 28 weeks. Its aim was to reduce the damage and pain done by backstreet abortionists, and for that reason I am pleased, but there is part of me that is very alarmed too."

I took a deep breath and nodded. I understood her concerns but felt too ill-informed to comment.

Sister said "Are you ok?" I managed a slight smile, nodding, and we then left the room, but inside I felt anything but ok.

Inside me was an acute pain that would not go away. I carried on working as if by clockwork; routine helped but the atmosphere on the ward was almost brittle; one wrong word or action and it felt as if the whole place would collapse into a paroxysm of grief. Every woman's sympathy was with Frances and her loss, yet it was more than that. The patients were afraid. It had happened to Frances, would it happen to them?

Somehow the day continued. Staff and Sister took over the care of Frances. Eddie arrived, pale-faced and looking terrible. He was ushered in to see his wife. The ward was silent as we tried not to listen to the muffled sobs from behind the screens. Later, he left, and Frances went to theatre as planned.

Sometime in that day, I saw a porter enter the clinical room with Sister and then come out carrying a black plastic bag. He whistled as he walked out of the ward; at the time, it seemed insignificant. It was only later, realizing that the foetus had disappeared from the clinical room, I remembered the porter. Later, much later, I discovered that a 23 week foetus was not recognized as "a life" and therefore disposed of with other clinical waste. There would be no funeral for

Eddie and France's little girl; No photos. It was as if she had never existed. Society, it seemed, felt that this was the kindest way to cope with miscarriage. How wrong it was later proved to be.

Chapter 12:
Almost there!

Classroom 1 looked no different than it did 3 years ago when we had first arrived in PTS; yet something had changed. This was our final 'Block' before our qualifying exams and sitting with the rest of our set; I realized that the change was within us. The women we had become were very different to the young women of 3 long years ago. Pregnancy, personal injury and better opportunities had taken their toll; set 175 had decreased from 53 to the 30 nurses, who now remained.

As a group we had matured and grown beyond recognition; each adopting our own styles and becoming comfortable with our own taste. Without uniform it was easy to distinguish between us but a feeling of 'togetherness' remained. We had evolved from being an anonymous part of the hospital machine, anxious to obey the rules and conform; to professional nurses whose experiences had taught them that, perhaps, life was not just a set of rules to follow.

The hospital's motto was 'Ratione Dirige Cursum': 'Let reason guide our course.' Our training had forced us to face many different ethical dilemmas and now we too had an opinion and would be willing to question our superiors, if necessary, to ensure we did the best for our patients.

Mary leaning back in her chair stretched "Well here we are. There were times when I never thought I'd make it, but we're almost there and I'm glad I've survived." A murmur of consent spread around the room. We were unaware that we were being watched until, from the back, came the sound of someone clapping slowly. We turned, startled, to see Frank Jones standing at the back of the room, smiling at us affectionately. His red hair was now peppered with grey but he still looked good. Making his way to the front he took up position leaning on the tutor's desk.

"It's good to hear you all being very philosophical and acknowledging your pride in how far you have come" he began. "However I must ask that you are patient. This study block is very important; we have a lot to do to prepare you for your final exams."

He explained that 'Block' was to be divided into sections. There would be lectures from both the medical and surgical Consultants, and these would be interspersed with practical sessions to ensure we understood what was required of us in our 'Practical Final'.

"Tomorrow" he said "We need to see your 'Practical Experience books, which I trust have been discussed with and signed by the Ward Sisters on each of the wards you worked."

A buzz went round the room and I wrote in my diary "bring GNC book". It was unlikely I would forget it. The buff covered book was the official record of our experience during training. It was updated at the end of each placement, when each nurse would have a one-to-one session with the Ward Sister. The types of patients we had nursed, as well as the procedures we had assisted with were listed and Sister would only sign if she considered us to be competent in caring for patients with these conditions. We also read her report which outlined how we had worked in that area. This was sent to the School of Nursing; any nurse receiving a negative report could expect to be called to see Sister Tutor to "discuss her future in her career"

As we completed our training, the book would be scrutinized by the General Nursing Council, and formed the legal record that we had received the recommended amount of experience. That little buff-coloured book provided a vital part of the proof that we were fit to qualify as SRN's.

Later in the week, Frank, looked troubled. "Ladies" he began "We have been studying your books and it seems some of you have not worked in the community. This experience is essential before you qualify." It sounded like bad news. Clearing his throat Frank continued "So we have arranged for the following nurses to spend a week on the District to rectify this." He began to read the list off and soon, as expected, I heard my name; "Nurse Cooper, to go to Camden Town to work with the District Nurse."

It seemed cruel to set the alarm for 6.30am during Block. My mood didn't improve as I struggled into the baggy gabardine mac with its matching hat that I had been instructed to wear over my striped uniform dress. Waiting for Camden bus, I saw my reflection in a shop window and could have cried. I looked a cross between a badly dressed mature student and a homeless lady who had just been turned out of a hostel.

"Morning Nurse" The bus conductor said with a grin. "Working in the District today are we?"

I nodded relieved that I was at least recognisable as a nurse in my awful attire. Arriving at the doctors surgery I was welcomed by Sister Higgs, whose ample figure was well suited to the baggy gabardine.

"Nurse Cooper? Lovely to meet you; today we hope to show you a completely different aspect of nursing." As I was ushered out of the surgery I was pleased to see a battered black Morris Minor. I had feared we would be on bicycles. "Hop in" she said unlocking the door. "Keep your fingers crossed the blighter starts, I had to get my husband out of bed to give it a push this morning." She laughed causing a coil of her mousey hair to escape from her hat and pirouette across her forehead like a spring. Brushing it aside she continued "Made his day, especially as he had been at the fish market all night."

Climbing into the car she turned the key. To my relief there was a gurgle and a groan as the engine was coaxed into action.

We stopped outside a shabby terraced house, with drab net curtains barely covering the windows. The paint was so old and faded it was impossible to determine its original colour. Sister explained "Our first patient is an elderly man, who is a diabetic. He lives alone, and to do this he needs our help. We call every morning, without fail, but without the support of his home help and his kind neighbours, I doubt if he could stay here."

I shivered as we stepped into the hallway of Ted Carter's house using a key Sister pulled from a grubby string tucked behind the letter-box. It was shocking to think that behind similar doors across Camden Town, numerous elderly people sat and waited for the District Nurse to arrive and begin the cycle of visits that punctuated their day. "How else could Ted let us in, nurse?" Sister asked as I was about to question her about the key. "He can't walk to the door can he?"

Ted was lying helplessly on a narrow divan bed, which his neighbours had kindly brought downstairs for him. The house, once full of love and laughter had now diminished. The once vibrant floral wallpaper in the living room had faded to an indistinct brown pattern and a damp smell which reminded me of autumn days hung in the air. Photos of his wife, Elsie, and twins stood proudly as reminders of better days, or as Ted called them his 'salad days'. Elsie had died, the twins had married and moved away from the area and Ted was left, marooned in the downstairs of what had once been his castle.

"Morning Ted" Sister called.

"Morning Sister" came a muffled reply.

I hung back, but Sister pointed to the kitchen, or scullery, as it was called. Filling the blackened kettle, I lit one of the cookers two rings; the gas made a soothing hiss as the blue flames flickered under the kettle. This was the only source of hot water in the house and served to provide water for a quick wash and shave for Ted and later, when he was dressed, a cup of tea. Sister helped Ted out of bed and into his armchair.

The remains of yesterday's fire lay smouldering in the hearth awaiting the attention of Brenda, Ted's home help who would be the next on his list of visitors.

I noticed Sister looking at Ted with concern. "Is everything alright?" she enquired. He shrugged "Think so Sister, just feeling a bit tired today."

Sister's nostrils quivered and she handed Ted his urinal. "Could you just give us a sample please so we can check your sugar levels?"

We retreated to the kitchen as Bert obliged. "I'm not happy with Bert today" Sister began once out of earshot. "There's a distinct sweetness coming from his breath and he is not his normal cheerful self."

She began to unpack her black leather bag, laying a shiny silver kidney dish on the scrubbed wooden draining board, and placed a glass syringe in it next to Ted's bottle of insulin. "I'll give him his usual dose of Insulin, its important he has that, but I bet his urine sample will show his sugar is too high."

She began to draw-up the insulin, but I could sense she was looking at me. "When you have been a nurse for as many years as I have" she began "you will probably notice that sometimes, you get a feeling that all is not quite right with your patient. You may not be able to identify for certain what it is, and you would not get any marks in an exam for mentioning it but, it is called a 'nurses intuition', and in my experience it is usually correct. Only a very brave doctor would ignore a nurse's intuition without good cause."

She left me to consider what she'd said, as she gave Ted his insulin. We tested his urine and, as Sister had predicted it contained a high level of sugar and some acetone. Ted was drinking his tea greedily when we went back to the room. He looked up expecting to see the small enamel bowl he used to wash and shave, but today it was absent.

Instead Sister pulled up a small footstool and sat next to him. "I think we'll forget about your wash this morning Ted," she explained "You don't look too well and your sugar levels are a bit high. Let me take your temperature." She slipped the glass thermometer into his mouth explaining as she did "That's right. It goes under your tongue. And no talking allowed."

Ted sat obediently quiet, looking as indignant as a schoolboy in detention. Sister winked before saying to me in a stage whisper "At last peace; it takes a lot to keep Ted Carter quiet".

The mutual respect between nurse and patient was obvious. After the statutory minute she took the instrument from his mouth and screwing up her eyes looked at the thin silver line of mercury. "Just as I thought" she began "Your temperature is 101 Ted. There is clearly something wrong. No wonder your sugar is too high." She knelt down until her face was level with his and taking his hand said "I think I'm going to pop to the surgery and ask Dr Blake to come and give you a once over".

Ted sighed "I wish you wouldn't Sister" he complained. "I'll be alright, I'm just tired, that's all". The silence in the room felt heavy and oppressive. Ted was the first to speak. "You know what that doctor will do don't you Sister?" he paused. "He'll want to put me in that hospital won't he. I've heard what they say about that place and I'm not going. I won't be put away. This is my home and this is where I shall stay."

Ted flopped back into his chair looking exhausted. "Ted." Sister said softly "Doctor might not want you to go to hospital, and even if he does, the stories you heard aren't true. They wouldn't want you to stay there either. They'd just find out what was causing this temperature and keep an eye on your diabetes then send you back home to us as soon as they could."

Ted said nothing as Sister stood "I'm going now. I'll tell Dr Blake what we've talked about, and I think he'll want to come to see you himself" She put on her mac, and turning to Ted said sternly "And if the doctor decides hospital is the best place, mark my words I shall certainly hear of it if you make a fuss."

Ted went to speak then changed his mind. As we entered the hall I heard him call out "Sister" She turned to face him. "Thanks" he said quietly "I know you care." his smile said more than words could.

"We're passing the surgery on the way to our next patient" Sister explained as we entered the car "I'll just call in and have a word with the doc." Changing gears noisily we pulled up outside the surgery "If you want to pop in and get yourself quick drink lass, I should. It might be your only chance all morning."

"Thanks" I replied, secretly thinking that a trip to the toilet was probably needed as well. If all the houses were like Bert's it might well be a while before I had the chance to go there too.

Back in the car Sister explained that the doctor had put Ted on his morning visit list so there might be more news at lunch time. She glanced first at her watch and then at her diary. "We must get on" she began "We've still got quite a list of patients to see".

Our next visit took us to a modern neat block of flats, surrounded by a communal garden. The smell of newly mown grass hung in the air as we climbed the steps to the second floor flat. A windblown pot of bright geraniums stood outside, their scarlet petals lying like confetti around the front door. Sister began to explain. "This is a first visit for me too nurse, so we shall both be in this together" she continued "Dr. Royce asked us to call. He has known Miss Sissinghurst for quite a few years. She has multiple sclerosis and is usually fairly independent, but when he visited last week he noticed she had a broken area on her leg. When he asked her about it she got very cross and refused to let him actually do anything. I think he is hoping she will have come to her senses and we might be a bit more successful. I'm not convinced but here goes."

Sister rang the flats bell; the door which wasn't locked swung open slightly. From within a voice said "Yes? Who's there?"

"It's the District Nurses Miss Sissinghurst." Sister replied.

There was a long pause then "I suppose you had better come in".

As we entered the lounge I was overwhelmed by the variety of colours. The walls were vivid green with purple skirting boards and doors. A huge Swiss cheese plant meandered up to the ceiling supported by a precarious structure of bamboo canes. From its upper leaves, painted wooden birds peered down at us and an assortment of drums made from animal skins added to the jungle theme. A white cat lay across the hand-crocheted bedspread, solemnly surveying us. It purred softly, like a metronome, which in other circumstances would be restful. But today was not a day for rest; today there was a battle to win.

Sister smiled kindly "Doctor asked us to call" she began "to look at your leg. He thinks you have an ulcer". I stood trying to look sympathetic, and not notice the debris of dirty crockery and newspapers that were strewn on the floor, covering the faded carpet.

Miss Sissinghurst's eyebrows rose alarmingly, threatening to disappear into her wispy hairline as she exploded "Huh, what does he know? The man's a fool. It's a tiny lesion that's all. An ulcer indeed." Sister tried to continue but was interrupted. "Do you know he wanted to put a bandage on my leg from my toe to my knee. I ask you. What was he thinking of?"

I had moved closer and was kneeling by the bed; I reached out and began to stroke the sleek white cat. It stared at me, with its ice-green eyes. "What a beautiful cat you have. Miss Sissinghurst. What's its name?" I asked "Sid" the answer was spat out as the tension in the room went up a notch.

Unperturbed I continued with the stroking as Sister speaking gently, addressed our patient. "The thing is, that lesions of this kind can take a while to heal; the circulation is often at fault and bandaging the leg, as the doctor suggested, does often improve things." Miss Sissinghurst continued to scowl at us, skirt pulled firmly down to cover the leg in question. "Perhaps we could have a quick look, just to see if we could do anything to help?" Sister asked.

The next moment was one of those times that only makes sense in retrospect. All I was aware of was a sudden flash of movement beside me; Sister, who had in her hand the patients notes, suddenly jumped forward. The notes hit Sid's nose with a sharp whack; meowing piteously he shot for cover under the bed. I hadn't even noticed that he had been about to attack me.

"He seems to know people I don't like." Miss Sissinghurst explained, glaring at us. Sensing our defeat, we started to retreat.

Sister sighed "There would have been repercussions if the cat had hurt us. Miss Sissinghurst, but we can't make you do anything."

Without warning, the patient lifted her skirt to reveal a pusey leg ulcer about 2 inches square. "It is an ulcer" Sister began "the doctor's recommendation was probably the best way forward."

The scowl on our patients face deepened "Forget it." she interrupted "I am not having a bandage covering my leg. Do whatever else you want, but not that."

Ten minutes later we left the house. The ulcer had been cleaned and covered with a non-adhesive dressing and we had arranged to return to review the situation in a week's time. The war was not over, but at least we had accomplished a minor victory.

"We will have to tell the doctor what's happened" Sister said as we drove away. "Don't forget to mention Sid." I reminded her.

She nodded "The incident will have to be reported. I should hate anyone else to be attacked."

The rest of the morning was uneventful. Leg ulcers were common among older people. They took a long while to heal, making it difficult for patients to get out and about which meant they became reliant on our care. District Nurses certainly seemed to spend a lot of time on their knees, bandaging legs, cleaning wounds and preventing further infection; the list was endless. I had considered myself broadminded but watching Sister kneeling on filthy carpets leaving layers of grime and dog hair on her uniform made me realize what a sheltered life I had led. At least in the hospital setting our surroundings were clean. Perhaps I did not have the makings of a district nurse. By lunchtime I felt grubby and tired. I longed to go home and have a bath, but the afternoon stretched ahead of us.

Back at the surgery, comforted by a mug of tea, my mood improved. Unannounced the door to the office flew open and a man with his mac slung over his shoulder came in. He had kind, blue eyes and blonde hair which was brushed off his face.

Sister's face lit up. "Doctor Royce" she began "How did you get on with Ted?"

He smiled and it seemed that the sun had come out in the tiny office. Perhaps there were some perks for working on the District. "You were right to be concerned. He has a chest infection. He wouldn't hear of going to hospital so I've started him on some penicillin and I was hoping you could visit again later to check his urine and make sure his Diabetes hasn't gone crazy. Let me know what you think. If his blood sugar gets too high he'll just have to be admitted."

Sister nodded "Of course, we'll go and I might see if we can get the night nurse to give him a call tonight as well."

Doctor Royce turned to me "I don't think we've met" he began. Sister interrupted "Oh doctor how rude of me. This is Nurse Cooper. She's here for just this week from the hospital. They want her to see what we get up to on the district."

He took my hand in his saying "Well I'm pleased to meet you Nurse Cooper and I hope you'll find your time with us worthwhile."

He smiled, lighting up the room for the second time; I smiled too, trying to think of something interesting to say, but no words would form; I just grinned, feeling like a fool. As he turned and left I looked around the room, fearing everyone would be staring at me, but no-one seemed to notice anything amiss.

The week started to fly by; the penicillin was very effective and Ted improved quickly and, much to his delight, remained at home. I felt ambiguous about the work. It seemed to be going well but I felt bored. In hospital, people had operations, doctors did ward rounds, and life had a definite buzz. I was finding my placement rather dull.

I tried to explain to my friends "It's good to get district experience Mary," I began "but to be honest it's not my favourite placement." I paused and Mary recognising that we might be in for a long haul disappeared into the kitchen saying. "I'll just put the kettle on"

I stretched, struggling to make myself comfortable. "It's nice not be rushed off of my feet" I yawned "But really there are some days I wonder if we ever achieve much at all. What's the point?"

Mary came and sat beside me, putting a steaming mug of tea on the floor. She seemed unusually quiet. "I can see you don't agree with me" I began, feeling slightly offended.

"Agree with you? What do you mean? Are you saying we don't need District Nurses?" She paused to take a big gulp of her tea "No of course I don't agree with you. That's stupid."

I pouted "Well you don't need to be a trained nurse to give someone a wash."

Mary shrugged "No perhaps not, but you're not just giving them a wash are you?" It was my turn to be silent. Mary stared at me then continued "I'm sorry if I sound sad but I thought when we washed someone we did a lot of other things at the same time. Like talk to them and find out if they have any particular worries: check their pressure areas and advise them how to stop becoming sore; look in their mouth and check it's clean and that their tongue isn't coated or black like shoe-leather...? I thought we called it holistic care. Care of the whole patient. I thought that was the point of training to be a Nurse. Forgive me if I'm wrong."

I noticed how pink she was and wondered what I had done to deserve such an onslaught. For a while we were both silent. I made the first move and picked up her empty cup. "I'll wash these" pleased to escape to the kitchen.

Suddenly Mary was by my side. "Sorry for going on like that" she mumbled. "I'm in a foul mood. I was listening to some guy on the radio earlier. He was talking about the NHS and the waste within it just like you were. He seemed to be talking about job-lots, not patients. He wasn't a nurse, he was an administrator and what's more he didn't seem to have a clue about what nurses did. I don't think he cared either. Put a bunch of administrators in charge of the NHS and that will just about finish it. It makes my blood boil."

There was nothing to say. I gave her a quick hug and we spent the rest of the evening listening to Bob Dylan; together perhaps we could change the world.

The next day, Sister was off and had left me in the surgery's office to catch up on paperwork. I was sorting through the files, when the phone rang. I answered expecting it to be for Sister.

"Hello nurse" the doctor's receptionist sounded wary. "I hope you don't mind. I know Sister has a day off, but we wondered if you could help?"

"I'll try" I replied, suddenly feeling very important "What's the problem?"

"We've just had a patient ring. She only lives round the corner, but she sounded really upset"...Hesitating she continued "Her husband is ill. I think he has cancer, and she just said that she can't change his bed".

My eyebrows rose, "Can't change his bed? That sounds odd."

Another pause "I agree. I've had a word with the doctor. He says its most unlike her, she's usually very capable. He wondered if you could pop round. We know you are only a student, but what do you think?"

I didn't have to think. Of course I would go. Taking the lady's address, I picked up the nursing bag and quickly glancing at the map, left

Minutes later I knocked on the heavy wooden door practicing what I would say. I was, after all, only a student. Eventually the door opened revealing a tall slim lady, her greying hair betraying her years.

Seeing my uniform she almost dragged me into the house. "Oh Nurse you've come. Thank goodness"

I started to launch into 'I'm only a student speech' but she wasn't listening and just kept saying "Please follow me. Oh thank goodness you've come."

We climbed a steep narrow staircase, in what was a pleasant Victorian terraced house. At the top of the stairs was a small landing and my escort knocked quietly on the dark wood of one of the doors "Muriel, Muriel, it's the nurse" from within I heard a soft "Come in" and I was ushered inside.

It took a while for my eyes to adjust to the poor light in the room, as the blue velvet curtains were drawn. Eventually I could make out a large double bed on the very edge of which, a gentleman, in blue striped pyjamas, was lying on his side with his back to the room. In the corner hunched in a small armchair and clutching a large handkerchief to her face was a lady, who I assumed was Muriel. I could see that she was sobbing silently.

I knelt by her chair in silence for a moment, but when she didn't speak I asked tentatively "Can you tell me what's happening?" To my dismay, the sobs increased, filling the room with their anguish.

At that point, the lady who had let me in spoke quietly "Sorry nurse. It must be hard for you. I'm so sorry."

Her voice faltered as if she, too, would start to cry. I moved towards her "Perhaps you could just help me with a few details. My name is Nurse Cooper. I'm only a student Nurse, Sister is off this afternoon, but I'll do what I can to help. What's your name?"

Her name was Agnes; she had been called that afternoon, by her distraught sister, Muriel. Muriel's husband, Len, had been discharged from hospital yesterday and Muriel was struggling to care for him.

I was about to ask what had happened at the hospital, when suddenly from the bed I heard "Too right she's struggling. I've wet the bed for God's sake; that's all and look at her."

I crossed the room and sat on the edge of the bed. "Is it Len?" I began "Its Nurse Cooper. The doctor has asked me to call. Can you tell me what the problem is?" He gave a big sigh and turned to face me. "It's me Nurse. I'm the problem."

His face now visible looked almost skeletal, his eyes appearing huge as he stared at me. I'd seen that face so many times, and it usually indicated that the patient was in the final stages of Cancer. "I've got the big C. You know what I mean I'm sure" he said angrily "It's in my Prostate, They've taken it out, but there's nothing more they can do." He sighed and turned away again. "My wife told the hospital that she could manage, and I wanted to come home. Now look at us and all I did was wet the bloody bed."

There was a murmur from the armchair and Muriel spoke "I've tried Nurse. I've called my sister and together we've tried to change the bed for 2 hours. For 2 hours. I can't leave him wet it's not right, and he can't help."

Len started to interrupt but Muriel continued "Len, Len love Please. It's not your fault. I know of course it's not your fault and I do want you at home, you know I do. Please Len please don't fight, not now" she lowered her head looking exhausted.

"Is the bed still wet?" I asked. Muriel nodded. I reached into my Nurses bag pulling out my tabard and pulling it on smiled confidently. "Have you got a clean sheet?" Agnes rushed forward sheet in hand.

Taking it I smiled "Well let's be changing this then."

Muriel hurried to my side "But Nurse he can't stand and how will you manage to change it on your own?"

Again I smiled "Nurses have a few tricks of the trade, just you wait."

Muriel and Agnes joined me as I stood beside the bed. "This is what we do" I instructed and began to roll the sheet lengthways until I reached the centre fold. Bending down I loosened the wet sheet that Len was lying on and rolled this until I reached his back. Taking my clean sheet, now also half-rolled, I placed it in position next to Len and smoothed it flat, tucking it in as I did so. "Len" I instructed "There's a bit of a bump for you to roll over. Can you do it?" Slowly Len turned, moving over the roll of the two sheets as he did so. I moved quickly around the bed and this time was able to remove the soiled linen replacing it with the fresh sheet as I did so. It had taken a couple of minutes. "There, done" I said standing up again.

Muriel looked incredulous," I can't believe it was that simple" she said "I've been struggling for hours."

Agnes took the dirty linen from me and left the room. "If you get me some warm water, I could change Lens trousers and give him a bit of a wash. If that's alright Len?"

He nodded and I knelt by his side while Muriel organised the warm water. Len looked very subdued "Are you ok?" I asked.

He nodded "Thanks Nurse, I'm not sure what happened. Its different being at home and when Muriel went to pieces like she did I thought that was it. Finito." He made a sign like someone tightening a noose around his neck, and I realised that both he and Muriel were very afraid.

A diagnosis of Cancer is very frightening, at least with the right help, there were many things that could be done to make life easier. Whilst washing Len, I discovered that in hospital, he had used a urinal but he hadn't got one at home, hence the current situation. I was surprised too that the doctor was not aware of Len's diagnosis because I thought he would have visited to ensure all was well.

When I mentioned this to Muriel she went red. "The hospital did give me a letter. They told me to drop it into the surgery but well" she paused before continuing "when Len came home I went to pieces. I've only just remembered it now." She indicated the carved wooden mantelpiece, where the remnants of a fire was smouldering and propped up next to Len's cards was a letter addressed "For the Doctor". She bent down and put her arms around her husband "Oh love. I'm so sorry. I do want you at home. I've missed you so much"

Len took her hand "It's ok" he said quietly. "It's not your fault. I'm only half the man I was. This bloody disease is the pits. I don't want to be too much for you."

I didn't want to break up their reconciliation, but it was important that they knew that they didn't have to struggle alone, so I said "There is a lot of help available. When I leave here I'll take the letter into the doctor, so he can visit and check that everything is going as it should. Also I'll organise a commode and a urinal for you and finally I'll get Sister to visit tomorrow to give you a wash and have a proper sort out to ensure you get all the help you need. Is that OK?"

They smiled "Yes, thank-you so much".

The door opened and Agnes entered carrying a big tray with a flowery bone china teapot and four pretty cups and saucers to match. I glanced at the large plate of chocolate biscuits which accompanied them. Muriel opened the heavy curtains allowing the late afternoon sun to transform the room as we sipped our tea seated around the bed; peace now restored.

Back at the surgery I was pleased to learn that Dr Royce was Len's doctor and I soon briefed him on the situation. Today speaking as a professional my awkwardness disappeared and he seemed impressed that I had visited alone and managed the situation as I had. Later, as I made my way home, I felt that now familiar feeling of warmth in the pit of my stomach; I had made a difference today, and was confident that with our help Len's last weeks would be as comfortable as possible in the circumstances. Mary was right; our patients weren't job lots. They were people who need to be treated with skill, understanding and professionalism.

Sister on returning to duty the next day was summoned to see Dr Royce. As she left his office, her eyes were shining. "Well done" she said "Our good doctor is most impressed with how you dealt with Len yesterday. It was an awkward situation and you handled it well."

I too smiled, enjoying my moment of glory. "I can't believe it's your last day here with us." Sister continued "It's gone so quickly. I have a list of visits for us to do this morning, including Ted Carter and Len, so that will give you a chance to catch up with them. Then after lunch we'll fill in 'The Book'. We don't want the General Nursing Council accusing you of not having experience of the District do we?"

I shook my head "No I certainly don't and, yes, that sounds like a good plan."

Back in the Morris Minor, I reflected on how the past week had changed my mind about District Nursing. Far from the mundane job I had assumed, district nurses offered lifelines to ill people, caring for them and their families with skill and professionalism and helping them remain at home wherever possible. It was a lesson I would carry with me throughout my career.

As promised, Sister completed the relevant paper work and gave me the usual 'report' needed when leaving each area. She smiled as she handed it to me to sign. "I know you have missed a week of your study block" she explained "and we have had some students who seemed to think our work is inferior to working in the hospital". I blushed, remembering my conversation with Mary earlier. Sister continued. "However I can only say what a pleasure it has been to work with you and that you have impressed us with your ability, kindness and compassion and I hope you go on to have a wonderful career ahead of you."

She smiled; watching with amusement as I glowed in the light of her compliments. Taking my hand she led me to the door "I think you deserve a bit of free time, so be off with you. Don't forget to come and see us if you ever fancy a job on the district." Assuring her I would I said my goodbyes but firstly was summoned to see Dr Royce.

Standing outside his office two minutes later I felt anything but confident. I knocked tentatively "Come in" a voice called and I entered the room.

Dr Royce looked up from the notes he was writing and smiled. "Sister said you wanted to speak to me?"

"Yes she said you were going" he began "and I just wanted to say how sorry I was that your stay with us was so short. You certainly impressed us all. Not least Len and Muriel."

I smiled and said "I'm glad to have had this time with you all. It's been great. Back to study now...final exam soon."

He hesitated and momentarily seemed uncertain. "I just wondered" Then clearing his throat continued "I know you don't really know me, but I have some tickets for 'The Last Night of the Proms' and I wondered if you wanted to come". Looking distinctly uncomfortable he added "I don't know if classical music is your sort of thing, but it's a great evening. You can't buy the tickets, you know, you have to apply for them and they run a lottery. I got lucky but now I've been let down by someone and I don't want to go alone or waste the tickets. It would be sacrilege."

His voice tailed off and I couldn't help feeling sorry for him. I smiled "Thank you. I'd love to go. It's something I've always wanted to do."

He jumped up and took my hand "Wonderful. Well I can't go on calling you Nurse Cooper can I?"

"It's Joy" I replied. "Simon" he said and we both laughed.

Sitting on the bus ten minutes later I replayed the events of the last hour in my mind. Not only had I had an excellent report from my work placement, I had a date; with a gorgeous doctor; to the last Night of the Proms. I could hardly wait.

❀　❀　❀

"You're going where?" Mary asked as I sat on her bed trying not to look too excited. She had just washed her hair and was wearing her pink candlewick dressing-gown; her hair hidden under a big striped towel arranged like a turban. It was hard to have a serious conversation with her looking like that. I was about to explain when she dashed from the room returning moments later with Jane in tow. "You can tell us both" she commanded slamming the door shut. "We want to know everything."

"It's not a big deal" I began but was silenced by the glare my friends were giving me, "Ok, well perhaps it is"…I took a deep breath. "Simon, he's the doctor at the surgery who was so kind to me, has tickets for the Last Night of the Proms. He said he had been let down by someone, but really wanted to go himself, so asked me." I shrugged my shoulders, trying to look as if it was perfectly normal to be asked out by a doctor.

Jane looked as if she were about to explode. "Please, please tell me you said yes?" I rolled my eyes as if I was trying to remember "Of course I said yes, you idiots. Do you think I'm mad?"

"No comment" Mary replied sternly "Now remind me. Is the Saturday in question, tomorrow?" I nodded.

Mary jumped up and took my arm. "Take us to your room immediately. This calls for a review of your wardrobe."

Standing outside the Royal Albert Hall the next day, I wasn't sure my outfit had been the right choice. The gold coloured pinafore with an orange blouse was a favourite, but against all the flamboyant clothes of the other concert goers I felt under-dressed. I hadn't realized that the Albert Hall had so many entrances; through each of them streamed a queue of people in every conceivable fashion. The 'seated audience' generally looked smart in their formal clothes for a night at a concert; The men in evening dress and the ladies, gowns of satin or silk shining with sparkling beading. Pearl or even diamond jewellery shone from the ample bosoms and slender wrists of their owners.

Strolling into the 'promenading area' was a strange mix of an audience wearing a cacophony of clothes. Anything seemed to go. Girls wore dresses made entirely of the Union Jack Flag, some full length, others more like a pelmet under which their long slim legs were displayed. Many of the men wore evening dress but it did not necessarily fit , in fact it seemed the baggier the better and the black bow tie was replaced by one made from the inevitable Union Jack . Heads were crammed into top hats and bowlers and none of the promenaders seemed to be without an umbrella or a balloon.

For a moment I panicked and thought about leaving. What if Simon was dressed in a costume or an evening suit? I hadn't thought to ask him what he was wearing. Besides time was passing, maybe he had changed his mind. I had just convinced myself that this was the case, when I felt someone tap me on the shoulder.

I turned to see him smiling at me, without a Union Jack in sight. "Sorry I'm late," he began as he steered me towards the entrance. "Have you seen all these costumes? Aren't they great?"

There was no time to reply, as we had reached the entrance. Tickets displayed we were carried along in swarm of people, and, like the tide crashing onto the seashore we landed, flushed and breathless, at the front of the arena just below the orchestra.

We had just a few moments to savour the scene. Far from being uncomfortable, having standing room only for us, 'The Prommers', made it special. The orchestra arrived and began to tune their instruments and suddenly a great hush descended on the hall, as the conductor for the evening, swept onto the stage, bowing low to his audience. The applause thundered echoing up to the huge vaulted ceiling and the orchestra began to play. I couldn't really identify the music; classical music had been sadly lacking in my education. All I knew was it spoke to a hidden part of me that I hardly knew existed. I felt as if I was drinking in the notes like a thirsty man craves for water in a desert. My soul, it seemed, was being fed and for a couple of hours all thoughts of illness, patients, exams, and suffering disappeared as I bathed in the emotions I was feeling.

Simon seemed to share my enthusiasm, but I could have been alone. In the interval, we sipped red wine and made polite conversation. "It's wonderful" I struggled to explain. "It feels as if there's been a great hole in my life and the music is slowly filling it. Did you recognise any of the music?"

He smiled kindly, "I think the soprano sang an aria by Mozart." He paused thoughtfully before saying "and one of the orchestra pieces was definitely Elgar's Nimrod. Have you heard them before?"

I shook my head. "Well Joy I'm glad I have been a part of this new experience for you. Perhaps you're going to become a real fan of classical music." I smiled; perhaps I was.

The second half was less intense and made us laugh. A prommer in the front row produced a big brassy horn complete with its black rubber bulb. Perhaps it had once been used in a carriage. The orchestra played 'The Sailors Hornpipe' and to everyone's delight the conductor, waving his baton furiously, bought the entrepreneur horn player, into the music at the appropriate time. Then it was our turn to clap in time to the music of Strauss's Radetsky waltz and, with the conductor as cheerleader, a contest developed as the orchestra and audience tried to race each other. The buxom soprano reappeared in a low cut red satin dress, to sing some sea shanties. She concluded with 'Rule Britannia' and 'Land of Hope and Glory'. I felt so patriotic it almost hurt.

Suddenly it was all over, but the euphoria took longer to dispel; I wanted the evening to continue forever. But, of course it couldn't. Simon had to get back to the surgery because he was on-call from midnight, so I thanked him for such a wonderful evening. He kissed me gently on the cheek and we parted; me on the tube back to the nurses home; and he back to answer any emergency calls from his patients. It was not the most romantic of endings, but I had had a wonderful time and for that moment, that was enough.

I knew Mary and Jane would demand I recall every detail of my evening, but as I travelled home alone I felt as if I was cushioned in a bubble of air. The evening had filled me with emotions that I didn't know existed. Being with Simon had been nice, but the music? Well that had been something more; it had awoken a hunger in me I didn't know existed. How would I explain that to Mary and Jane?

Chapter 13:
Exams; Exhaustion and Grief

"Good luck on Monday darling. We'll be thinking of you. Just relax and do your best. You're a good nurse". Mum waved me good–bye on a blustery Maundy Thursday morning as the daffodils blew in the breeze. It was the week-end before our Final exams and I was returning to the hospital after a break at home; I was terrified.

I waved back, trying hard to be positive and believe her. We had been preparing for our finals for three years, yet I felt I would never be ready. I wasn't sure if it was a good thing to be on duty the week-end before or not. I wasn't much good at last minute revision.

After a hectic shift I rang home for some last minute encouragement. "Hello". The voice on the end of the line sounded strange. It wasn't Mum; it was my sister. "Ann?" I replied, puzzled. "I didn't know you were going to be at home. Is everything ok?"

There was a pause; I realised something was wrong. "Joy" Ann began tentatively, and then in a frightening rush continued "Its Mum. She's had a brain Haemorrhage. She's in hospital."

"When?" I struggled to assimilate those terrible words.

"Yesterday. In the afternoon, Dad found her."

"But why has no-one told me?" I blurted out.

"It's your exams on Monday." Ann explained. "We didn't want to upset you." Exams, Exams; How could exams matter? Mum; Kind, loving, generous Mum was ill. I must go to her.

"I'm coming home" I gabbled into the phone. "I won't be long". Ann tried to protest but I didn't hear. Slamming the phone down, I willed my professional capacity to cope with emergencies into action and organised myself.

Sitting on the train later I watched the familiar stations come and go, and finally let the tears that had been threatening since my phone- call, splash down my face. It was not the thing to do; to cry on the District line. There were embarrassed giggles from the two youths opposite and a well-meaning elderly man, noticing me, lowered his newspaper and patted me on the shoulder saying "Don't worry dear. It may never happen." But it had happened.

Mum died half-an–hour after I arrived at the hospital. She didn't regain consciousness; I noticed her pulse rate was increasing and blood-pressure falling. I watched helplessly as the doctors consulted with each other, deciding how to treat what they presumed was the recommencement of her sub-arachnoid haemorrhage. There was nothing that could be done; her death was inevitable.

Back home, surrounded by family, we tried to comfort each other. Everything seemed unreal. It was as if our world had stopped, yet time continued to pass. In a state of numbness I arrived back at the flat on Sunday; sent by the family who were determined that I should continue as planned with my Finals.

"It's what Mum would have wanted" they insisted; they were right. She would have wanted that for me. But how? Feeling as I was: How would I cope?

Back at the flat, I was surrounded by my dear friends. We clung together and wept. There were no answers to be found; our experience as nurses had taught us that. But somehow in the midst of so much pain, my flatmates rallied to support me.

Jane took control. "We've rearranged the bedrooms so that you're sharing with me. It's quieter and more private and if you wake in the night, promise me you'll wake me. You don't have to do this alone."

I nodded gratefully. Jane had suffered a terrible bereavement too during our training. She understood about grief. Now she was standing with me despite facing the dreaded exams. I could not find the words to thank her. Mary arrived with a tray of tea and biscuits and we sat in a solemn circle to prepare for the next day.

On Monday, barely aware of what was happening; my friends led me into the exam room. All the desks were named; mine was halfway down the long rows of single desks lining the room. Jane handed me a supply of pens, pencils sharpeners and mints to suck and gave me a quick hug, before slipping into her place.

"You may turn your papers over." Frank instructed, and willing my mind into action, I studied the questions in front of me. The exam was scheduled to last for 3 hours and we had to answer 4 of the 6 questions. The first 3 were compulsory, and covered anatomy and physiology and the illnesses associated with the different systems involved.

"Describe the anatomy and physiology of the respiratory system and demonstrate the changes that occur when a patient develops pneumonia. Outline the care and treatment of a patient with this condition." The words floated in front of me and I began to write automatically recalling as I did so the lectures I had attended; the doctor's rounds I had been on and most of all; the patients I had cared for with this condition. Somehow I chose and answered the necessary questions and in what seemed no time at all Frank was instructing. "Time up. Put your pens down".

I had done it; I had completed the written "Finals". I tried to feel excited but all I was aware of was a horrible feeling of numbness.

How can you explain the grief of losing someone you love? There are no rules; for each person it is different. At the time I was too busy just trying to survive. Life was a battle to be fought. Everything seemed unreal, like some terrible dream. I kept hoping I may awake and find it had all been a terrible mistake. I felt like 2 people. Feelings of numbness clashed with periods of intense pain, when I would suddenly remember what had happened and be overwhelmed by a spasm of actual pain that came from somewhere deep inside and spread across my chest, in great suffocating waves, until I thought I might choke. Yet on the outside this strange being, which was me, joined in conversations, laughed, ate, drank and went to the toilet.

We got lots of letters from friends, and some I found impossible to read. Mum had a strong Christian faith and some letters would try to comfort by saying Mum was in heaven, and so I shouldn't grieve. But I missed her so much. Was I being selfish? A few people tried to convince me of a purpose for her death.

'It's all mapped out; you'll see, one day, why it had to be?'

This thought troubled me deeply. Who was this God who had planned this terrible thing? It wasn't that I had stopped believing in God, but I didn't know who or what He was any more. He became a tyrant who would punish me if I did wrong. Is that why she had died? Was it something I had done? I longed for someone to talk to about these things; but there was no-one who knew any answers at that level; no support; just my wonderful friends without whom life would have been unthinkable.

On the days following the exam, life settled into a strange routine. We had to prepare for the 'Practicals' which were to be held the following month so we spent the rest of the week in the School of Nursing. It was ideal for me, allowing me the regular hours I needed to commute home each evening. In that way I was able to support Dad and help with the practicalities of arranging Mum's funeral. I tried to keep busy as I seemed able to cope then. Travelling home alone on the tube though was a real struggle. The nearer I got to my destination, the more the pain of loss grew. I missed Mum so much. I couldn't see a future without her beside me.

One day as I entered Classroom 1 Sister approached me. "Just a quick word Nurse Cooper". She led me to a quiet corner and smiled kindly. "I'm so sorry to hear of your loss". She took my hand and my composure began to crumble. It was always the same when anyone was kind to me. "How are you coping?" She asked.

I nodded fighting back tears. "You did very well to manage exams in such circumstances" she continued. Again I nodded, unable to speak.

"Well" Sister's tone changed and she became more business-like. "Life goes on?" I managed another nod.

"We have made you an appointment to see Sister Scargill, the Allocations Sister. We have told her of your mother's death and she will arrange an appropriate ward for you at this time. I managed a weak smile before replying "Thank you Sister." She squeezed my hand gently before saying "Good luck Nurse Cooper". Then turned and walked away.

At 9am the next morning I sat outside the Allocation Office. The corridor was bare and comfortless. There were no pictures on the wall or vases and magazines on the shelves just an old wall clock, reminiscent of one described in a Dicken's novel. It ticked loudly, as if reminding me that life was ticking past. I felt anxious. Sister Scargill was notorious for being manipulative. Her sole function in the hospital was to allocate nurses to particular wards, ensuring as she did so, that each nurse gained the experience required by the General Nursing Council. However it was also her job to ensure that wards were adequately staffed; a daunting task I must confess. Hers was the hand that provided the notorious 'Change List'.

Every nurse had heard the account of how one of the hospitals most confident nurses, on finding she was to go into Night Bank for the third time, had demanded an interview with Sister Scargill. She was determined she would not conform and had told her friends she would rather leave, than do Night-Bank again.

Apparently after her eloquent plea Sister had replied. "Nurse I know I am asking a lot of you, but may I tell you a secret? I am desperate. The hospital needs someone professional and competent to cover Nights for the next month, and your name came to mind. Now if you are not quite up to the task, I shall be disappointed but I shall understand. What do you think?"

The nurse was, of course, flattered and had agreed to do as asked; only later realising she had been used.

The door opened and a pink- faced nurse exited and said "You can go in". Sister Scargill sat behind a huge oak desk; a sheet of foolscap paper lay before her and she held a blue fountain pen, poised, as it were for action. She peered at me over the top of the gold-framed spectacles that were perched on the bridge of her nose. She didn't speak and when the silence became too oppressive, I began hesitantly.

"It's Nurse Cooper... Sister O'Reilly asked me to see you because..."

"Yes, of course Nurse I remember" she interrupted, staring at me intently. "I understand you have had a bereavement." I nodded, not trusting myself to speak. She was studying the paper in front of her. "Your Mother died?" Again I nodded and she continued briskly. "Bad luck. May I just say the same happened to me, during my training. My father died."

She linked her fingers together pyramid- like, and looked thoughtful. "Do you know what I think?"

She paused before continuing "Keep busy. That's the best thing. Don't dwell on what has happened....I am putting you on Ward 37. Men's Medical. Nights. It's very busy there. Cardiac. That will keep you on your toes."

No words would come, so again I nodded, trying to wrench my face into some semblance of a smile. "When's the funeral?" she asked.

"Friday" I replied.

"Good, good" she continued "Nights start on Monday. You'll have the weekend to recover. That's all sorted." Dismissed, I left the office and the next Monday, two days after the funeral of the most important person in my life, I started night duty on a men's cardiac ward.My world had turned grey but Sister Scargill was right, I was too busy to think and surprisingly, on the surface I coped. I was too tired to acknowledge my grief and the pain that flitted in and out of my life. I tried to keep it all locked inside, afraid that if I let my defences down, I would be overwhelmed; swallowed up by sorrow and loss.

A couple of weeks later, we found ourselves sitting, in our uniforms, outside another examination room. This time it was to take the practical assessment of our nursing skills needed to become State Registered Nurses. Mary, Jane and I fidgeted nervously outside the Practical Room. In what seemed a lifetime ago, Classroom one had been a familiar place where we had learnt how to make beds and give injections. Today it seemed alien territory.

"Nurse Cooper". The voice which summoned me sounded stern, and as I entered the room, the examiner, in the fitted navy dress and frilly cap of a Tutor, did not smile. "Number?" she asked and, with trembling hands, I passed her the printed examination number I had been given. It seemed to take her a long while to find my name on the list and tick it, but eventually she said. "Please go to Station one"

Station one was manned by a similarly dressed female clutching a clipboard. She spoke. "Nurse please lay a trolley with all that is required to bathe a new-born baby. You have five minutes." The room was flanked with a series of wooden tables, loaded with instruments and equipment associated with every conceivable area of Nursing. Suction machines bereft of their rubber tubing stood next to old-fashioned drip stands which looked as if they could have been used by Florence Nightingale herself. Shiny steel theatre instruments reflected the chipped enamel jugs we used to give enemas. I found myself wondering if it would be appropriate to use the words "High, Hot and a hell of a lot." If asked how to give an enema? I forced my attention to the task in hand.

The trolleys were standing next to a washbasin, so working logically I began by washing my hands, the automatic response to any nursing procedure. Cleanliness was paramount and our tutors had empha-sised the fact that you could give 100% accurate answers to any questions, and fail the exam because you had not washed your hands when you should. Next, I cleaned the trolley all the time my mind returning to the time I spent in the Obstetric hospital. I had bathed numerous babies there and even led a teaching session for new mums before they returned home. Yet my mind seemed frozen; unable to recall a single thing. All I could sense was the examiners eyes watching every move I made.

Relief flooded in when I noticed a large plastic doll lying on one of the theatre tables and nearby was a plastic bath; my mind seemed to be thawing. Soon I was loading the trolley with towels, cotton wool, baby soap, surgical spirit and all the necessary paraphernalia needed to bathe a new-born child. I stood back to examine my handiwork just as the examiner said "Time is up Nurse."

She held her face in neutral as she approached and examined the trolley, taking notes as she did. Turning to face me she fired a volley of questions. "What temperature should the water be?"

"Show me how you would care for the umbilical cord." I poured surgical spirit into a galipot and filled another with sterile cotton wool and with trembling hand began my demonstration, using the doll as my model. The questions continued, then suddenly, with an abrupt nod, I was dismissed. "Go to station 2 please Nurse Cooper."

Station two was based in a far corner of the room, by a large window, and was presided over by a male examiner; a white coat covered his casual cord trousers and pale cotton shirt. Despite his appearance, his face, as he stared at me over his dark-rimmed spectacles, looked stern. He clutched the inevitable clip-board. Outside, the grey sky was weeping angry rain and it splashed noisily onto the window. "Number please Nurse". Handing him a card containing my number, I tried to control my shaking hands.

He entered my details carefully onto the clipboard, then instructed; "Nurse Cooper please assemble all the equipment you would need to assist a doctor perform a Chest Aspiration." I relaxed. At last a situation I had dealt with frequently. I washed my hands with a flourish and as I selected the trolley and began to clean it, in my head, I was running through methodically the list of things I needed for my trolley. Skin cleanser, local anaesthetic, syringes, sterile bowls…I began to assemble my equipment noticing, as I did so, that the rain had stopped and the sun was appearing from behind the clouds. Could this be a good omen? In no time I was pushing the trolley towards my examiner and answering his questions with ease. I felt almost smug, but was soon beginning again; this time assembling the equipment needed for a blood transfusion and answering questions regarding a patient arriving in Casualty vomiting blood. What might be the cause? What investigations might be needed? How would you care for a patient receiving a Blood Transfusion? Time stood still until eventually, dismissed, I found myself in the corridor. An arm grabbed me; it was Mary. "How did it go?" she asked.

I thought for a moment. "OK, I think"

I sank into a nearby chair realising that another part of our ordeal was over. All that remained was "The Viva"; a one -to- one question and answer session with one of the Consultants.

Two days later, we had an anxious wait outside yet another exam room. This time it was a smaller, more intimate affair, and somehow even more terrifying. Inside, preparing to quiz us on our medical knowledge for five long minutes was a one of the hospitals consultants. Consultants still maintained their God-like status and 'The Prof' was no exception. His reputation preceded him. Despite wearing a conventional suit, a huge purple silk bow-tie and gold-rimmed pinc-nez spectacles gave him an air of flamboyance. Although he was a brilliant surgeon, he did not tolerate fools gladly. Many a junior doctor had been reduced to a quivering wreck by this man. What chance had we?

With racing heart I heard myself summoned to the room. 'The Prof' sat at the large oak desk, on a worn leather chair which he swivelled slowly.

"You may sit" he instructed as I hovered above a standard wooden chair on the far side of the desk. I had barely done so when the questions began.

"Name the 12 Cranial Nerves." He stared at the ceiling. I willed my brain into action. I found the neurological system the hardest to remember; it was so complex. Then I remembered that next to the toilet in the flat we had posted a list of those particular nerves with a rhyme to prompt us.... 'On old Olympus towering tops a Finn and German viewed a hop.'

I began... "Olfactory....optic..." counting each one on my fingers as I did so. With a sigh of relief I counted 12; the final nerve, but the questions continued to come. "What are the causes of high blood pressure?"

"Describe the specific post-operative care of a patient who has had an abdo-perineal re-section."

"Name 3 types of Insulin in common use?"

"What are the signs and symptoms of Pulmonary Embolus?"

"A patient has returned from theatre following surgery for a fractured jaw, which has involved having his jaw wired. Describe how you would care for him."

"What are the normal levels of haemoglobin?"

"What is haemoglobin?" The expression on the Prof's face did not change at all and just as my brain felt it would burst he stopped. "Thank you nurse. You may go." It was over. I stumbled to my feet and mumbling "Thank you sir" left the room.

"How did it go?" Mary was staring at me.

She looked concerned. "OK" I shrugged my shoulders wearily. The truth was I scarcely knew or cared.

Mary gave me a quick hug. "At least it's all over" she whispered, then in a louder voice continued "In fact they are all over. From now on I see an exam-free year ahead." She smiled kindly and I didn't have the heart to voice my thoughts. Inside my head, revolving like a record was the phrase 'That's if I don't have to re-take them....'

As we waited for our results, spring became summer, and without the restrictions of endless revision we were able to enjoy the long, warm evenings. The flat, so cold and comfortless in winter, became full of light and warmth. We would people watch from our windows, wondering about their lives. If it was warm enough we would walk to Parliament Hill Fields; after 20 minutes the dust and traffic were left behind as miles of open heath land stretched before us. A short climb took us to the summit of the hill and we would sit on a bench, watching the buildings of London glistening in the evening light; Our eyes always drawn towards the GPO tower, the landmark nearest to 'our hospital'.

It was on one of these evenings that Mary, voice full of emotion said "I don't think I can bear the thought of losing you all."

"Losing us?" Jane queried "Whatever do you mean?"

"Well" Mary continued "We have done so much together over the last three years. Just think of all the things we've seen and how much we have changed." We nodded, waiting for her to continue. "Well providing we all pass Finals..."

"That's a big 'provided' Mary" I interrupted.

"Oh Joy. I know; but whatever happens we are all going to be split up. I mean we'll Staff here at the hospital for a bit, but not for long."

It was Jane's turn to interrupt, as trying hard to sound like Miss Barnett she quoted "Nurses. We are very proud of our training, but we do not feel it would be good practice for you to remain here, at this hospital. Of course gain experience as Staff- nurses, but I suggest you look to the future. Move to a different hospital; consider further training. This is just the start of your career and you need a variety of experience to become the calibre of SRN's that we expect from our training school. Of course, our greatest joy would be for you to gain the relevant experience, and then apply for a Sister's Post here." We burst into applause as she came to the end. "That was brilliant, Jane. You're wasted as a nurse. You could be on the stage."

The sun was going down, as we returned to the flat. I think we all shared an acute sense of loss at the realisation that our time together was coming to an end. We sat quietly sipping coffee. "I don't know what I'm going to do without you all." I mumbled, my eyes filling with tears as I spoke.

Mary put an arm around my shoulder. "I'm sorry Joy. I'm so sorry for being such a misery. I'm sure it will all work out in the end." She was quiet for a moment, and then said brightly. "Why don't we have a dinner party?"

We all stared at her. "A dinner party? Are you being serious?"

She nodded "The last couple of months have been tough and it's almost 6 weeks before we get our results. It looks like we will all be working hard on the wards;

now we have taken our exams we'll probably all be covering for when Sister or Staff Nurse are off. You know what it's like".

We nodded. She was right. Mary's enthusiasm increased as she continued. "I vote we do something nice. Just for ourselves. We could invite some people who have been special to us..." her voice trailing off.

So it was settled. Arrangements went ahead to plan for our party. Jane's dad had a friend who thought we were all angels. She had often sent gorgeous homemade food to sustain us, and was easily enlisted to make a huge apple pie. Mary had spoken to a local butcher and he had promised to get her a leg of lamb, which she was going to roast. Jane fancied a trifle, so agreed to produce one. The rest of us were put on vegetable duties.

"No roast is complete without lovely veggies and, of course gravy." Mary declared and we all nodded in agreement. Our next task was to decide who to invite. Helen was first to decide. "I'm inviting Rob" she began "he really helped me organise my studying. I couldn't have done it without him."

That was one place decided. We needed to work out just how many people we could seat, and after a lot of discussion, and some furniture moving, it was agreed that we had room for 10 people. That meant we could each invite one person. Gradually names were floated and the pretty notelets with butterflies on, which were to serve as invitations, were written and sent. I was struggling to think of a guest, when Simons name popped into my mind. I hadn't forgotten our trip to the Proms. So without further ado, I sent him an invitation, care of the surgery, because I didn't know his address. Now we just had to wait for the responses.

Two days later I was alone, struggling to cope after yet another night disturbed by a terrible nightmare. It was always the same; I would hear Mum calling "Joy... Joy. Where are you? I need you. Where are you?" Her voice was so familiar. Tormented by her distress I would wake sweating and anxious. Then I would remember.

I stood huddled in a dressing gown. I was filling our red enamel kettle to make a cup of tea, when the phone rang. I picked it up. "Hello".

There was a pause. Then a voice I couldn't place said "Joy?"

"Speaking" I replied rather curtly.

"Joy, its Simon". He sounded concerned. "Are you ok? You sound different." Simon, of course. I had sent him an invitation to our dinner party. I began to explain but it was too much.

"Oh Simon. No I'm not really ok. Sorry...." I took some deep breaths, struggling not to cry.

He seemed to understand and was saying softly. "Just take it easy Joy. No rush. Can I help?"

His kindness caused the tears to stream down my face as I continued "I'm sorry...It's just that my Mum died suddenly a few weeks ago and I've had a bad night." I stopped unable to continue but Simon didn't seem to mind. "Oh Joy, that's awful. I'm so sorry. Is there anything I can do?"

When I didn't reply he continued "It's alright to cry you know. It helps grief. It's ok." Clutching the receiver to my face, the sobs gradually subsided with the relief of being given permission to cry and the knowledge that someone who cared was willing to listen.

"Simon" I managed eventually, sniffing as I spoke "are you still there?"

Of course he was still there and he didn't think I was crazy. To think I hadn't seen him since our night at the proms. He felt so close at this moment. "Well" he continued "What I rang to say was, yes please. I would love to come to your dinner party and feel very privileged to have been invited." It was confirmed. Simon was coming. I felt my spirits lift.

In the weeks between our final exams and the official results we chose the ward we would eventually like to 'Staff' on. If the Sister agreed, and there was a vacancy, we were given a narrow strip of blue Petersham, which we attached to our striped belt with pins. With this came the title 'Acting Staff Nurse'. It announced to everyone our status of being 'almost a Staff Nurse' (providing of course we passed our exams), and provided the hospital with a supply of should-be competent nurses. Most enjoyed this dubious pleasure and were often left in charge of the wards over the weekend. It was good experience, but could be harrowing. Patients and their families did not care what title you held; they just wanted the care to be competent and compassionate. Being in a new role often meant we stayed on–duty just a bit longer, if it meant when Sister returned, she would hear good reports of us.

Weeks of working hard to make a good impression had left us tired and a little stressed. It was then we sat down to make the last minute plans for the dinner party. We tried to look enthusiastic when Mary arrived with the inevitable pad of paper. The food, of course had been organised so I was sure there was really not much to do. Mary thought otherwise. She looked around critically before saying. "First we need to tidy up. We can't have a dinner party in a flat that looks like a pigsty."

Helen groaned and Jane with a large yawn said "Mary don't stress, it will be ok. Joy and I are off tomorrow and we'll have a day of cleaning. You won't recognise the place." Mary looked sceptical, but succumbed when Helen made her a big cup of hot chocolate and declared the meeting over.

Tuesday came and it was hard to believe it was the same flat. Not only did every surface sparkle; we had re-arranged the furniture and the lounge had been converted into a room fit for a restaurant. The table, extended to its limit, was covered with a cream linen cloth, borrowed from Mary's parents and in its centre stood a shiny silver candelabra (also borrowed) boasting 3 deep red candles. Candles flickered from around the room in the hope that their soft light would give the romantic look we were hoping for, and hide the motley combination of chairs around the table.

Our taste in music was undergoing some change as we had recently 'discovered' Classical Music. Tonight we had selected Mendelssohn to begin, followed by some Beethoven and after that it was back to 'The Beatles'. The aroma of roasting lamb wafted from the kitchen, reminding me I had missed lunch. I was starving.

The doorbell rang and our guests began to arrive. Simon was last. He kissed me gently on the cheek and handed me a bottle of wine. Helen's head appeared around the door. She grabbed the wine and introduced herself finally saying "I'm in charge of the drinks. What can I get you?"

Armed with a drink we joined everyone else now seated at the table and before long were piling thick slices of slightly pink lamb onto our plates, together with crispy roast potatoes, peas, carrots and parsnips. There was homemade mint sauce for those who wanted it and a huge jug of thick gravy. For a while, conversation stopped as we all tucked into the feast, but gradually compliments to the chef began. It was lovely to see Mary looking so happy.

Surrounded by my friends, I felt warm and comfortable and accepted. How quickly the last 3 years had gone. How would I cope when we all went our separate ways? The thought made me shudder. Simon seemed to sense how I felt.

"Do I dare to mention exams to you?" he asked.

"No definitely not" I replied, "I honestly don't know how I have done." I paused. "In fact, I don't seem to know much about anything at the moment."

He smiled "In the circumstances that sounds about right." He took my hand and said "Thanks for inviting me here tonight Joy. Your flat-mates seem a great bunch." He refilled my wine-glass; this time with a red. I sipped it thoughtfully before replying. "They are wonderful. I don't know what I would have done without them."

Our plates were empty and there was a general scraping of chairs as we cleared the table. Jane stacked the plates and took them through to the kitchen. Helen opened a bottle of Chianti.

She held it up. "Just so you know; I bought this because I love the bottle." Its lower half was bulbous and was enclosed in a woven basket. "You are welcome to the wine but if anyone pinches the bottle they have me to deal with" She looked fierce as she continued "I'm going to make it into a lamp."

As we laughed the kitchen door opened and Mary and Jane paraded in; Mary carried a large blue striped jug of home-made custard in one hand balancing an apple pie in the other. Jane followed, the cream of her trifle threatening to overflow onto the floor. A big groan went from us all. They placed the dishes in the centre of the table and we all clapped.

Mary glowed with pleasure but stood waiting for us to be quiet. When she was sure she had everyone's attention she began. "We had this party tonight because we wanted to say thank-you to friends who have helped us through the last 3 years in various ways." She paused and looked at each of us before continuing. "It seems to me we are entering a new phase of our lives. Our exam results will soon be here" Helen and I groaned loudly but Mary persisted. "Then we will all have some decisions to make. It seems impossible that we may have to give up the flat and even," she struggled to find the right words to say. Eventually she managed "I imagine we, as a group, will be splitting up. There will be lots of goodbyes."

Her voice broke as she finished and to our dismay large tears poured down her cheeks. Jane flung her arms protectively around her and we sat very still; not knowing what to do next.

Simon saved the day "Can I speak?" He stood up "I've only just met you all but it is obvious what a lovely group of friends you are. Being the oldest person here." He drew himself to his full height; but Helen prodded him and said "Get on with it Granddad. The custard's getting cold." A ripple of laughter ran around the table and the tears turned to smiles.

Unperturbed Simon continued. "As I said you are wonderful friends who have been through a lot together and in my experience friends like that, remain friends; things may change but I bet you will always be there for each other, no matter what."

He sat down self-consciously but we knew in our hearts he was right. Jane took control. "Thank you Simon. I think you're right. Shall we have a toast?" She raised her glass "To friends. Wherever we find them".

We followed "To friends..."

Helen jumped up "I suppose you all need more wine now! Are we ever going to get that apple pie?"

She rushed manically around the table filling everyone's glass. Everyone laughed and Mary and Jane got to work, dishing out the puds. It had been a wonderful evening; just what we had all needed.

That night there were no nightmares.

Chapter 14:
Results

Time dragged although life was busy. As Acting Staff Nurse I had lots of responsibility on the Men's surgical ward I had been assigned to. The Sister in charge was keen to have me and I was flattered. I was enjoying the challenge.

In addition to ensuring all the patients received good nursing care, the task of a trained nurse was to ensure everything was in place to run the ward efficiently. This included ordering all the basic stock needed on the ward. It was essential to have my finger on the pulse of the ward ordering drugs and lotions from Pharmacy; dressing and items such as suction catheters, syringes, needles from stores; basics for the ward kitchen; the list was extensive.

Also, all equipment had to be regularly checked. Each ward, for example, kept its own stock of Oxygen (02) cylinders, which were often in constant use, for example, for patients with respiratory conditions and those returning from Theatre. An O2 cylinder and suction machine were placed, ready for use, next to each of their beds. If the level of oxygen was low or almost empty we would summons a porter, who would arrive, pushing on a little trolley, a black and white painted cylinder, nearly as tall as he was. There would be a loud hiss as he, after changing the flow meter from the old to the new cylinder, would open the screw with a large spanner allowing the pressurised gas to flow. At first sight the whole process was intimidating, but it soon became part of normality. It would only become a problem if not available when needed and that, for a trained nurse, was unthinkable.

Such new responsibilities were challenging and I loved them, however, hovering always at the back of my mind, was the question 'What if I've failed the exam?' I felt increasingly anxious.

As flatmates we had worked out our strategy for 'Result Day.' They were due Monday or Tuesday and would arrive at the flat in envelopes we had prepared earlier, in what seemed a lifetime ago. Our off-duty meant that I would be at home if they arrived Monday and Jane on Tuesday. We had agreed that we would open each others' and ring with the results. Rumour had it that if the envelopes were thin it was good news, and if thick, bad, because they would contain the forms needed to apply to re-take the exams. I had dreamt about thick envelopes for weeks.

I was working an early shift the Saturday before, the ward was not too busy and I was just deciding to go for coffee when the phone rang. "Men's Surgical. Acting Staff Nurse Cooper" I replied automatically.

"Good morning Staff Nurse" a familiar sounding voice began. Then the line went silent.

Puzzled I tried again "I'm afraid Staff-Nurse isn't here at the moment. Can I help?" This time the voice needed no introduction.

"Joy. It's Mary. You idiot! You passed!" She sounded close to tears.

"Mary" I began, hardly daring to believe what she had said. "But the results aren't due until Monday."

"Well that's what they said." She replied "But I assure you they are here and your envelope was very thin. You've passed. You are an SRN."

Momentarily stunned into silence it occurred to me to remember my friends. "But what about you?"

There was a moments silence then "Yes. I passed too. And Jane."

"Oh I'm so pleased" I said hardly able to stop jumping up and down even though I was standing in the middle of the ward. Then I realised that Helen or Anna had not been mentioned.

"Helen and Anna?" I enquired suddenly feeling apprehensive.

This time Mary was subdued. "No, sadly they failed. I've just told them. They've got the forms to resit, but they're pretty upset. They're at home for the weekend. So they will be getting lots of tea and sympathy from their parents. Poor things. Anyway must go. See you on Monday. Well done again." she concluded.

I put the phone down feeling deflated. How awful that they would have to go through the whole exam business again. I couldn't imagine how they were feeling. When I turned round several of the nurses on my shift had noticed me on the phone, perhaps even the 'almost dance' and were looking at me expectantly. "Was that call what we think it was?" asked the striped belt.

I nodded. "Yes...I passed" I added.

A cheer went up "Well done." They shouted. "You'll make a lovely Staff- Nurse. Well done."

The patients noticing the change in atmosphere asked what was happening, then as the news spread around the ward, there was a volley of applause. And so the day continued. Every time I tried to settle down and do some work, I would hear of another result and the whole process started again. I lost count of the number of hugs of congratulations I received. It was exhausting.

Eventually, shift over; I pulled my uniform off in the changing room and realised I had told none of my family yet. Then I remembered Mum. How she would have loved this news. She would have been so proud of me. Tears started and although I struggled to hide them it wasn't long before a little group of nurses were consoling me. "Oh Joy. Did you fail?" said one kindly, then before I could explain said "Don't worry pet. You can retake. I think about 25% failed so you're not the only one."

I shrugged silently; unable to get myself together and explain. I had passed after all; what of those who had failed. What would they think of me? To make matters worse I realised that I was the only person in the flat that evening. We had made our contingency plans for Monday and Tuesday, the days we expected the results.

Sadly I made my way to the public phone box and rang Dad. He sounded pleased, but he was on his way out so there was little he could do. My sisters, so close previously, had left home. At that moment I felt so alone. I had enough change to make one more phone call, and was soon dialling Jane's home number. Her dad answered the phone. "Joy. How lovely to hear you. Well done you. Jane has given me all the news and she's out shopping. I told her to get herself a new dress and then I'm taking her out tonight. We're going for a meal. This calls for a celebration."

"That sounds lovely" I replied, trying to sound convincing. "Enjoy yourselves." "What about you love?" he continued "Are you going home to celebrate with your Dad?"

"No, he's busy" I began, "can't be helped. I'll just have a quiet night in. I'm on-duty tomorrow anyway."

There was a short pause before he continued "Now look here. Tonight is not the night to stay in on your own. Where are you? At the Nurse's home? Well how about this." he continued "Get to the tube and come here. It only takes about an hour. I'll pick you up from the station. We'll go out for our celebratory meal. Don't say you've got nothing to wear; you can borrow one of Jane's dresses. It will be my treat. Jane will be ecstatic. She doesn't want to go out alone with her boring old father anyway, and you know me; a girl on each arm. What more can I ask."

I felt my voice wobbling "But..."

"No buts Joy. Do as I say. We'll see you soon".

"Thank you" I whispered.

I did as I was told, and we had a lovely evening. I don't think Jane's Dad ever really knew how much his kindness meant to me that night.

The round of applause died down and we sat quietly waiting for the Chairman of the Nursing Committee to begin her welcoming speech. The month following our results had been quite frantic. On the wards it was clear cut and easy to take our place with the trained staff, assisting in running the ward. We wore our blue Petersham belts with their silver buckles with pride, although it took some time for the fact that I was finally qualified to sink in. I constantly was surprised when addressed as Staff-nurse. It was both wonderful and scary. Only today, at our official welcoming ceremony did it feel real.

With good news came change as Mary had predicted. Mary had been the first of us to announce that she had applied to do her Part one Midwifery, at a hospital near to her parents' home in Surrey. "I dread leaving" she said. "Perhaps I should have staffed for longer; but you know how I've longed to do Midder, and everything just clicked into place. I couldn't turn it down" she sighed.

"Of course not" we had chorused "You'll make a lovely midwife. Go for it."

We had all smiled and wished her well, but inside we knew it was the beginning of the end. Decisions would soon need to be made about the flat. We couldn't afford to keep it with one less person to pay the rent, and somehow we found it difficult to envisage replacing Mary. How could we? Anyhow, we assumed, within a few months we would all be finding new jobs. At least that's what the hospital had advised.

Mary was accepted; the course started in two months. Soon it was decided to give notice on the flat and move, for our last few months of work, back into the Nurses Home. Sadness aside, it was a sensible decision.

Anna, although studying to re-take her exams was to marry in the summer. The last thing she needed was to start married life working shifts, and besides they were renting a flat in South London. Commuting would be out of the question; so she was actively looking for a job in out-patients in hospitals closer to home.

Helen, who also had to re-take finals, wanted a career in Ophthalmology, and applied for a post at an eye hospital in Manchester as a State Enrolled Nurse.

As she had trained for three years and despite not passing her exams to become a State Registered Nurse, she could work as a State Enrolled Nurse, which was a fairly new, more practical course, lasting for two years. Helen decided she would probably retake the State finals but, by working at a lower level, she would at least be doing a job which interested her.

That left just Jane and I. Jane's dad became our removal man and it was a sorry pair who unloaded their belongings from the car, outside a rather smart looking building on Tottenham Court Road, which was the residence for the hospitals trained–nurses.

We were to share a room. It was a huge square room with high ceilings and a general feeling of airiness and it was lovely to share with Jane. We were well looked after; our laundry was done; we could eat in the canteen should we choose; work was only a five minute walk away; I even got up too late to make my bed one day and when I returned it was all made with my old Teddy sitting upright against my pillows. It was everything I needed, but I gradually became aware of a dreadful feeling of desolation. I wasn't sleeping very well; the old nightmare was recurring with worrying regularity and when the alarm went off in the morning it as becoming harder and harder to get out of bed. I felt exhausted; everything seemed too much effort. I tried hard to not let my concerns affect my work; I think I managed to hide it quite well, but something wasn't right.

Mary had a weekend off and came to stay. She was enjoying her training and looked relaxed and happy. Jane was working, so Mary and I took the tube to the embankment and crossed the river to have coffee and scones at the Royal Festival Hall. The sun shone brightly making the river sparkle as if a thousand will o'wisps were skating on its surface.

I closed my eyes and relaxed and when I opened them again, I found Mary surveying me anxiously. "Tell me Joy" she began "How are you? You look tired." "Been busy on the ward." I said automatically "Being a Staff-nurse is great, but sometimes it's all a bit much."

"I bet." she laughed. "Are you enjoying it though?"

"Yes" I began "I've always wanted to be a nurse and now I am. Sometimes I have to pinch myself to make sure it's true."

For a while we didn't speak. I didn't quite trust myself to admit what I was really feeling.

Eventually Mary spoke. "Jane was telling me she thinks she might apply to do her Midder too." I nodded miserably. That just left me. What was I going to do? "How about you? Any plans for the future?" she continued. It took me a while to reply. A toddler on the next table spilt his orange squash and screamed until his harassed mother managed to placate him with a piece of her biscuit. I was glad of the distraction, but when peace eventually reined, Mary still sat awaiting my reply.

I sighed. "Oh Mary. I don't know what to do. Every time I think of Midder; I go cold. I just can't face it." I paused for a moment before admitting "In fact the thought of everything makes me go cold."

It was said. My concerns were out in the open. Sitting with Mary I had opened the door to the locked room inside my heart and now its contents were in danger of spilling messily out. I stumbled on, feeling my eyes fill with tears. That was new too. For weeks I had felt devoid of any emotion except tiredness. Now the tears started rolling slowly down my cheeks.

"Oh Mary. I'm sorry. I just don't know what to say. All I ever wanted was to be a nurse; and I am; and I love it, but it's not enough." I took a deep breath before continuing. "When I started at the hospital I was part of a strong family. I had Mum, Dad, all my sisters around. But it's all changed and I miss it so much. I don't feel anyone really needs me anymore. I miss Mum so much. I miss all of you too."

I couldn't continue and Mary reached across the table and took my hand as I blurted out. "I used to have such a strong faith and I just don't know what I believe anymore" "Joy."

She whispered "You've had a horrible time. No wonder you have all these questions; you've done so well. Be kind to yourself." I looked around suddenly self-conscious; Fancy crying like that in public. Mary sensed my feelings and stood up. "Let's go for a walk" she suggested. "It's lovely outside."

We walked along the embankment arm in arm and the soft breeze soothed me. Coming to an ice-cream van, Mary searched in her bag for her purse, saying "Chocolate. That's what we need. I'm having a '99'.

You?" "Of course" I replied "you know I can't resist chocolate."

We sat on a nearby bench and as Mary wiped the last of the chocolate from her chin she said "Perhaps you just need some time to get answers to your questions. Have you talked to a Pastor or anyone about how you feel?"

I shrugged "I can't think of anyone to talk to. Working shifts has stopped us getting really involved in any church. You know that's true." Mary nodded sympathetically. "The hospital chaplain? I don't think so." Again Mary nodded

"I've tried the churches at home but they seemed to be saying that Mum was in heaven and so I should be glad. Christians don't get bitter and ask awkward questions apparently. That's why I'm not sure I am a Christian anymore." Mary tutted.

"I'm sure that's not true. I think you just need some time and space for yourself. When are your 6 months staffing up?"

"In a couple of months." "Well, my dear Joy. Something will turn up. It always does. Just hang in there and I'm sure you'll work out what you want to do." She gave me a quick hug. I hoped she was right.

Jane and I were drinking hot chocolate in our room. We had both just finished late shifts. Holding her mug in one hand she was sorting through the post in the other and paused holding an official-looking letter in a brown envelope. "Something special?" I asked.

She looked embarrassed. "Joy. I've been meaning to tell you...I've been putting out feelers for a midwifery course. It's near to Dad. I thought I might go and live at home for a bit. That's if I get in."

Opening the letter she scanned it briefly. "I've got an interview in 2 weeks. I'll probably get turned down."

"Jane it's ok" I smiled. "You don't have to worry about me. Why shouldn't you get in? You're a great nurse." She turned to me and put her arm around my shoulder. "But Joy. I don't want to leave you behind. Mary told me that you weren't sure of what to do. Are you alright? You could apply too if you wanted?"

I paused; following my friends would be the easy option but it didn't feel right. "Oh Jane thank-you, but I really don't want to do midder. Anyway, I've had a few thoughts too. It's time to move on isn't it?"

"Oh Joy. You dark horse. Tell me all about it" She clutched my hand.

"There isn't much to tell" I began "Do you remember when we went for a few days to that holiday centre in North Devon?"

She nodded "The Christian one? Lee Abbey?" "Yep. That's the one" I replied continuing "I loved our time there. It was peaceful and the scenery was beautiful..." Jane butted in. "And you fancied one of the blokes who worked on the farm." I ignored her "You see its run by a Community, and I remember talking to one of the girls. She was a nurse. She told me they like to have a nurse there, in case of emergencies. Anyway, after seeing Mary, I had a think and that place popped into my mind. Don't ask me why. She said I needed a bit of space and a place to find some answers. So I thought. Why not? So I have written to them asking if they need any more Community Members."

"So you'll give up Nursing? Are you sure?"

"It could be just a short term thing. I want to feel part of something. I don't like feeling as I do now. This may be my chance to learn more about music and drama and get an answer to all these questions in my head. I feel as if I just need that at the moment."

Jane gave me a hug "Well if that's what you think. Well done. We'll both be looking out for the post then."

A few weeks later, Jane and I sat outside Matrons Office waiting to hand in our notice. Jane had been accepted for Midder as she had hoped and Lee Abbey had invited me to join their community. It hardly seemed real that being part of this great hospital was coming to an end, yet it felt right. My childhood dream of being a nurse had been fulfilled; for the moment I was stepping aside from progressing in that career. I was making time for myself; finding space to feed my soul. Perhaps I would return again to nursing in a hospital. I hoped so.

My life now was not as I envisaged but as I had learnt; change is an inevitable part of life. I was moving forward, to find new dreams and hopes. All I could wish for on my journey was that I would find friends and companions, as dear to me as my flatmates, to accompany me. And I added one last wish; that these friendships, so precious, would not be lost but be woven into the very fabric of my life.

I didn't recognise it at the time, but although I thought I had lost my faith; God had not given up on me. He was with me in my new venture and honoured those wishes, blessing me with more than I could ever imagine. And did that break mean an end to a career in Nursing? No; it was really the beginning but that, of course, is another story.